After d Dark

ADERONKE MOYINLORUN

Starling Romance
Indianapolis.Chicago

Starling Romance
Indianapolis,
IN 46224
812-233-3638

Cover designed by Pixel studio
Edited by John Briggs

Dedication

This one is for every woman out there who is living with a painful past. Who has been through abuse and tragic times. I pray every one of you finds your own Vincent who will love you even with all your flaws and imperfections.

This book is also for the 276 schoolgirls that were kidnapped, tortured and raped in the town of Chibok in Borno State, Nigeria.

CAUTION:

This book contains adult situations some readers may find offensive. This is a story involving some disturbing scenarios, child rape, explicit sex and violence. Not intended for readers under 18.

"When we think we have been hurt by someone in the past, we build up defenses to protect ourselves from being hurt in the future. So the fearful past causes a fearful future and the past and future become one. We cannot love when we feel fear.... When we release the fearful past and forgive everyone, we will experience total love and oneness with all."

— Gerald G. Jampolsky

Chapter One

It doesn't always happen like that, but I'm happy today. If there's anyone that can put a smile on my face, it's Vincent, the love of my life.

More and more lately, Vince has been the reason for my happiness. He's proved to me over and over again that he exists only to make me happy. His whole existence is controlled by the expression on my face, whether I'm smiling or frowning. And because I know myself well enough, I know how much work it takes to make a woman like me happy, I know how much effort it takes to put a smile on this face of mine. It's a hard thing to do.

I can describe myself in few words. I'm beautiful, broken, and damaged. Vince has told me over and over again to stop calling myself damaged, but that's the truth. He doesn't believe I'm damaged because he doesn't know my past. He suspects I might have had a difficult childhood, but he doesn't know for sure what happened to me. No one does. Except for me. And no one can know about it till I die. I'm taking that secret to the grave.

Today is a happy day, so I need not remind myself about the darkness that has haunted me since my teenage days.

My phone signals that I have a text and I quickly pick it

up, pushing away my breakfast.

Vince: Hey, Ice, you're doing sexy today?

Ice is what everyone calls me—my 500-plus employees, my two friends, and even Vince. Actually, Vince named me Ice, and the reason he did that is obvious. When he first met me, we didn't get along. He is a lawyer, and I hate lawyers. Not just lawyers, I don't like a lot of people. I hardly smile, and keep my conversations strictly professional. Simply put, I don't have a lot of friends and I don't get along with many people. Not because I'm a bad person, but because I want to be alone. In the last few years, I've learned that I'm the only one who can't hurt me. Every other person can and will. My mom, she hurt me. My dad, he disappointed me big time. My two friends, Lola and Jessica, both of them are a huge package of disappointment. My ex-boyfriend, he hurts me so much that I think hell is made for only him. Vince is the only one who hasn't hurt me until now. And as each day passes, I'm beginning to trust him.

I finish reading the text, smile to myself and decide to write back.

Me: I don't do sexy.

Vince: Why not? Try a short, sexy dress, six-inch heels, hair straight from the salon and see if clients don't rush to do business with you.

Me: Hmmm...Good idea. If a bikini will have the same effect, I'd prefer a bikini

Vince: You want to wear a bikini to work? I'm sending you my job application asap. Lbvs

Me: Application not accepted.

Vince: Y?

Me: You already have a lot of naughty thoughts about me. Don't want to add to it.

I hit the send button, still smiling like an idiot; I pick up my plate and throw it into the sink. My housekeeper will take care of it. I cook my own food, but doing dishes and housecleaning is just not my thing.

My job, the CEO position I'm occupying, takes so much of my time that I have no time for anything else. It doesn't exactly take all my time—I decide to give it all my time so that I won't have time for other stuff.

As fast as I can, I walk into my bedroom to get dressed. Unable to suppress the temptation, I walk to my window to take a quick look at the beautiful view of the city. I do that every morning. I live in a penthouse on Constitution Avenue in Abuja, very close to the Downtown Mall. I especially love the view from the window in my bedroom. A fountain, beautiful flowers and... I just love nature.

I'm enjoying this view when Vince texts again.

Vince: Lol. Whatever. I can't imagine you will ever wear a bikini, anyway. So I'm not disappointed.

Me: Really? One day, I'll surprise you. I'll come to your place at night in my sexy nightie and with two bottles of red wine.

Vince: Wow! We're going to get drunk. I'm in, but only if it ends with me doing **bad things** with you. Lol.

I smile to myself as I read the text. Talking sex with Vince just excites me in ways that I can't explain and if we start, I'm going to be late for work. I drop my phone, deciding against a response.

Very quickly, to my wardrobe, I choose my outfit: a grey blazer teamed with a white cowl-neck blouse over grey-colored pants.

When Vince said I don't dress sexy, he was right. I don't show cleavage; don't expose too much of my thighs either. But I dress sexy enough to attract the responsible men who know women don't have to be nude to be sexy.

From my closet, I choose a four-inch heel and a Prada purse, and then I sit in front of my dressing mirror to put on a quick, slight makeup. In a few minutes, I'm done. I stare at my reflection and decide I like what I see.

I reach for my purse, and then a folder that has been lying on my dressing table. The last thing I pick up is my phone. As I walk out of my bedroom, it's time to text Vince back. I look at my phone and realize Vince had sent three more messages.

Vince: Ice?

Vince: Baby...

Vince: U there?

Me: I'm here, Vince. So what do you mean you want to do bad things with me?

Vince: You really don't know? Hold on a second.

Standing in my living room, even though I know I should be rushing to the office, I wait for Vince's text.

In a twinkling of an eye, a text comes in. I open the text and discover it's a picture message. Opening up the image, I'm so surprised at what I see. Vince took a picture of his penis and sent it to me.

Me: Ewww. Pervert!!!!!!!! Lol

Vince: Lmao. You see what you've been missing.

Me: Lol

Let me quickly say I have a problem with penis-related issues.

It's unlike me, but I'm tempted to take a look at his penis again. I know I sound like a biology teacher calling it a penis. I'm aware others would prefer I call it something else, but, yes, I'm old-fashioned.

So I'm tempted to take another look at his penis. I open the image and feel my inside quiver. His penis is thick, thicker than any I have ever seen, and believe me, I've seen plenty of them. But this, it looks so good I don't mind staring at it for the rest of the day. My imagination runs wild, a tingling sensation building up between my legs.

I smile to myself. Things really seem to be getting better these days. Trust me, the fact that I'm smiling at a penis is as good as the whole world signing a peace treaty and ending a war.

Still smiling, and thinking of a response for Vince, I walk to my front door. It's time to go to work.

When I open my front door, I see my mom standing there and the smile on my face disappears immediately.

"Mom?" The sight of her takes away all the happiness I've been feeling since waking up this morning. "What are you doing here?"

Her brows wrinkle in a frown as she slightly pushes me aside and walk into the house. "Is that how you greet the mother you haven't seen in such a long time?"

"Two months is not a long time," I snap.

Don't get me wrong, I don't have mommy-daddy issues. I'm an only child and Mom and Dad pampered me in their own little way. I had almost everything I wanted. They gave me a good education. I went to school with the children of kings and queens. I have a degree in Business Administration from the best private university in Nigeria. My mom and dad, they were great in their own way. They did their best, so they thought, but when I needed real love, they gave me tough love. When I needed someone to stand and fight for me, my parents made me fight for myself.

My mom starts to say something, but I don't want to listen. I take my phone and begin to text Vince.

Me: Something came up. Gotta go.

Vince: K. Lunch, right?
Me: Yeah. See you at lunch.
Vince: K. Bye. Love you.
Me: Me too.

By the time I finish typing the last message, my mom really has grown impatient.

"Miki!" she yell my name.

I shudder and cast a look at her. I can see the frustration behind her face. I know I've tortured her enough. I've spent the last fourteen years torturing her like this. She has spent every second of her life wondering why I'm like this.

Oh! And my mom hates it when people call me Ice.

I look at her and see the frustration on her face. I feel a deep tightening in my heart and tell myself to be nice.

"What?" I ask, my voice now a little gentle.

"I'm talking to you about how you've grown and you need a man in your life. But I don't see you dating anybody right now and..."

I raise a palm to her. "Mom, Mom... you don't get to talk to me about things like that." See, I give her a mile and she wants ten miles. I'm nice for one second and she's already taking advantage of it. "Besides, not now. I'm late for work. I've got to go."

"Well, can I wait till you get back?" she asks, her voice gentle, too.

I shrug. "If you want to."

I'm about to step out of the house when I hear her voice again.

"Miki, your dad said you've been ignoring his calls. He wants to see you."

"I'm only ignoring his call for the moment. The company I'm buying today belongs to his friend. I don't want to talk to Dad because he will persuade me to give them a franchise or partnership instead of buying the company. And I don't do business like that."

She nods. "I understand, but talk to your dad."

"I'll stop at the house before I go to work."

I'm a little more comfortable with my dad than my mom. Well, both of them hurt me, but I'm more angry with my mom. That's only because I love her more. I expected more from my mom, and she let me down.

I walk out of the house to the garage and into my Lamborghini. I know I have a meeting at 9:00am. And I have only fifteen minutes to make it. If I stop at my parent's house, I will be late for the meeting. The good thing about my life is that people wait for me.

I drive very quickly and make a stop at my parents. Walking really fast on my four-inch heels, I'm panting by the time I reach the front door. My parent's house is big and luxurious. I only moved out of it about two years ago.

"Dad," I call as I push the door open.

I see him sitting on the chair and reading the day's copy of *The Punch* newspaper. Reading newspapers in the morning has been his routine since I can remember. He lowers the newspaper immediately upon hearing my voice.

"Miki, how are you?"

I walk closer to him and give him a quick hug. "I'm okay."

Releasing myself from the hug, I sit beside him on the couch. "You sent for me?"

"Don't you have a meeting with Cashmit PLC today?"

"They'll wait."

My dad cast me a chastising look. "You won't always be invincible, Miki. In business, you should learn to respect people. Don't keep them waiting."

"Yes, Dad."

He nods and then calls out to the help, telling her to prepare me a meal, but I decline.

"Well, then, let's go straight to business." He clears his throat and then continues. "What is your plan for Cashmit? You know, my friend owns that company."

I cut him off. "I thought he was passing on the business to his daughter."

He shakes his head. "No. He passed it on to his son. So it's his son you'll be meeting today."

"Oh! Really?" My face drops and I can't even hide the disappointment I'm feeling. Have I not been enough evidence to these old men that daughters can also flourish in business?

"Yes, really. So I'm just going to tell you to do what you have to do. Don't try to be lenient because you think the business belongs to my friend."

"Dad, you know I don't do business like that." I lift my purse from the floor and stand. "I've got to run. But no worries, Dad. To me, business is business, and friends and family are separate."

"I trust you."

Chapter Two

I park my Lamborghini in the executive parking lot at Daniels Group. As soon as I step out of the car, my personal assistant and so many other staff members are already waiting.

"Good morning, ma'am," Sade brightly greets me, holding out her hands to help me with my handbag. Sade has been a very good personal assistant, and she puts up with all my crap without complaining. I have a bad habit of working late into the night, say 10:00pm. I make changes to big projects at the last minute, which means she has to rewrite and reprint about sixty pages of reports every time I make a change.

She is a beautiful young girl. I don't call her a woman because she is barely twenty. She is in her sophomore year at college and only works with me to pay for school. From experience, I know being a woman doesn't come with age. Years ago, in some African cultures, they had rituals done to transition young girls into womanhood. Once a girl passed the ritual, "Congratulations!" she could call herself a woman. But since those cultures have gone extinct in 21st-century Africa, I guess I can say a girl becomes a woman when she loses her virginity. If that definition applies to me, that means I was barely even a child when I became a woman.

Needless to say, I slid my handbag off my arm and hand it to Sade. Without returning any greetings, I walk very quickly to my office.

Pushing open the door to my spacious and beautiful office, I turn to her.

"What's on for today?"

"Um…" she begins. "As usual, you got a gift from Father Paul, and he sent a note, too. The notes says…"

I wave a hand at her to tell her to skip that part. She doesn't have to read me the notes, I know what it says.

To err is human, to forgive is divine.

The priest has been sending me gifts and that same note once a week for the last five years.

Forgiveness, my black ass!

If apology and gifts were enough, there wouldn't be a need to hate those who hurt us.

"What did he send this time?" I ask, showing the least amount of interest.

"A flower, two books about forgiveness, and a check of two hundred thousand naira."

"You're a Christian, right?" I ask.

She nods yes.

"Keep the books, trash the flowers, and send the money to the orphanage."

"But, ma'am," she stutters. "Please, ma'am, my tuition…"

I see her hands shaking, and I'm sure if I listen well, I will be able to hear her heart beating real fast. I know what she wants, but I keep looking at her, waiting for her to say it.

"Ma'am, my finals are here. And the school won't let me

write exams if I don't pay up. I don't know if... you know... the money for the orphanage."

"Send. The. Money. To. The. Orphanage," I say in clips, almost biting my lips in anger. My reason for not helping her is simple: why should anyone else have it easy when I had it hard? No one was there for me, so why should I be there for anyone else? I have worked for every single thing I have. Let others work for theirs.

"Yes, ma'am..."

I cut her off. "What's on my schedule for today?"

She drops my purse in the drawer and opens the folder in her hands. "You have a meeting with Cashmit PLC for 9:00am, and they've been waiting for more than an hour."

"Get the files for Cashmit and let me have it in the conference room."

I walk out of my office and toward the elevator. The conference room is on the 7th floor. I wait few seconds, and as soon as I step into the elevator, Sade catches up with me and hands me the file, standing in the elevator with me.

I just love how fast she does her job. I really appreciate her hard work.

Opening the file and reading through the first few pages, I've already lost interest in the proposal Cashmit turned in. I close the folder and give it back to her.

"Remind me again why we're even talking to Cashmit at all?"

"Um..." she stutters a little, opening the folder I gave back to her. "Daniels Group is venturing into the business of producing sanitary pads, and Cashmit is one of the tops in the field..."

The elevator stops and the door open. I take the folder back from her. "Go back to the office and be busy."

She bows gently and walks away while I push open the

conference room door. Their heads turn toward me as my eyes scan the room and their faces. Throwing the folder on the table, I extend a hand in greeting to the person that looks like the boss.

Don't ask me how I could tell.

His suit looks expensive, his skin looks different, and he has the kind of bold aura that is easily noticeable on people who can boast of millions.

"Miki Daniels," I confidently introduce myself. "Welcome to Daniels Group."

He takes my hand in a handshake. "Ola Mathews, for Cashmit PLC."

I manage to feign a smile.

"We've been waiting for…"

I cut him off and without sitting, I continue, "I've read through your proposal, but I'm not impressed."

And because I don't like being dishonest, I decide to tell it as it is.

"Actually, I read only the first two sentences of your proposal, and I don't like it. So you have sixty seconds to prove yourselves to me."

He laughs and relaxes his elbow on the table. "C'mon, Miki."

Arrogant much? How dare he address me informally?

"Take a chill pill. Tell me, how's your dad doing?" he asks, smiling.

Hmmnn…trying to prove familiarity.

Without batting an eyelash, I tap my well-painted artificial nails on the table. "Sixty seconds…" I emphasize, trying so hard to suppress the itch to raise my feminine voice at him.

A puzzled expression spreads across his face and for one long second he seems dumbfounded. And then he regroups and begins "It's no longer a secret that Daniels Group will be starting the production of sanitary pads. Cashmit, being one of the tops in this business with over five million and five hundred..."

"I know the numbers," I interrupt.

"And numbers don't lie," he smiles, and winks at me.

Oh, no! If only he knew me well, he would know that flirting only irritate me. If he's been getting his business deals by flirting, well, he's lost it this time.

"Here's what I propose," he says as he stands up from his chair to maintain the same height as me, and then he buttons up his suit jacket. "A partnership between Daniels Group and Cashmit PLC. You have the name and publicity, I have the market. I think we'll make a good partner."

His eyes jerk to mine and I shoot him a stern look. "And what makes you think I'll like a partnership?"

"Because you're starting a business, and I've got the market, factory, and tools." He breaks our gaze and takes a slow look at me, staring from the first strand of my hair to my boobs and then he slowly licks his lower lip.

He can eye-fuck me all he wants, but he's lost his damned mind if he thinks I'll share my company with any-one.

"You don't think that I can afford to build my own fac-tory? And you don't think I'm capable of hijacking the market you already have? The only fun in business is shut-ting down the competition. So where's the fun if I become partners with my competitors?"

He stands there for a second. From the way he's closing and opening his palm, I know he's so angry he wants to punch something.

Better not be me.

Seriously, I don't know who let this kind of person

handle business. Business is not meant for people without backbone. Their very first mistake is waiting for me for more than an hour. It tells me they are desperate.

If I have a meeting with someone and the person dares to show up a minute late, I'm gone. That's the way I've been able to command respect for myself in this business.

Slowly, his butt goes back to the chair, trying very hard not to look at me. "Maybe a franchise. We're ready to re-brand our products into Daniels Group, if you're willing to negotiate a franchise..."

I rest my hands on the table and cut in. "Let me make this clear, Mr. Mathews. The only thing we'll be negotiating today is the price I'm willing to pay to buy your company."

His eyes flash with vicious anger. His palm becomes a fist and hits the table at the same time as he jumps to his feet. "No way! There's no way I'm selling my father's hard labor over to you." Leaning over the table, he makes eye contact with me. "Listen, you spoiled brat! I don't expect you to understand anything about hard labor or hard work because you've been pampered and spoiled. Mommy and Daddy paid your way up, and everything you've ever owned was handed to you on a platter of gold. Daddy is rich and Mommy has everything. You are a silly little girl who cries if Mommy doesn't give you everything you want. And now you decide the thing that you want is my father's company, what my father gave his soul to build, and what I've worked and sweated for. You think buying more companies will score you more points with daddy; that it will make you into the son your father never had. Well, you're wrong, little brat! You're not getting your hands on what is mine!"

Suddenly, hurtful tears burn my eyes. Anger bubbles inside me. Can he misjudge me any further? This is the story of my life. People always misjudge me. No matter how tough I act, people only see a twenty-nine-year old girl who inherited Daniels Group from her father. Last I remember, the company was worth nothing when I took it from my father. See what I've done with it? But no one sees that. My parents gave me everything, but everything they gave to me, I paid for in my own way, I bled for it, literally. I still suffer the pains in ways no one, and I mean no single soul, will ever understand.

Holding back tears, I grab the folder on the table and turn to leave. I shouldn't give him the dignity of a response, but after taking two or three steps, I change my mind. I stop for a second to clear the tears that had built up in my voice. Now sure of myself, I turn and look at him. "You know, it would be a mistake to think you won't regret turning down my offer to buy your company now. Because whether I have your company or not, I'm going to start the production of sanitary pads. All I have to do is do a few ads, and your market will be mine."

"It won't work. People are not stupid enough to believe everything in an ad."

"If the ads don't work, all I have to do is reveal your secrets and tell the public about how you've been ripping them off by using cheap materials which scientific studies reveal can cause cancer."

He shakes his head. "I don't use cheap materials. You won't do that."

"Oh, believe me, I can and I will. I can do anything that is absolutely necessary to make my business flourish. And by the time I take over your market, your company is going to be worth nothing, and you will be begging people to buy it from you. People not as nice as me will offer to buy it for one penny. Your father's hard work and your sweat will be priced at one penny. So before it gets to that, take my deal. Fifteen million US dollars for your company. Think about it. Nothing is really changing, except that instead of you being the boss, you will now work for this little brat. Me." I finish my speech and let out a deep breath.

For one long second, the room is dead silent.

I keep looking at him, watching his hands shake with impotent anger, trying desperately to suppress his anger and calm himself. "There are about 150 million people in Nigeria," he finally says, his voice sounding so defeated. "1.11 billion in Africa altogether, which means there is about 600 million female potential buyers. Miki, the market is big enough for both of us to play a fair game."

I raise a shoulder in a shrug. "Still… unfortunately, I don't play fair. And with the way you attacked my personality earlier on, I know you don't play fair either. So what's it going to be?"

He stares at me with intense resentment. And then he lets out a deep breath. "Twenty million US dollars."

"Fifteen million. Take it or leave it."

He sighs again and nods. "Okay."

A sweet smile spreads across my face. "Thank you," I say, picking up the folder on the table. "It's been nice doing business with you." I extend my hand in greeting, but he doesn't take it. He just keeps staring at me. "Very well then. My lawyer will meet with your lawyers, and we will conclude the buyout. Once again, welcome to Daniels Group."

Chapter Three

With a sly smile plastered on my face, I go into my office and celebrate yet another victory. After a few seconds of enjoying my mental happiness, I grab my phone and plug in my earpiece.

Time to work some more.

Earpiece in my ears, I go to the music app on my phone, trying to decide what to listen to. Well, I don't have too many artists on my phone. In local music, I love me some 2face Idibia songs and Beautiful Nubia. Those two guys are talented. And in international music, I like Rihanna, Jennifer Lopez, Taylor Swift, and Bruno Mars. That's all I ever listen to.

Today I'm kind of in a Beautiful Nubia mood, so I hit one of his albums. And as Beautiful Nubia's *Seven Lives* blasts at full volume into my ears, I grab my laptop and begin to work, studying and cracking my head to make sure the numbers add up.

I've been working for almost an hour when the music stops and my phone signals I have a text message.

Vince: I'm sorry, baby. Can't do lunch. Last minute client.

Me: That's okay.

Vince: I'll make it up to you, I promise

I'm not at all angry that Vince is cancelling lunch. In fact, I'm going to skip lunch anyway. If I don't finish the necessary work, I don't eat. I'm like that. That's how I'm able to make Daniels Group into a multibillion-dollar company. It's my hunger, my pain, my sacrifice that makes this company thrive.

I work for two more hours, and when I check my watch, I realize it's almost 2:00pm. There's somewhere I have to be. My therapy session is 2:00pm every Monday and no matter how busy I am, I never miss it.

I save all my work and then shut down my computer. Pulling the earpiece out of my ear, I throw my phone into my handbag, exchanging it for the little makeup tools I have in there: eye liner, lipstick, and hairbrush.

I don't want to be recognized at the hospital. The last news or publicity I want right now is people finding out that Miki Daniels is seeing a psychiatrist.

I use the dark eye liner to darken my eye a little and then glide on the matte red lipstick. After I release my long human hair from the ponytail, brush it out and let it flow over my shoulder.

The makeup is fit for my black skin color, but it's too much for me. I've always lacked the patience for heavy makeup, except for special events.

Putting on my big sunshade, I almost don't recognize myself in the mirror. That's the purpose, anyway.

I grab my handbag and head for the door.

Opening the door, I see Sade at the front desk laying her head on the desk. From the way her shoulders are moving, I know she's crying, whimpering like a wounded animal. I've shed enough tears to last me a lifetime; so much so that I don't care if anyone decides to cry herself to death.

"Sade," I call out.

She lifts her head up. Very quickly, she wipes her tears

and jumps to her feet. "Yes, ma'am."

"I'm out for the day. Reschedule everything else I have today to tomorrow."

"Yes, ma'am," she says. A tear betrays her and slides down her cheek. She quickly wipes it off.

"Our lawyers are meeting with the lawyers from Cashmit PLC. Tell them to close the deal today. And let me have the report first thing tomorrow morning."

"Yes, ma'am," she replies.

I begin to walk away until I hear her say, "Have a good one, ma'am."

"Thanks," I reply and turn to her. "And it's unprofessional to cry at your workplace. If you still want your job, cry in your bedroom."

That's what I do.

She nods.

And then I walk away.

****

At my therapist's office, I sit opposite her.

Dr. Lara is everything I'm not. She's nice, smiles more than a thousand times every day, and goes out of her way to please people. And much more, she's beautiful and sexy. Her skirt is never beyond her knees, as she likes to show off those appealing thighs. Her blazers are always very tight, squeezing her boobs and showing cleavage.

Without being told, I know she's a very sexual person.

I don't know her full story, but I'd do anything to exchange lives with her. Every time I see her, she reminds me of what I would have grown up to be if my teenage years weren't marked by intense darkness.

"Let me guess, Miki," she says with her overly monotone yet feminine voice. "You still don't want people to know you're seeing a psychiatrist?"

I remove my sunshade and smile. "Yes."

"You know, not everyone who talks to a psychiatrist is insane."

"Well, we might not all be insane to the point of walking naked on the street of Abuja, but seeing a psychiatrist? People know your mind is sick. I accept that, but I like to keep my private affaire private."

She looks at me, eyes narrowed. "Your mind is not sick, Miki," she says softly. "You've just been through too much, more than what anyone should have to go through."

It's moments like this that make me like Dr. Lara. I never told her about the darkness that haunted me, but still she's the only person who has come close to understanding me and my ailment.

I nod and she withdraws her gaze. Opening a drawer, she brings out a paper and gives it to me. "Fill out the form, please."

Dropping my purse on the floor beside me, I take the form from her. It's a questionnaire that I answer at all my sessions. It has simple questions like Do you sleep well? Do you drink alcohol? Do you eat regularly? They're all questions I don't have to lie about.

I answer the questions as fast as I can and give it back to her. She reads through it very quickly and smiles. "Looks like you're doing okay."

I nod and smile back.

I usually don't smile this much, but her smiles are infectious.

She relaxes her back on the chair. "So, tell me, what's new? Any improvement?"

"Yes," I say, more than anxious to tell her about my improvement. "I saw a penis. And I smiled."

Dr. Lara sits up and rests her hands on the table. "Really?"

"Yes, really. I saw a penis, and I love it. I didn't panic, I didn't scream. I smiled."

Right now, my therapist and I seem like 16-year-old girls discussing their boyfriends. She smiles genuinely at me and appears very interested in what I have to say. "Tell me more."

I rest my hand on the table, too. "Okay. So Vince and I were texting back and forth. And then we get a little dirty and then he sent me a picture of his penis."

The smiles and the excitement on her face disappear as quickly as possible. She relaxes her back again on the chair. For one long second, she says nothing. Finally, she looks at me again and says; "Miki, you do know a reaction to a picture is always different?"

"I know... but..."

She cuts me off. "Miki, I'm telling you the first thing you need to do is to fix your relationship with people. Trust people. Be nice. Love people. And the rest will come. You will find it very easy to make body contact with others."

Her words make my heart—the one I didn't know I had—hurt. "How can you even ask me to trust anyone after everything I've been through? After all the pain I've had? My childhood was taken away from me. I was just a child... and..." I stop and struggle with tears for a second. "I've lost everything. Everything was taken from me. I was just a child... I was..."

I stop talking and glance away.

"Please, continue. I'm listening."

Still, I'm quiet. I hurt. My life has been like this; every bit of it a daily fight. I fight with myself, and the hatred I feel toward people. I fight the darkness that is spreading over me. I know I'm a strong person. I'm strong, but I've got too much baggage from the past.

"Miki," Dr. Lara says, "we've been having this session for how long now? Almost two years if I'm correct. And you've not opened up to me about the past that made you into this."

Still, I remain quiet.

She continues. "I can't make you tell me. You have to be ready. But I want you to know things will get better if you trust one person with your past—and it doesn't have to be me."

Her words get to me, but...

"Miki," she calls again, her voice laced with worry and concern, "I know you're sick. But your sickness started because you shut down your feelings and stopped relating with people. To fix your sickness, you've got to fix the real problem."

I'm frozen, staring at her without saying one word.

"You know this is therapy. You're supposed to be talking with me."

"I don't know what to say," I reply. It's the truth. I don't want to talk about my past. And since talking about it is what she needs me to do right now, it means there's nothing left for me to say.

"Tell me more about the man you're seeing now."

"Vincent?" I ask.

She smiles at my enthusiasm. "That's his name?"

I smile back. Now I won't stop talking. She has chosen the one topic I love to talk about.

Chapter Four

Vincent Ali

I still can't believe I canceled lunch with my girl. It's just that this client shows up at the last minute and I can't just turn her away. It's not as if I rate my clients over my girl. Hell, I can never do that. I can never rate anyone above my Miki.

She means the world to me. I love her more than words can explain. What I feel for her is genuine and completely different from anything I've ever felt with any woman. I've loved once before, but death took her from me several years ago.

After I lost her, I became a shadow of myself. My life went downhill. I drank from one bar to the other, fucking whores in every club around the street of Abuja. I was like that for several months. As time passed, I knew I had to get my act together and be strong for my little daughter. I stopped drinking, but I didn't stop fucking any available pussy—until I met Miki.

From the first moment I laid my eyes on her in that conference room, I knew she was it. I knew I'd found love again. This time, the love is more intense than anything I had ever felt. You know, when you love so much it feels like your heart is going to explode. That's exactly the way I feel about Miki.

I met her to discuss my client. She was taking over my client's company. She came into the conference room that morning bitching at me, angry that I had changed the terms of an agreement she had made with my clients earlier on.

From that very moment, even though she was raging as hell, my heart went out to her and I couldn't take my eyes off her. She was the most beautiful woman I had ever seen. And no, it's not just her pussy or her boobs that I wanted because she wasn't even flaunting any of it. She was professionally dressed and covered up, but, it only takes a man like me an instant to see the beauty behind it all.

She's a small woman, about five feet five inches. She's a slim and slightly curvaceous woman. Her boobs are well-rounded above a tiny waist and her ass, well, my dick hardens every time I see that ass. Her dark skin is beautiful and her smiles lights me up inside. She's the only person capable of that.

I chased her for several months, trying to make her mine, only to discover that she's a coldhearted bitch who barely acknowledged that I existed, let alone accepted me into her life. Bitch or no bitch, I love her like that. I've heard people say a lot of shit about her, but I don't care. I fondly called her Ice. Even with her terrible attitude, she is flawless to me. She is perfect for me and I love her like that, just the way she is.

It's only been three months since she gave me a chance, and the last thing I want is to screw that up. So believe me when I say I can't rate a client above my girl. I really can't.

It's just that this client is different. She comes into my office, crying and explaining how her boss sexually abused her. There's no way in hell I can turn a blind eye to a case like that. I have a daughter, too, seven years old. And if any man ever tries that with her, I'll make sure he rots in prison—and then rots again in hell.

So I can't turn the client away. I have to at least help dry her tears.

But I'm trying to make it up to my girl. Immediately after I finish work, I drive to Tantalizer to pick up dinner for two. And then I head to Miki's apartment. She isn't home when I get there, but I know the passcode and let myself in.

I had everything all planned for this beautiful night. The best food, the prettiest rose petals covering the floor, the brightest candles lighting the room, and mood music set to her favorite song, Bruno Mars' *Just the Way You Are*.

I'm not doing this for my girl because I want anything in return. I'm doing this to put a smile on her face. She's an amazing woman, and she deserves every bit of happiness.

But I sure as hell won't mind getting laid tonight. Damn, I haven't had sex over the last several months. Miki said she wasn't ready for it, and I can't do it with anyone else. I guess that's the difference between me and any other man. It has to be Miki. There can be no one else.

****

Miki

I pull up in the parking lot and glance around only to discover that my mother's SUV is gone. I let out a breath of relief.

Thank the Lord the woman's gone.

I'm in no mood for her drama.

I walk into the building and take the elevator to my floor. When I get to the door, I type in my passcode and the door opens.

Walking into the room, I'm surprised at what I see. The only light illuminating my living room is from a candle at the center of a neatly set dining table. One of my favorite Bruno Mar's song is playing in the background.

Before I can say jack, Vince appears from the kitchen, walks over to me and gives me a hug. "Hey, baby."

I can't hug him back. I stand there, frozen.

He releases me from the hug and then glances around. "You like everything?"

Like? I love it.

No one has ever shown me this much attention before. I'm the girl who never received any Valentine's gift from a lover. I'm the girl who never felt loved for one second of my life. How can he even ask if I like this?

Tears lace my eyes and I'm short of words. I don't know what to say. I just throw myself in his arms. "Thank you," I say, resisting my sobs. "Thank you very much."

I don't say it to him, but the truth is I've never knew love like I know it with him. I know I'm going to tell him that one day.

He releases me from the hug and places a small kiss on my lips. "Go, baby. Take a shower and let's eat dinner."

I nod gently and walk very slowly toward my room. I can't help glancing back and staring at him every now and then. He stands there watching me as I leave, a proud smile on his terribly handsome face.

I go into the bathroom and have the quickest shower of my life. Still in my lovey-dovey mood, I rush back to join Vince for dinner.

His suit jacket and tie lie somewhere on my couch, and his blue shirt, slightly unbuttoned, reveals the muscles of his chest. It's been three months since we started seeing each other and I haven't seen him like this before. We haven't been this intimate before because I always avoid it. But this night... avoiding it is not on my mind. I want more.

Vince pulls the chair for me and I sit. "So, what are we eating?"

Opening the plates, he flashes me a smile that pulls at the depth of my heart. "Jollof rice and fried chicken."

He serves my meal before taking a seat opposite me and serving himself. I grab my spoon and take my first bite. "Hmmm.... delicious."

"I'm happy you like it, but I didn't cook it. I bought it at Tantalizer."

"Still, the intention is delicious." I smile and wink at him.

He winks back, his wink a lot sexier than mine.

"So, how was work today?" he asks after a brief moment of silence.

I drop my fork and glance at him, excitement written all over my face. "I closed the deal. I bought Cashmit PLC today."

"Wow! Congratulations, baby." He grabs the bottle of red wine on the table. "Let's drink to it."

He opens the bottle, grabs a glass, and pours one for me and one for himself. And then he raises his glass as I raise mine. "To my baby, for her success today."

Glasses clink and I drink mine with one gulp. "What percent alcohol is this?"

He gives me a side glance. "About 13%. Why do you ask?"

"That's a lot. Are you planning to get me drunk to-night?"

"No, I don't want you to get drunk," he replies.

"Why?" I ask.

"Why?" he asks again, the barest hint of a smile playing at the corner of his mouth. "Because if you're drunk, I might take advantage of you."

I laugh, reach over, and smack him on the arm. "That's sexual assault."

He laughs. "I know. I'm the lawyer here, remember?"

"Speaking of which," I say, swiftly changing the subject. "How was work?"

"No, don't ask about my job." He grabs his cup of wine and drinks. "Unless, of course, you don't mind talking about murders, crime, and shit for the rest of the night."

I shake my head. "I don't want to talk about crimes."

With that, I begin to eat my food. A few seconds later, I raise my head and look at him. "Still, Vince, I don't under-stand what you do. I thought you are a corporate lawyer, not a criminal lawyer. When we met, your firm was repre-senting a company I bought."

He finishes chewing before he starts. "My firm has some kind of incentive program where clients pay every month whether they have a case or a need for a lawyer. At any point in time, if they have a need for a lawyer, maybe for divorce, crime, business or anything, my firm repre-sents them. That's because we carry all kinds of lawyers. It's a large firm."

"Okay. Maybe Daniels Group and I can get on the incen-tive program, too. What do you think?"

He leans in a little bit, offering me a better view of his slightly haired, muscled chest. "It's my job to defend you whether or not you join my incentive program. I will defend you."

"Really?"

He nods and continues to eat.

"That means you can't take any client that are an enemy of Daniels Group."

"That means I can't take any clients at all."

I cross my arm and scowl. "Meaning?"

He gives me a sarcastic smile. "Everybody is against Daniels Group. In case you don't know, a lot of people don't like you. Why do you think I call you Ice?"

I close my eyes and grimace as if in pain. "Ouch! That hurts."

"I meant that in a good way."

"You're the only one who can turn an insult into a compliment. But..." I say as I try to flash him one of my cute smiles, "...I don't care if people don't like me, as long as you like me. You're enough for me."

He keeps staring at me as if there's a lot of a feeling bubbling inside him right now. I think again about what I said. *You're enough for me.*

That's about the nicest thing I ever said to anyone.

Anyway, Vince keeps staring at me, his gaze starting a spark, maybe even a fire, inside of me. "I'm made to be enough for you," he finally says, his lips curling into a sly smile.

After we finish eating, Vince takes me by the wrist and leads me to the living room. And then he goes back to the dining table and pours more wine.

Holding out a glass of wine for me, he says, "Drink up, baby."

I hesitate. "Vince..."

"Come on," he says, and in a twinkling of an eye, his glass is empty.

Like him, I gulp my wine and empty my glass. I feel kind of dizzy, like I have to pee, as if the whole drink went straight down there and threatens to burst my bladder. But I'm sure that's how people feel when they drink, right?

I've never had this much wine before. You may begin to wonder what I did as a teenager. Yeah, I never had any fun.

Vince pours another drink, but he doesn't give it to me. He sets it on the table and then walks slowly over to my CD player. He puts in a disc which I'm absolutely certain does not belong to me. He must have brought it with him.

Damn! The man was well-prepared for this night.

Picking up the remote control, he walks back to me, smiling. "You ready to show me all your dance moves?"

My heart caught in my chest.

I don't dance. That's just not me. Even when I go to church and everybody is happy dancing, I just try to move my body back and forth so I don't seem like a tree planted in the center of the pews.

I roll my eyes at Vince. "We can't play loud music up in here..."

That's me giving excuses.

Before I finish, he cuts me off. "I'm sure your neighbors won't mind."

"Vince... we both have work tomorrow."

"Good thing we're the boss. We can go to work any-time. Or we could just boycott work tomorrow."

My heart speeds up. I'm as nervous as a schoolgirl about to recite a poem in front of a crowd for the first time. "Vince..." I press on, trying to convince him to stop this before it becomes a disaster.

"Oh! Come on, Miki, live a little," he says as he leans in closer. "You have everything. A good job, a good family, and a man who loves you more than anything. You're an impressive woman. You're beautiful, charming, smart, capable."

He's looking deep into my eyes as he says all these things. His words, plus the remnant of his masculine co-logne, is making my head swim...

"All these things are worth celebrating. So, relax, and have some fun."

Grabbing his glass, he finishes the wine he had previously poured, takes the remote control and in a split second, my speakers are blasting at full volume. The song playing is Dbanj's *Oliver Twist*. That song is irresistible; it topped the UK Singles Chart for several weeks.

"Vince!" I'm shouting now, trying desperately to be heard above the loud music.

He takes two steps back with a smooth dance move, and then touches his ears to gesture he can't hear me over the music. I need not be told he's only pretending not to hear me.

I laugh as I watch him do the *Oliver Twist* dance moves. Like I said, I'm not much of a dancer but I've seen little kids dance to that move.

"You're a bore!" he says, and with that, he breaks into a huge laugh.

I snap up straight, totally jerk out of my own skin. "What?! I am not!"

Actually, I'm kind of a bore, but I'm not about to admit that to him. I'm capable of fun, too.

I drink my share of the wine he previously poured, and then drop my glass on the table. I can't explain how, but I know I step back and do my *Oliver Twist* dance move, laughing hard as I do.

Vince laughs and cheers me on.

And I do it again. And again. And then again.

Gosh! I can't believe how free-spirited I feel right now. I feel light, as if the weight of the world has just been lifted from my shoulders.

Vince moves closer to me, his hands on my waist as we laugh, dancing easily together with no boundaries, no embarrassment.

And that's me having the most fun of my life.

Chapter Five

Vince

I swear I've never seen my baby have this much fun. Hell, I'm sure she hasn't even had this much fun in her entire life.

I thought a little bit of alcohol and attention could help her lighten up and it worked.

She's laughing hard and dancing hard. I wish she could see herself right now.

My Miki might be uptight and maybe a little bit cold, but behind that steely mask she wears daily is another soft, kind, innocent woman who is just wishing to get some love.

I really do wish she could see herself right now. I wish I had a secret camera pre-installed somewhere in this house to catch this moment. I know some moments like this are better if it's just a memory, but I'd like to remember it forever. It arouses more cravings for it.

I'm not keeping track of time, and I don't know how long we've been dancing. All I know is my baby is tired and should be going to bed soon. She's wearing a pitch-color nightie, made from that soft, silky, transparent fabric that women like to wear.

The whole night has been torture for me as I can't help staring at her firm breasts in that see-through nightie she's wearing. And now, as she collapses into my arms, her breasts rubbing against my bare chest, my dick turns to stone.

I feel my hard-self touching her. She probably feels it, too, because she draws slightly back and looks me in the eye.

I don't shy away from her gaze. I stare into her big brown eyes. I let her see my true feelings—no teases, no playful flirtations—just a true, hungry desire. I want her. More than I've ever wanted any woman my whole life.

I lean in, still staring at her. She's holding her breath.

And I like it.

I slowly hold her face in my palm. I can feel her whole body trembling beneath my touch.

Damn! That turns me on.

I lean in closer and kiss her.

Her lips are so soft. And GOD, she tastes sweet. So sweet I want to taste her all over, find out if the whole of her is that soft and sweet.

I hold her tightly in my arms. And then I begin to kiss her everywhere. Her cheek... her chin... and then I grab her hair, gently pull her head back and place hot, wet kisses at the hollow of her neck.

Her whole body shivers.

Slowly, she opens her mouth to me and I conquer her lips with a kiss... so soft... so sweet. Her lips are full. I feel as if those lips are made for me, made to kiss only me.

Just as I'm about to tilt my head and deepen our kiss even more, she surprises the hell out of me.

Arms wrap around my neck, she pulls my face down to hers and completely takes over the kiss. More aggressive... more sensual... as she moans right into my mouth.

Fuck, that move drove me wild.

It's one of the biggest turn-ons I've ever experienced in my whole damn life.

Just as her aggression increases, mine increases.

I lower my hands and feel her curves and my hands slides to her ass— GOD what an ass! My imagination runs wild, and I swear I feel my temperature rising now, more than ever.

I grab her ass in my hand and force her against me, pressing her hard against my dick, which is now harder than ever.

Ever so gently, her hands go down below my belt... and she begins to caress me.

Oh, fuck...

She keeps tracing her fingers around my dick, sweat greasing her palm as she presses it against my dick as if she wants to feel it, hold it, caress it.

Her hands feel amazingly soft on my hardness.

I moan.

I sure as hell haven't felt this way in a long time.

The whores I've been fucking have never been this passionate. They're much more interested in my money than my desires.

I put both my hands on her ass, lift her up, and place her on the couch.

****

Miki

I don't know how long I've been dancing, but I know I'm tired as I collapse into his arms. I'm fully relaxed until I feel this hard pressure between his legs, between me and him. He has to be aroused. That's the only explanation.

I pull away a little and look at him to check if I'm right.

And I'm damn right.

When I look into his eyes, I see the fire of unstoppable desire burning in there. He leans in and I hold my breath.

He holds my face in his palm.

His touch makes my whole body quiver.

And then he leans closer and kisses me in a way I've never been kissed before. Hell, I've never been kissed before.

His lips press against mine, firm but gentle.

Gentle, but all consuming.

He holds me tightly in his arms, crushes me against him. And then he begins to kiss me everywhere. My cheek, my neck... and then he grabs my hair, gently pulling my head back and placing hot, wet kisses at the hollow of my neck.

My whole body shivers with raging desire.

I know I should be scared, but I'm not. I've had sex with countless men. But Dr. Lara told me what they did to me was not sex. It was an act of violence. She said sex with someone you love doesn't hurt. It feels good, better than anything you've ever felt. For some reason, I know Vince is the man who is going to show me exactly what feeling good means.

His kisses on my neck send me over the cliff. I don't know how, but I open my mouth to him, taking over the kiss. My hands are all over him, from around his neck down to his chest and then to his back. God, his body is hot, sexy, firm, and strong.

His hands move quickly around my waist, and then he grabs my ass, squeezing it and pressing me against his dick.

I feel something hot but wet between my legs. Lord help me, my panties must be soaked by now. I'm soooo fucking wet.

My hand moves slowly down below his belt, where I let my fingers play with the very hard, very long thing hiding under his pants.

I want to remove his pants. I want to hold him. I want to feel him grow bigger and harder in my hand.

I'm so turned on, my legs grow weak. I can barely stand, his strong arms all that are keeping me up.

Just in time, with both of his hands, he grabs my ass, lifts me up, and places me on the couch, towering over me.

And then in a split second, everything changes for me. Maybe it's the way he is right above me that triggers it, I don't know. All I know is that my heartbeat begins to sky-rocket.

I'm sweating.

I'm shaking.

I can't breathe.

"Miki,"

I'm hearing my name, but I don't know who is calling.

I'm trembling.

My eyes are closed; I can't see anything.

But I can feel the pain. I can feel the metal cutting into my flesh. I can feel blood crawling out of my lady part.

"Miki," Once again, I hear my name.

"Leave me alone," I manage to say.

Despite the blood flowing, I can feel him pounding his dick up into my hole. Another one deep down my throat, so deep I can't breathe.

I open my mouth, coughing, trying desperately to catch my breath.

And when I do, my eyes focus on Vince.

"Get out!" My voice is harder than I intend it to be.

"Miki…"

"Get out!"

I can't let him see me like this.

"Did I do something wrong?" he asks, my heart tightens at the innocent, confused look on his face.

But I can't stand for him to see me like this.

I push him off me and shove him toward the door.

I open the door. "Leave!"

"Miki…"

"Get out!" I say before slamming the door in his face.

And then I break into a loud sob as my butt hits the floor and my back rests on the door. My heart aches too much.

I'm still trembling. Dr. Lara was right. I'm not ready for this.

I thought I was ready. I was doing okay for the first few minutes of our make-out. His touch felt so good I thought I was in paradise.

But it turns out I'm not ready. And maybe I'm never going to be ready.

More than that, though, I feel more pain now that I've lost Vince. He's never going to see me again. What kind of man wants to be with a woman like me? I've been alone since I can remember, and I'm going to be alone forever.

Chapter Six

Miki

I wake up this morning to a headache that threatens to split my skull in two. My stomach feels very uneasy, mostly from the excessive alcohol I had last night.

My whole body aches and that's probably because I didn't sleep on my soft bed. I slept on the hard floor. I cried myself to sleep on the floor by the door where I threw Vince out of my house.

I raise my eyes and look at the wall clock. It's 11:00am. My God! I can't believe I slept for so long.

I rush to the bathroom. It feels as if my bladder is going to burst. I pee very quickly, and then take a quick shower.

After dressing as fast as I can, I move to the kitchen to make some coffee. That's all I can take right now. My stomach has been acting funny since I woke up this morning. Not just my stomach, but my brain is acting funny. I'm afraid I'm not going to see Vincent again. He hasn't called or texted me this morning. What did I expect? Call me after the way I treated him last night? Somewhere in my heart, I'm hoping he does. I'm hoping he doesn't leave me. I'm hoping he sticks with me through it all. Because, honestly, he's all I've got. I'm scared of being lonely. I'm scared I'll go blind with me soaking my pillows with tears every night. I'm scared I might die of heartbreak because this heart of mine can't handle any more pain. It has endured too much hardship and can bear no more.

As I sit to take my coffee, I pick up my phone and try to call him.

I get no response.

My heart is beating really fast, afraid that I am right: Vince is done with me.

I call him about six more times. I know, it's too much but I can't just accept it that Vince won't give me a chance to explain. Not that I'm ready to tell him the truth to him anyway. I can't. If he learns the truth, he sure as hell will dump me. No man can be with a woman like me.

But still...

I want Vince. I call him two more times. And then I decide to send him a text.

Me: Vince, please, pick up. I'm sorry about last night. I'm sorry. Please, talk to me.

There's no way I'm sending that text. I need not be sorry for anything. I'm not the first girl to push a guy while making out with him. It happens. So I need not be sorry. I'm just going to send him a text, pretend as if nothing happened last night.

I delete the first text and write another one.

Me: Good morning. How u doing? I called u several times but u didn't pick. I'm worried about u. U okay?

I read it again and decide I like this text better. That sounds more like me, more like Miki Daniels. I send the text to Vince.

With that I know I'm back to being me. I've just shut down that needy, desperate, lovey-dovey mood I've been in since last night.

I act tough, but I'm miserable.

Even worse this morning, I'm angry. I pity a lot of my employees who are going to get fired today. I'm angry that my life is miserable. And who says I should be the only miserable person in the world?

I finish my coffee, throw my cup in the sink, and then rush to work.

It's well past noon when I get there.

"Good afternoon, ma'am," Sade greets me with a very bright smile, but I ignore her.

"What do I have today?" I say as I push open the door to my office.

Very quickly, she follows me into my office and hands me a bunch of folders. "Report from the buyout of Cashmit PLC," she begins. "I've sent copies to your email, but printed it out just in case you want a hard copy for recordkeeping. Also, you're supposed to have a meeting with our pasta production company today at 10:00am. They've been waiting for you."

"Reschedule the meeting. Tell them to come back tomorrow. What else?"

I can tell Sade knows I'm in a bad mood. She's shaking now.

I don't want people to be afraid of me. I just want to be able to vent all this anger I'm feeling inside. It's not as if I exactly love to ruin other people's lives, I just have too many emotions bottled up inside of me and...

I need to stop psychoanalyzing myself and listen to Sade.

"Umm..." she stutters, her voice shaking. "You're conducting an interview today."

"What interview?"

"To hire a new computer analyst. You fired the old one, ma'am."

"I know. Let me have her files and send in the applicant."

She gives me another folder and then hurries out of my office. Sitting down on my luxurious and comfortable armchair, I take off my heels and cross those beautiful legs of mine. I begin to read through the programmer's application and I'm impressed. It appears she knows the job. I just hope she's able to impress me in person.

After a slight knock on my door, it opens, and in walks the applicant. She's almost as tall as me. She's beautiful. She's neat. But she's nervous as hell.

She bows slightly. "Afternoon, ma'am."

"Take a seat," I reply.

She sits on the armchair opposite me. "I was told my interview is at 9:00a.m. I've been waiting for more than three hours."

She's nervous and she still stands up for herself. Good. But today is not a good day to mess with me. Not when I haven't heard from Vince, try as I might.

I rest my elbow on the table and look straight at her. "Your name is Titi Idris, correct?"

She nods her head.

"Look, Miss Idris, this is the working condition of Daniels Group. I say sit, you sit. I say stand, you stand. I say jump, you ask how high. I make changes to work at the last minute. I make employees work late sometimes. I'm a very busy person, so people wait for me a lot of the time and I don't apologize for it. You won't like me, and I don't expect you to like me. But as long as you do your job well, we'll be alright. So, do you still want this interview?"

"Yes, ma'am," she says.

"Good," I reply and relax my back on the chair. "Now, I've read through your files and I'm impressed. You graduated the best student in computer science at the University of Lagos. And you've worked for so many big companies. But you got fired at your last job. Why?"

"I wasn't fired. You bought the company and lay off some workers. You said you didn't have a need for us. I'm one of those workers."

"Really?"

"Yes, ma'am."

I read the documents again. Now, I remember. I actually did buy the company she used to work for. The company was running at a loss. They were spending far more than they were taking in. I bought the company and made the big decision they couldn't make. I cut down the expenses, which meant some workers had to go.

"Okay. Like I said, I'm impressed. You're good, and it looks like you know the job. But give me two reasons why I should hire you."

"Two reasons?" she asks again.

"Yes, two reasons."

She's quiet for the next few seconds, probably thinking of the best answer.

"The first reason you should hire me, I'm the best computer analyst..."

I cut her off. "No, you're not the best. I admit you're good, but if I continue to look, I'm sure I'll find someone way better than you."

She's quiet for another long second. Her hands are sweaty. She's shaking and I can see movement on her neck that tells me she's swallowing hard. God, I didn't mean to put her on a hot seat. I just want to know she's able to take all the pressure that comes with working for me.

"Please, I need this job," she begs.

And I don't want her to beg.

"It's been four months since I lost my last job and it's been hard..."

She suddenly stops talking. I don't know why until I hear the tone from her phone. Her phone is ringing.

Damn. People can be funny sometimes. Can she not switch of or silence her phone for just a few minutes during this interview?

She takes a brief look at her phone. "I'm sorry," she says as she drops the call. "As I was saying, the situation in the country is hard. It's hard for me to get a job. It's hard for anyone, no matter how intelligent. It's hard out there."

Her phone rings again and she stops talking to take a brief look at her phone.

"You know what?" I say, getting irritated. "Just go ahead and pick up the call."

"I can?" she asks.

I nod yes.

Smiling, she takes the call. "Hello? I'm sorry, the interview started later than I expected. Please, can you watch her a little bit more? ...Just thirty minutes... Please...I promise I'll be back soon. Okay, thanks."

With that, she hangs up and glances at me. "It's my nanny. I'm supposed to have returned home to get my kid by now. I'm a single mom. I have a one-year old who is depending on me. That's why I need this job."

"You have a baby?"

She stares on, confused about why I'm asking her. "Yes."

I wish she hadn't said that.

"I'm sorry, Miss Idris, I can't hire you."

I can see the disappointment and the sadness on her face and my heart breaks. "Why?" she asks.

"Your life is in a mess. You can't work late into the night because you have a child to return to. Your nanny might screw you over sometimes and you might not be able to work. Your child will need your attention, and I believe you should give it to her. I can't hire you."

"You can't hire me because I have a baby?"

"No. Because you're not organized. It seems you can't handle raising a child and having a demanding job."

She stares on, shakes her head in disbelief. "How can you even say that? Don't you have a child?"

"I can't have children," I reply with no hard feelings.

Tears lace her eyes. "I see why God didn't give children to a person like you."

She stands up and leaves, shutting the door loudly behind her.

She can think whatever she likes about me. She can say whatever she wants. I can't have a baby. Years ago, after some terrible events happened to me, I was down with a terrible, infectious disease that affected my ovaries. It was causing me so much pain the doctors had to shut down my ovaries to save my life.

So now, I'm twenty-nine years old and I'm at menopause already. And if I remember very well, I was about twenty-two years old when the doctors had to force me into menopause to save my life. I can't have a baby, but that's not my greatest nightmare. That's not even the secret I dread revealing. Being a mother isn't on the top of my list. I don't want to fail my child like my parents failed me.

One hour later

I can't eat anything because I still have a roller coaster in my stomach, but I'm hungry as hell. I didn't even have much to drink last night, so I wonder why I feel terrible.

It's been one hour since I got to work. My mind goes back to Vince, not that he ever left my mind anyway. I grab my phone and check if he's called or texted me back.

Nothing. It's after 1:00p.m and he hasn't called me. This is it. Vince is going to leave me.

He will leave me if I do nothing. And I can't let that happen.

He's all I've got. Without him, I'll be lonely. And I'm scared of lonely.

I pick up my phone and call him again.

Answer the damn phone!

A few seconds later, my phone signals that I have a text from Vince. Hurriedly, my heart beating real fast, I read it.

Vince: Stop calling my phone!

It feels as if my heart just stopped beating. To be honest, I don't exactly know what I'm feeling right now. I'm not expecting Vince to be nice, but I'm not expecting him to be such a big asshole.

****

Vince

I park my Bentley in the parking lot of Daniels Group. If you ask me, I don't know exactly what I'm doing here right now. I'm angry as hell, and my brow is all wrinkled up in a big frown. Yet I can't seem to stop myself from caring for her. She had more to drink last night than she ever had in her life. Maybe she had a slight headache or troubles with her stomach. It's my fault she had that much to drink. I have to fix it.

I walk into the office building and then to her office. Sitting at the entrance is Sade, Miki's personal assistant.

"Hi, Sade," I greet her casually.

"Afternoon, sir," she replies, and from the expression on her face, I know she's surprised by the frown I'm wearing on my face. "You don't look fine, Mr. Ali. Is everything alright with you?"

I nod. "Is she in?"

"She's in, but she's in a bad mood. Let me check with her..."

I cut her off. "Don't worry."

I walk past her and push the door open. And right in front of me sits Miki in her huge, black, luxurious armchair. Her office is painted white, with a floor covered in red carpet, a tall refrigerator at the far right of the room and a large couch.

"How dare she let you in without my permission?" she asks, her voice hard as hell. My last text must have angered her. Still, if I can brush my own anger aside and come for her, she better be ready to suck up hers.

"That girl is fired." she continues. "Sade! Sade!"

"Leave the girl out of this."

She stands on her feet, confronting me. "What do you want?" Her voice is as cold as ice and I can tell she's angry as hell.

"Come with me," I respond without betraying any emotion.

"What?"

Hell! I don't have time for her questions. I have so much work on my desk that it was hard to even gain these few minutes. Walking over to her side, I grab her wrist and drag her along.

"What? Where?"

I notice she looks a little shorter than she usually is and I glance down at her. Oh! She took off her heels. I let go of her and go back to her chair to grab her shoes. And then I walk back to where she's standing. Getting on my knees, I lift her foot and begin to fit it in the shoe.

"What...?"

I cut her off. "Shut up!"

She's gazing at me, confused. I look back at her, and even though I'm furious, holding her, touching her skin like this makes me feel so... much calmer, so much more re-lieved. She's like the river that calms my soul. She's a for-tress, and now I'm angry that she means all that to me even when I mean nothing to her.

I'm done putting on her shoes for her, and I rise to my feet. She must have noticed I'm not in a good mood be-cause she's suddenly gone silent. And I can tell she's dying to understand me right now, but I'm in no mood to talk a lot.

Again I grab her wrist and drag her from her office down to the parking lot. When we reach my car, I let go of her, open the front passenger's seat and gesture for to get in.

She refuses to get in. Instead she folds her arms across her chest and gives me that attitude.

"Get in!" I yell.

She shivers and jumps into the car.

Hell. I didn't mean to raise my voice at her, but for once she can just be quiet and do as I say.

I slip into the driver seat and drive off.

About three minutes later, I park in front of the Mama Pot Restaurant.

Mama Pot makes the best pepper soup in Abuja. I visit her once in a while if I have too much drink. Her pepper soup always calms my stomach, cures my hangover.

I glance over at Miki and gesture her to get out of the car, which she does. Quietly, no questions asked, she fol-lows me into the restaurant.

I pull out a chair for her and then order one bowl of soup.

"Eat the soup. It will help your stomach." And that's all I can say as I sit opposite her, watching her slowly devour the soup.

****

Miki

I eat the pepper soup in silence. Once in a while, I'll take a random look at Vince and every time our eyes meet. He's staring at me. My heart is beating fast. I've never seen him this angry. I've never been this afraid, been this quiet, and let someone else take the lead.

But it's not his anger that keeps me quiet. It's the fact that he still cares. Yes, he's angry, but despite that, he's still worried about my well-being because I had a lot to drink the night before.

As we drive back to the office, he's quiet, and I am, too. But as I stare at him, I can see the hurt behind the anger on his face. I can see the way he keeps swallowing hard, as if he could swallow all the emotions building up inside him.

"Vince," I finally gather the courage to say something, "I've called your phone about one thousand times since yesterday. I texted you and..."

He cuts me off. "Don't talk about that," he says without taking his gaze off the road.

I can feel the silence tearing us apart and it feels as if something is tearing my very heart from my body, as if something is pulling my soul away.

"Vince," I press on, touching his shoulder.

Before I can say more, his palm becomes a fist and he hits the staring wheel. "Dammit!"

The next second, he's swerving off the road and parking the car.

"What are you doing?" I just had to ask.

He opens the car door. "Giving you time and space."

Without giving it much thought, I open the passenger's door and run after him as he walks to a quiet, small park across the road. "What is wrong with you?"

He makes an abrupt stop and glares at me. "What is wrong...?" He looks as if he wants to say something, but then he changes his mind. "Nothing is wrong with me."

He continues to walk.

I run after him. "You're angry because I pushed you away last night."

He stops and looks at me again, still giving me a glare. "No, I'm angry about the way you did it."

Confused, I raise a brow. "How?"

"You could have told me to stop. I would have stopped. I would have understood. But instead you pushed me away, pushed me out of your house in the deep of the night. And you know so well how dangerous this city can be at night. I was outside your house for more than an hour. I left my car keys in your house. Thank goodness, I had my cell phone. That's how I called a taxi. Who knows what would have happened to me by now? Hell, I could have been kidnapped or shot dead."

My God! How can I be so cruel? When I pushed him out, I was thinking about myself. I didn't think about him, I didn't think about the consequences of my action. I only think about me, my problems, my pains, my tears, my job... just me, me, me!

I walk closer to him, try to touch him. "Vince."

He draws back slightly, avoiding my touch.

He won't even let me touch him. I can see the signs. Vince is going to leave me. I didn't exactly know how much he means to me until I'm about to lose him.

"You don't get it, Miki. I used to find your 'I don't care' attitude very attractive. But now I realize I can't be with a woman who doesn't care about my life, who doesn't think twice about risking my life."

Hearing that, my heart breaks into a million pieces as tears lace my eyes. "But I care, Vince."

He shakes his head. "No, you don't."

On a second thought, maybe he's leaving me because I refused him sex and all of his big talk is just a flimsy excuses to leave me. I want to be sure. So I shrug and say, "You're not leaving me because I pushed you out. You're leaving me because I haven't let you get into my pants since we started this relationship. Is sex all you want me for?"

Oh, no. I wish I hadn't said that.

He's so surprise he shuts his eyes for one long second. When he opens them, the anger in them is gone. Everything in those eyes is just pure hurt.

"How dare...?" He stops talking and lets out a deep breath. "Do you even know I love you?"

"Vince..."

He cuts me off. "Do you even know how it feels to love you?" he asks, almost yelling with tears in his voice. "I love you so much it feels as if my heart is going to explode. So much it feels every bone in my body is going to break if I don't hold you in my arms. It feels like a part of me dies every second I go without you. You're my life support; I can't even breathe without you. I'll do anything for you, Miki. I'll dry your tears. I'll fight for you. Hell, I'll even give my life for you, but you feel nothing for me."

He stares at me earnestly, tears in his eyes. I've never heard anything so beautiful in my life.

Tears flooding my face, I just want to run into his arms. But I can't. I'm afraid. "Vince... I feel something," I manage to say.

"No, you don't. You know how many times I've told you I love you. Your response is always me, too. You never say 'I love you' back. You never even show that you love me. It feels like I'm the one making all the effort here, and it gets tiring, Miki."

I stand still in front of him, shaking, tears running down my cheeks as my heart breaks over and over again. I want to say something, but I can't. I don't know what to say. My heart is too heavy for words.

But he's right. Every time he says he loves me, I see the sincerity in his eyes. I see that he means it. But... I never say I love you back. When I reply by saying "me, too", it feels as if I don't mean it. The feeling called love is so strange to me, and I fear I may never get to know it better.

Chapter Seven

Miki

"You were right. I'm not ready."

Dr. Lara leans forward and rests her hands on the desk, looking deep into my eyes. "I'm so sorry you had to find that out. Tell me, what happened?"

My eyes are looking at her, but I'm not really seeing her. My eyes are just staring into nothingness. "I lost him. I lost love."

"How? Tell me how it happened."

I don't know where to start, but the beginning is not an option. I decide to start with the one that's easiest to bear. "I came home that night to what seems like it's going to be the best night of my life. Vince made..." Tears fill my eyes, but I hold them back strongly. "He made everything perfect. Candle light, beautiful flowers, my favorite song, and a delicious dinner. Everything I've wanted—some love, some affection, he was willing to give it all, but..." Tears build up in my throat and I swallow hard to continue. "...I ruined everything."

Dr. Lara sits there looking at me, listening intently as I pour out my heart.

"When he touched me, his touch felt soooo good, like I was in paradise. But before I knew it, it felt like... it felt like years ago when..."

I stop talking. This is it. This is how far I can go before I start to speak about the beginning, how it all started. And I want to forget everything, never to speak of them again.

Dr. Lara takes a deep breath. "Miki, you know that whatever happened in the past stays in the past right? You can't change anything."

"Don't you think I know that?"

"You don't, because if you did you would move on and face the present and enjoy this good life you have."

My voice hardens. "I know, okay? I'm trying to move on. I'm trying to forget..."

She interrupts me. "You don't have to forget it. You have to move on from it, but you don't have to forget it. It's two different things. When you're ready to move on from your past, you share that past with people you love. You forgive the past and start a new beginning. Start from a new page."

"A new page?"

"Yes, a new page. What happened to you in the past is gone. It can't happen again."

My palm becomes a fist and hits the desk. "Oh, yes it can! He's still out there somewhere!"

Dr. Lara draws back slightly and narrows her gaze at me, her face all wrinkled together in worry and confusion. "My God. What did he do to you?"

I raise a brow. "What did who do to me?"

"You said he's still out there somewhere."

I didn't know I said that much.

"Miki, are you afraid someone who's hurt you before is going to come back and hurt you again?"

I seem not to have the right words to respond.

"He hurt you so bad, didn't he? So much that his existence still scares you to the bone. Your brain has re-created him in your mind, re-created his fear in your mind. You see him. You see him in every man you've ever met. That's what has been messing with your brain."

She looks absolutely certain about what she's saying.

"If you have it all figured out, can you at least prescribe me some medication to calm my nerves?" I ask.

She relaxes her back on her armchair and all the stress on her face suddenly disappear. "No. I'm not going to prescribe any meds."

"But why? All the psychiatrists I've seen in the past have all prescribed me some meds."

"And did it work?"

I didn't respond.

Standing up from the chair, she walks slowly toward a small refrigerator at the corner of her office. "Iced tea?" she offers.

"Yes, please."

She walks past my range of view, but I don't turn around to look at her. I can hear the opening and slamming shut of the refrigerator door. In a few minute, she walks over to my side and hands me a small mug.

"Thanks," I say as I take the mug from her.

Slowly she walks over and sits back on her armchair. I watch her sip her tea as I sip mine.

"So let's talk about Vincent," she says as we both set our cups on the table at almost the same time.

"Why?" I ask.

"Because you love him more than you think you do."

"How can you be so sure?" I give a small smirk. "I don't even know what love feels like."

She smiles, more like to herself than me. "We've been having this session for almost two years, Miki. And we've never gotten this far before. Within the last couple weeks, you've shown more emotions than ever. You've smiled. You've cried. Today, you even got angry, and something from your past slipped out of your mouth. Now the only thing that I'm sure brought these changes on is the appearance of this man in your life."

Her words sink my shoulder and make me feel tired from the inside. "He won't even talk to me anymore."

"Then talk with him."

Thinking about Vince easily brings tears to my eyes. I'm a strong woman. I know I am, but when it comes to Vince, I feel so weak, as if I won't survive one second without him. I have to swallow up these tears to keep them from running down my cheeks. "I can't talk to him. He said we're over. He said he used to find my 'I don't care' attitude very attractive, but not anymore. He said..."

"From my experience, he doesn't mean everything he said to you. I mean, from everything you told me about him, I can tell he cares about you. He probably said all that to get a reaction out of you."

"Really?"

"I think so. So go back and talk with him."

"Why should I go back to him? That would be selfish of me to go back. He has everything to offer. Love, affection... but I've got nothing to offer him. What do I do the next time he tries to... you know... share some intimacy with me..."

"That's why you should talk with him. Trust me, I'm sure he will understand. I don't expect you to throw all your past at him all at once—just embrace it as it comes."

"What if he tries to... you know..."

"Make love with you?"

I nod, my heart beating fast at the mere mention of it.

She smiles. "Tell him you want to take things slow. I don't think you're ready yet, but if it does happen, take a deep breath in and out, eyes closed. You're at the beach and the sand is soft. The ocean waves are small and make little noise. Remember, only the good memories and shut out the bad ones.

****

Kikiola Daniels

I've hired people to follow and watch my daughter, and I received the most shocking news of my life today. My daughter is seeing a psychiatrist. For what? Since when? I don't have all the facts, but I have to find out by any means necessary.

I'm driving toward the National Hospital. I'm going to talk to Dr. Lara, the doctor in charge of my daughter's case.

I know it's wrong for me to have my daughter followed. It's wrong for me to go into the hospital and ask questions. It may even seem like I'm a bad mother. But before you judge me, try to understand me.

I'm desperate. It's a desperate situation, and desperate situations demands desperate measures.

I've suffered like this for more than ten years. My daughter has tortured me for that long. I've watch her grow cold, with feelings for no one. I've tried reaching out to her in every possible way, but I can't. It's like she's in her own world and has shut everybody out. She's made it clear she doesn't want me interfering in her affairs, but I can't just let her be.

Miki used to be such a cheerful, lovely little kid. The last time I saw that little cheerful child was twenty-two years ago when she was seven.

As a seven-year old, Miki was bright, smart, and loved by everyone—and she loved everyone, too. And then she turned eight and everything changed. First, I noticed she stopped speaking with her daddy. When her dad was in the living room, she was in her bedroom. She started avoiding him. And then at sixteen, I totally lost that cheerful, bright child. She stopped talking to me. Not just me— she stopped talking to everyone. She stayed in her room all day, reading or listening to music. She had no one.

I tried to reach out to her, but she made it clear she wanted to be alone. I tried, God knows I tried. I can't count how many times I tried to talk to her, let her know she can talk to me, but she hated seeing me. You don't know how much I've suffered watching her like that. She's my only child. Her dad and I have tried our best to provide her the best things in life, and we don't deserve such treatment from her.

Her dad and I sent her off to the best private university in the country. She graduated and did a short internship at one of the best corporations around. We didn't hear from her for four months during the internship. The next time I saw Miki, the silent girl had changed. She was talking now, but too much. She had become brutally honest. She didn't mind looking people in the face and telling them how much she hated them. She didn't care about hurting people's feelings. She didn't care about destroying people's lives as long as it served her purpose. She's lost all compassion.

The only thing she cares about is Daniels Group. While I appreciate what she did for the company, I don't appreciate having an ice queen for a daughter.

She's alone, and I can't just sit here and do nothing. I want her to be happy. She's got a good job. She has money that can last her for the next three generations. She needs someone in her life. I mean, money isn't everything.

And now that I've been told that she's seeing a psychiatrist, I'm thinking she has a psychiatric condition I missed all this while. Were her mood swings as a child some kind of psychiatric condition? I don't know, but I need answers.

I park my SUV in front of the hospital and walk straight to the front desk.

"Hello, ma'am, how may I be of service?" the nurse sitting at the front desk asks.

"I'm here to see Dr. Lara."

"Do you have an appointment?"

"Yes," I reply.

"Let me see your ID."

I look into my Gucci purse and bring out my National ID card. She types my name into the computer in front of her. A few seconds later she gives me back my ID and a small paper. "Walk straight down, make a right, the last room to the left. Dr. Lara will be there to see you."

"Thanks."

As I walk down the hallway, my heart is beating fast. I don't know what to expect. I pray my daughter's condition is not something very terrible.

I open the door and see Dr. Lara sitting in the center of the room. She looks like a woman in her early forties, and she looks like she's a nice woman.

"Please, come in," she says with a beautiful smile. She's very friendly, too. For a moment, I'm happy my daughter is in good hands.

I walk into the office and take a seat opposite her.

"Good afternoon, ma'am. How are you doing?"

I smile at her. "Except for the hot weather, I'm doing alright."

"I know, right? It's so very hot these days. I think we're expected to have rain today, anyway."

'That will be a nice relief." I reply.

"Yeah. Rain will do this city much good. We need some cool air."

I smile back and give her the small paper I received at the front desk. She looks at it and the smile on her face disappears. "You're Kiki Daniels?"

I nod. "Yes, ma'am." I try to be respectful even though I'm way older than her. I'm a woman in my early sixties, but I can pass for a forty-year-old woman. I've taken good care of myself over the years.

No doubt, Miki takes after me with her beauty and sexy shape.

"Let me guess, you're not here to discuss your medical condition. You're here to discuss Miki."

I relax my elbow on the desk. "I'm aware my daughter is seeing a psychiatrist."

"I'm afraid I can't answer yes or no to that."

"I don't want you to answer. I know it for a fact. But what I don't know is why she's seeing a psychiatrist. What medical condition is she suffering from?"

"I'm afraid I can't tell you."

"Why?"

"Because I'll be breaking the patient-doctor confidentiality."

"But I am her mother."

"Need I remind you that the patient we're talking about here is twenty-nine years old? I don't have to tell you anything, whether you're her mother or not."

I didn't plan on the fact that she might refuse to talk to me about Miki. But I'm not giving up that easily. "How much?"

She pulls her brow together in a big frown. "What?"

"How much? I'll pay you any amount for you to talk to me about my daughter."

Her lips tighten in anger, and she looks at me with disgust. "I can't be bought."

"From my experience, everybody can be bought. We all have our price."

She sits back and folds her arm across her chest. "Tell me, how much money did it take for you and your husband to neglect your duties to your daughter?"

I scowl. "I did not neglect my daughter." My voice hardens, anger taking over my sense of self. "Did Miki say I neglected her?"

"She said nothing of the sort. But I'm not a fool."

"Well, I did not neglect my daughter. My husband and I, we worked very hard to provide Miki the best things in life. She's our only child."

"Good. If you're convinced you did everything for your daughter, you have no business with me. Go home and talk with your daughter."

I let out a deep breath. "She won't talk to me."

Dr. Lara releases her folded arms and looks me in the eye, letting me know she's not afraid to say what she's about to say. "The only thing I'm going to tell you today is you've spent time working hard to give your daughter what she doesn't need, and the real thing she needed, you've neglected to do. You failed her."

My heart pains with big shame and I place my palm over my chest. It hurts to hear that.

Chapter Eight

Miki

I don't feel like working today. I'm sad and a little depressed. It's been several days since I last saw Vince and I still don't know how to adapt to living without him.

I miss how he makes me laugh. I miss his beautiful eyes looking at me and telling me over and over again that he loves me.

I look at my watch. It's a few minutes to 12:00pm. I decide I'm going to work a little more and leave at noon. Sade can push all my appointments to tomorrow.

A few minutes later, I hear a soft knock on the door and then Sade walks in without needed permission.

"Ma'am... your friends..."

Before she can complete the sentence, I hear laughter.

"Girl, loooong time, no see!"

The two leeches I have as friends welcome themselves into my office and give me a hug. I don't hug them back.

"Girl, we've really miss you," Jessica says as she pecks my cheek.

I'm wearing a chiding expression. "Next time, you should let Sade warn me of your arrival before you barge into my office. That way I can run away, or just have her tell you I don't want to see you."

Lola rolls her eyes at me. "Are you going to insult us while your assistant is still standing there?"

I glance over at Sade. "Thanks, Sade, you may leave now."

As soon as the door closes, Jessica sits on the chair opposite me and Lola sits on my desk, glancing at my wrist.

"Oh, my God! Is that a Rolex?" She gushes over my watch. "My God! This is worth about 20,000 US dollars, right?"

I keep staring, giving no response.

"It's so beautiful. Can I have it?"

I take my hand off the desk. "No, you can't."

She sticks her tongue out at me. "Stingy ass."

"Broke ass," I reply.

"Whatever," she replies, stands up from my desk and walks toward my refrigerator. "What do you have in there?"

"Everything. But please don't break my cups."

"Ugh..."

She opens the refrigerator and grabs a bottle of 1986 from the stack I have in there.

"That's for my guests only."

"Last time I checked, I'm your guest," Jessica counters.

"No, you're the pain in my butt I can't get rid of no matter how hard I try, and I only let you drink my expensive wine if we have something to celebrate. So what are we celebrating?"

Lola pours a wine for herself. "Trust me, we've got plenty to celebrate." She winks at me and drinks her wine.

And then she pours one for me and one for Jessica. I set my glass on the table, I don't even take a sip.

"So why are you here?" I ask as soon as Jessica takes a sip of her own wine.

"C'mon, Ice, we're here because we miss you. Don't you miss us?" Jessica replies.

"Hell, yeah, I miss you like a toothache."

I'm not a fool. They're not here because they miss me. They want something. That's what this friendship is about. If they're knocking on my door, they need my help. Once I've helped them, they don't care if I need a shoulder to lean on, too.

We've been friends since high school, or let me say we've been pretending to be friends since high school.

Jessie's family is close friends with my family. Her dad and my dad are close friends. Her mom and my mom are close friends, so it only fell into place that Jessie and I became friends. We went to the same school, where our parents practically forced us together. They went as far as setting up a playdates for us. If I want to be honest, it was my family that was sucking up to them.

Jessie's family was very rich at the time. They owned the famous Jamal Corporation which was the controlling power in the business world at the time, just like my Daniels Group is now the controlling power in business throughout the country. The Jamals were rich and my parents had to suck up to them as a ladder to the top. My family back then was middle class.

Even, presently, when Jamal Corporation has lost all its influences, the Jamals are still one of the richest in this country. Her dad, Hon. Jamal, went into politics and is presently the senate president of this country.

Jessie is about 5 feet 6 inches tall. She has the body of a model. She's light skinned and I'm sure she thinks she's the most beautiful girl that ever walked the earth. Her hair is always done in neat, big braids, the length of it going as far as her waist. Despite all the money available for her, guess what kind of job Jessica does.

She's an escort!

Escort is the classy name for whores or prostitute, but Jessie isn't doing it for the money. She has all the money she needs. She's doing it for fun.

Lola's family on the other hand does not belong to the big league. Her family is not poor, but they're a little less than middle class. She sucked up to Jessie and me in the hopes of joining the big league. She's a sucker for everything I own. That is, for all the expensive designer brands she can't afford. Prada and Gucci. Hell, she's still eyeing my Rolex.

The good thing about her is that she's always in a happy mood and is better at making friends than Jessie and me. Lola is about five feet four inches, almost the same height as me. In childhood, Lola was dark-skinned, but now, thanks to all the cheap bleaching creams, she's a light-skinned woman. Ever since we graduated from college, she hasn't been able to get a job. And yet my jobless friend wears more expensive stuff than people who have jobs. My gifts and castoffs.

"For the last time, why are you here? How may I help you today? What do you need me to do for you?" I glance at Lola. "Do you need me to be your bank today? Do you need me to loan you some money you will never pay back? Do you want me to pay your hairstylist or maybe pay for your mani and pedi?" I glance at Jessie. "Jessie, do you need me to pat you on the back and say that you're doing the right thing being an escort? Do you need me to encourage you? Do you even need me to help you choose a dress you want to wear to a club tonight?"

Jessie raises a palm to shut me up. "Fine. You're right. We're here for something."

Lola interrupts. "But it's good news."

"Good news? Well, then, let me hear it."

"I got a job!" Lola screams out loud.

I must say I wasn't expecting that.

"Wow! That is good," I reply.

"Wait, Miki," Jessie says. "You haven't even heard the best part."

"And what's the best part?"

Lola rise to her feet, cat-walking up and down my office and grinning like a mad woman. "This sexy lady... just got a job with ABJ TV station. I'm going to have my own talk show!"

"That's big!" She rushes over to me and into my embrace. "I'm soooo happy for you."

"Thank you," she replies.

"This really calls for a celebration," I say as I grab my cup.

"Wait," Lola says. She rushes back to the bottle and pours more wine for herself. And then we raise our glasses.

"To Lola, for her new job, and for more money, fame, and wealth coming to her," Jessie says.

"And for the start of her independent life," I add.

Lola rolls her eyes at me before she smiles, and then we jam our glasses together and gulp our wine.

Lola drops her cup on my desk. "But I'm going to need your help."

"Why didn't I see that coming?" I ask rhetorically.

The room is silent for a while. I glance at Lola, and then to Jessie. "Please, don't ask me to sponsor your talk show."

"No, no, I'm not asking that," Lola says and in the twinkling of an eye, her eyes go from happy to sad, which I guess is supposed to make me feel pity for her.

"I've been asked to only bring influential people to the show, but since I don't know anybody influential..."

I interrupt. "Not me. You're not using me to boost your show."

"Miki, please," Jessie pleads on her behalf.

"No, Jessie. I'm not going on that show. If you're such a good friend, why not talk to your dad and let him appear on her show? Last time I checked, he's the senate president. Or maybe you can be on the show. You're a famous socialite."

"I can't be on the show—you know that. I can't command good ratings like you can," Jessie admits.

"Oh... I forget that the only thing you're known for is that you have a rich daddy. Apart from that, you're nothing," I reply, devoid of any emotion. Trust me, I just had to rub in her failure one more time. It makes me feel good.

"Miki!" Lola tries to caution me.

"What!" I glare at her. "I only said it as it is."

"No, Lola, don't stop her," Jessie says. "Let Miki be," she continues as she glances at me. "You forget that you and I both share the same thing in common. We both got money in our blood. Born to a rich daddy."

"No, don't change history. I don't have money in my blood. I wasn't born to a rich daddy. My father sucked up to your father for years and still never climbed the ladder. I made it happen. I made Daniels Group."

Lola frowns. "You girls should stop this now."

"What? I'm telling the truth. Have you forgotten how my family licked her family's ass for years?"

"Whatever," Jessie replies.

If there's anything that is good about me, it's that I'm an honest person. I'm not afraid to tell the truth even if it's unfavorable to me. And like the saying goes, it's better to laugh at yourself before others laugh at you.

"Please, girls, don't make it about you. This is about me."

Without really looking at her, I say, "About appearing on your show, I'll think about it."

"You don't have much time. My first show is airing live in few hours, 8:00pm tonight, and you're my first guest."

I don't think I heard her correctly.

"What? And you're telling me now?"

"Miki, please," she pleads.

"Don't you know anything about running a show? When you're bringing a guest to a show, you have to advertise, let viewers know way beforehand."

"I know, but I'm trying to pull a Beyoncé."

I fold my arms across my chest, studying her face. "Meaning?"

"You remember how she dropped an album without any prior advertisement?"

"Dammit, Lola, it won't work. I am not Beyoncé. I'm not a celebrity."

"All the more reason it's going to work." She sounds like she's sure of what she's saying. "You are the CEO of a multibillion dollar company. Your name is everywhere. Youngest African billionaire. But you've never really granted an interview to the media. Do you know how fast word will spread that you're live on TV?"

"Lola!"

She goes on her knees. "Please, Miki."

How do I say no when she's begging like that, making herself so low by kneeling in front of me? "Anyway, if you don't get a lot of views, it's your failure, not mine."

"Yay!!!" she rises very quickly from her knees and throws herself into my arms again. "Thank you."

Jessie cuts short the excitement. "Can we go shopping now? She needs something good to wear on her first show."

"Who's paying?" is the first question I ask.

They stare at me.

I had to refrain from cursing at them. "Lola, you remember when I said we toast to the start of your independent life? I take that back."

She playfully smacks my shoulder and smiles.

I know I'm indulging them, but that's the only way to get rid of them. No matter how much I insult them or treat them badly, they won't let me be. But helping them today will rid me of them for the next two months until they have another problem.

****

We go from one shopping mall to another shopping mall to get all our shopping done. At a few minutes to eight, Lola and I are at ABJ TV station prepping for the talk show. I'm wearing a knee-length fitted black dress and silver-plated five-inch-heel sandals. The crew spends several minutes on my makeup. My long hair, which is wavy at the ends, is left flowing down my shoulder, almost touching my left breast.

By the time I look at myself in the mirror, I have to admit that I like the me I'm seeing right now. I look so different. I guess I'm used to seeing myself in a blouse and a dress-up pants suit that I had forgotten how curvy and beautiful I can be in a dress. I guess I should do this dressing up thing more often.

One... two... three

Click.

The camera starts rolling.

I'm not going to bore you with the show details, but I have to say I struggle through every bit of it. And it has nothing to do with Lola. She's fantastic. In fact, I didn't know she was this good at hosting a show.

The problem I have is that I'm pretending to be nice, I'm pretending to be who I'm not, which is too much work for me.

Lara asks me the next question. "So, how did you make Daniels Group into a success?"

I let out a deep breath. "Honestly, I don't know." I smile. "I've put in about eight years of hard work into Daniels Group."

Actually, I've put in a lifetime of hard work, but I dare not say that or she'd ask me what I mean.

So I keep pretending?

"I guess my eight years of hard work paid off."

She nods in agreement and smiles, but is still not convinced by my answer. "But how did you do it? What steps did you take? I'm sure many of our viewers would like to learn one or two things from you."

"Actually, the very first thing that I did was to have a strong drive to succeed. I'm not talking about just a mere dream to be rich. I have to succeed or else I have nothing to live for. It's either I succeed or I succeed. I had no other option. After that, I began to think about how to make it happen. At that time, Daniels Group was still Daniels Bottled Water. It was owned and managed by my dad. And what they do is make, you know, bottled water. It was a good business, but not enough for me. So I began to think about what I wanted to do. Eventually I think, why not produce something that everybody will have no choice but to buy, whether rich or poor, young or old? I rebranded Daniels Bottled Water into Daniels Group. That's only because I know I'm going to be doing a lot of things, producing and doing different types of business under that one umbrella. So I start producing salt and then sugar, noodles, spaghetti, and then, when I began to make more money, I ventured into other business. Construction, oil, movies and currently I'm trying to start producing sanitary pads which has a very wide market, I believe."

She nods as if she's hearing my story for the first time. "So what's your advice for young ones who wants to become like you?"

If I'm not pretending, my honest response would have been I don't want anybody to be like me. My life is full of intense unhappiness. But since I can't tell the truth, I modify my response.

"My advice to young people who want to become an entrepreneur is that they should have a drive to succeed, and then they should sit back and think of something that they're good at. Then, work very hard and make it happen. But I must warn you, it's not an easy road. There are times you will have to make difficult choices. Sometimes you make decisions that make you look like a bad person. Along the road, I've shut down so many competitors. So many people have lost their jobs because of some of my decisions."

She interrupts me. "Speaking of which, I believe a lot of our viewers want me to ask you this: you've said there are times you've had to make choices that didn't go down well with many people. In that case, how are you giving back to society? Believe it or not, they kind of contribute a little to your success. What are you doing to give back to them?"

"I'm trying my best," I reply.

"But you won't define yourself as a philanthropist."

My friend is grinding me in front of millions of people. I try to be calm. "I can't call myself a philanthropist, but I'm doing my best."

"Really? Because there's been rumors around town that you don't like to help people when they ask you for help."

Damn! I've got to stop pretending.

"You know what? You're right. Maybe I don't give people money when they come crying of hunger at my door step. I'm not looking down on the poor. Believe it or not, I know what it means to be poor, to be on the other side of life. Believe me, I know. Now I may not be able to give you money to feed yourself, but I can employ you. Thousands of citizens of this country have a job because of me. Thousands of people are able to feed their family because of me. Thousands of people have a smile on their face because of me. So if that's not giving back to society, I don't know what is. I'm going to do my best for Daniels Group, and with that, I'm also doing my best for the people, to put food on the table for so many people."

Lola smiles and stops pressing.

A few minutes later... *click... click...*

The camera stops rolling.

Lola hugs me and thanks me for being on her show. And then she says, "We have a small entertainment prepared for you."

We walk out of the room, and outside is a small gathering of about twenty people. As we walk into the gathering, all eyes are on me. I meet so many of their gazes, and they flash me a smile. I smile back, trying to be diplomatic.

Lola is standing beside me when a waiter came by and serves us drinks.

"So what do you think? How was the show?" I ask.

"For now, I don't know, but Ice, thank you so much for coming on. I owe you huge."

I sip my drink. "It's nothing."

"Seriously, Miki, why do you do this much for me? You always help me. Why?"

I stare at her for one long second, then I manage a small smile. "Because I owe you," I reply. I wish I can explain further, but I can't. Trying desperately to change the subject, I say, "Jessie is not here?"

"Yeah. She couldn't make it. She had to go to the club."

I roll my eyes at how ridiculous that is. "You mean she can't give you a few hours today. She just had to go fuck a stranger today."

"It's not what you think."

"Then what is it?"

"Jessie wants to quit being an escort, but she's looking for someone. She said she had a one-night stand with this man and she's somehow convinced he's the man for her. She's trying to find this man again. That's why she doesn't want to miss one day at the club."

I stifle a grin. "Well... good luck to her."

Few people in the gathering join Lola and me. They introduce themselves and try to form acquaintances with me. As we keep chatting, someone who I presume is the big boss of the TV station walks in and joins the gathering. He thanks me for being on their show and blah... blah... blah...

I'm not very good at socializing. I'm bored already.

Fortunately for me, Lola takes all the attention from me. "Boss, how did I do?"

"The report on the show is not in yet, but you pulled in many viewers. Millions, I guess," he replies. "Congratulations, Miss Lola. Your talk show is here to stay."

I've never seen my friend this happy in her entire life. She smiles genuinely and tears lace her eyes. Tears of joy, I suppose. I had to tell myself that I made this happen for her. I owe her that much.

I'm in the midst of a crowd, but I feel alone. Making sure no one notices, I withdraw from the gathering. Lola is happy. I've got to go find my happiness, too. I just hope it's not too late.

Chapter Nine

Miki

I park my car in front of the Vincent Ali & Associates office building. As I walk in, I feel a kind of boldness that tells me I deserve to stand before Vince. I have to give us a try again. But as soon as I step into the conference room and set my eyes on him, all the boldness flies away.

I had talked to his personal assistant on the main floor, and he had told me he's doing some business in the conference room.

When I opened the door, my eyes fell on Vincent standing at the center of the room. Maybe it's my wishful thinking, but when he looks at me, he looks like he's happy to see me. Or he's surprised to see me. He stands there for one long second, looking at me, forgetting that we're not alone.

Breaking the hold of our gaze with a glance at the two people sitting there in the room, he says, "Alright, guys, this is the end for today. We'll wrap it up first thing tomorrow morning."

The men stand and pack their documents into their briefcases.

"Excellent job today, guys," Vince continues. "Have a good night, and I'll see you tomorrow."

The men smile at him. They shake his hand and leave.

As soon as the door closes, our gazes meet again.

I take a few steps toward him, butterflies dancing in my stomach. "Hey..." I say quietly.

"Hey..." he replies, his voice calm, gentle, and steady.

"I came to talk to you."

He doesn't respond. Slowly he glides his hands into his pocket, never taking his eyes off me.

I'm almost shaking. I try to finger my purse as I stare down. "I had an interview at ABJ TV station today. I was asked how I made Daniels Group into a success. My response was that I had a strong drive to succeed. Using my own words, I said…"

"I had to succeed or else I have nothing to live for…" he finishes my statement for me.

My eyes widens in surprise. He actually watched me on the TV today. Somehow, that encourages me to talk to him.

"About four or five months ago, that was true. Until…" I have to stop because it seems my voice is shaking. "Until… I mean, I used to live only for Daniels Group. These last few months, I suddenly have something else that occupies my mind. And it wasn't the company. It was you."

I look at his expressionless face. I can't figure out what he's thinking.

I manage to continue. "Vince… if there's anything I've learned in the past few days, it is that I can't be happy without you. I can survive without you, but I can't live without you. And going through life is more than just surviving. The woman I am without you is nothing… but you, Vince, you're everything. And maybe you're right—maybe I'm so screwed up that I don't understand what love means. But I know that when I wake in the morning, you're always on my mind. I wait for your call. I wait for you. My happiest moments are when I'm with you. And when I'm not with you, my heart feels like it's going to explode. The same way you feel. And maybe this is not love, but…" Tears fill my eyes. "Is that not enough for now?" I ask, my heart beating really fast. A tear drops down my cheek and I slowly wipe it off with my hand.

"Come here," he says with a deep voice as he removes his hands from his pocket.

I hesitate.

He holds out his right hand for me. "Come here," he repeats.

I slowly walk toward him. Grabbing my hands, he pulls me into his arms.

Relief brings me close to tears, and for no reason—no reason at all—I burst into a loud sob. His arms just make me feel so good. There's nowhere in the world I'd rather be than here right now.

With his arms still wrapped around me, he kisses my tears away. And then he stares deep into my eyes. Holding me tightly in his arms again, his hand caresses my hair.

"Was it hard?" he asks.

"What?"

"Telling me how you feel. Was it hard?"

"Yeah. A little."

"I'm sorry. I didn't mean to put you through that."

I don't know what to say. So, I just wrap my arms around him even tighter.

"Vince... I..."

"Shhh..." he cuts me off. "Say nothing. Just let me hold you like this."

I stop talking. My head resting on his chest, he holds me tightly as I hold him back.

"I've missed you."

****

Vince

The last few days without Miki have been hard. Really hard. I haven't gone a minute without thinking of her. So many times, I was close to calling her and saying, "You know what? Forget everything I said about us being over." I wanted to say it didn't matter if she doesn't love me back; that my love is enough to sustain the relationship. I had to use all my strength to refrain me from calling her.

I have to be sure that I'm with a woman that feels that this whole relationship is happening. That it's not just happening in my head, and that I'm not insane because the love I have for this woman is almost driving me to insanity. These last few days that we haven't talked, I can't count how many times I've been tempted to stay at a distance and watch her. But then again, I had to refrain myself. I don't want to stalk her.

So when she walked through that door this evening, and when she walked into my arms, it felt nice holding her, even though every one of her tears cut right through me. Holding her in my arms and having her talk sincerely about her feelings made me feel better. She had never cried in my arms like this before. I feel like I'm finally getting somewhere with her; that I'm finally breaking through the wall she's built around her.

"I've missed you," I finally say.

She releases herself from my hold and look into my eyes. "You left me all alone."

Her words feel like a direct hit to the gut. "I'm so very sorry."

"That's okay. I've missed you, too." She smiles and places a kiss on my lips.

The kiss is short, but it's enough to make me smile. My baby is changing real fast for the good. When we first started dating, Miki will never initiate a kiss.

Arms wrapped around her waist, I draw her closer, looking so lovingly into those amazing eyes of hers. "So what have you been up to?"

Smiling, she raises her shoulders in a shrug. "Nothing really. I had this talk show with ABJ TV today. It's my first."

"I watched the show. You were great, and you looked gorgeous."

I see the excitement on her face. She can't hide her smile. "Really?"

"Yes, really. C'mon, turn around and let me see you."

She takes two steps back and turns around with a smile on her face. What an ass! That's the most fuckable ass I've ever seen. That dress actually does justice to her shape.

I hug her from the back and kiss her neck. "You're sexy. I think you should dress like this more often."

"Okay."

And I sure as hell can feel that ass resting on my dick, and my dick starts to ache. I can only hope she doesn't feel how hard I am.

The moment passes, and she turns around and rests her head on my chest. "It's been a long day. I have to go home and rest and prepare for tomorrow."

I bend a little and take my lips close to her left ear. "I just got you back. I'm not losing you again."

My breath on her skin makes her shiver.

And I like it.

"So?" she says, while looking at me, her voice low and breathy.

"Do something with me tonight."

My words must have frightened her. I feel her jumping out of her own skin. "No, it's not what you think. I mean, let's go eat together, go to the cinema... you know, just do something together."

And then her face looks relaxed.

My eyebrow goes up. "Miki, is there something I should know about? Something you want to tell me?"

"Vince..." She says my name in a calm but disturbing voice. And I can see the rising and falling of her chest.

As much as I want to know why she's scared at every hint of sex, it's against my nature to force someone to tell me something she doesn't want to. Everybody has secrets. Everyone has a right to keep secrets, and I respect that right. If she wants to tell me, I'll listen, but I'm not going to force her.

"Miki," I try to modulate my voice to sound reassuring. "I'm your man, and that means you don't have to tell me anything you don't want to. I'll still love you."

She nods in agreement and smiles.

"So, how about we go to the cinema tonight?"

"Okay."

Ten minutes later, I park the car at Silverbird Cinema. As we step out of the car, I hold out my hand for her. She stares at it in surprise. I continue to hold it out for her. She gazes into my eyes and slips her hands into mine.

"You like public displays of affection?" she asks.

I lean closer and put my mouth close to her ear. "I want to shower you with affection just so the ladies can get jealous."

"Really?" She pushes her lips forward at me. "Then let me get a kiss."

"As you wish, ma'am." I lean in and kiss her as my hand slightly moves to her ass. I just love that ass.

She smiles a genuine smile, and her smile pulls at the string of my heart.

We are walking into the building when we meet this young lady staring at Miki.

"Miki Daniels," the stranger yells with excitement.

Miki glares at her.

"I saw you on TV today. You're my role model."

Miki didn't smile, didn't even say a word. She just gives her the cold shoulder.

I can see the disappointment rolling across the young lady's face, and before the situation gets any more awkward, I smile at the lady and increase our pace as we walk off.

"What did you do that for?" I ask.

She frowns. "What?"

"That lady was saying hi. You didn't respond."

"I don't know her. I don't have to greet people I don't know."

"It's called courtesy, Miki. Someone smiles at you, you smile back. Even if it's a fake smile."

"Alright. Alright. I will smile back next time. Happy now?"

I shake my head. "Just when I thought the name Ice doesn't fit you anymore, you show me it fits like a second skin."

She playfully smacks my shoulder and laughs.

And then we get to ticket booth. "Hi," I greet the lady. "What movie is playing tonight?"

"Local or international?" she asks.

I turn to Miki. "Baby, what do you want to watch?"

She considers for a while. "Let's do local," she says and rests her head on my shoulder.

"Okay. For local movies, we have *Last Flight to Abuja*, *Tango with Me* is also playing tonight."

I turn to Miki again. "Which one do you want to see?"

"I'm in the mood for romance. Definitely, *Tango with Me*."

Chapter Ten

Miki

I'm sitting in my armchair in my office when my phone signals I have a text. I know its Vince. I can just feel it when it's him texting. Quickly I grab my phone.

Vince: Hey Ice.

I smile to myself.

Me: You should be working now.

Vince: Can't stop thinking about u baby. It feels like I've known u for years.

Me: And you don't even know the first thing about me.

Vince: 34-28-34

Me: What?

Vince: That's the first thing about u. Boobs 34, waist 28, hips, 34.

I smile as I read the text. He knows my measurements. He probably stares at me too much. I'm guessing he has eye-banged me so many times.

I'm still thinking of Vince when I hear a voice yelling, "Hello, ma'am!"

I glance up. "Oh... Sade, what is it?"

"I had to yell because I've been standing here for almost a minute. You didn't notice."

"I'm sorry. I was carried away."

She stands there, frozen.

"What?"

She blinks like twenty times in a second. "You apologized."

She looks very surprised. I'm surprised, too, so I try to change the subject.

"What did you say you want again?" I ask.

"Oh… I just want to remind you of your 3:00 clock appointment."

"Okay."

She bows slightly and walks out.

Now I can go back to texting Vince.

Me: Lol

Vince: What's your cup size?

Me: Really? You're asking me that?

Vince: Yes, really.

Me: Only if you tell me your penis size.

Vince: my erection is 9 inches.

Me: Lie. You wish.

Vince: Not a wish, babe. I sent u a pic once, right?

Me: You mean that image you sent me. Believe me, I thought that penis belongs to a porn star

Vince: Lol. Oh! I forgot to tell u I was a porn star in my previous life.

Me: Hell yeah. Seriously. Penis size?

Vince: I'm serious. I can let u verify if u want to. I'll let u play with it.

My heart begins to race.

Me: This sexting just got to a whole new level. I think my temperature is rising.

Vince: I've got a bath in my office. U can come for a quick shower.

Me: I know your wicked ploy.

Vince: Lol. I promise I won't disturb. I'll just watch u naked and probably try not to caress your soft, naked body.

Me: Moan.

Vince: Oh baby, I'd like to hear u moan right into my ear.

I can feel the heat rising inside me, and I have to press my thigh together to keep a throttling grip on it.

Me: How about you and me shower together? Cuddle under the showers with you, kissing you, breathing you in like pure air and licking all your body and licking that huge man down there.

I can't believe I just wrote that.

Vince: Hell. My body temperature is exploding. Baby, don't make me embarrass myself in front of my assistant. That huge man is hard and my assistant might think it's for her.

Me: Lol. Hmmm...tell her I don't share.

Vince: Do u even know u're the sexiest woman on earth?"

No, I didn't. Not until I met him.

Me: hmmm

Vince: Have u seen yourself in d mirror? That ass of yours is to die for.

Me: you make me feel sexy.

Vince: And I can make u feel so much more if u let me.

Me: What kind of sex do you like?"

Did I write that? I'm dying of embarrassment right now.

Vince: I like wild, intense sex. Sex so aggressive that it brings out d animal in u. Sex without boundaries or controls.

Vince: I like fiery, fast sex that's so passionate that d whole room feels upside down, your vision blurs and one foot of d bed is broken as a result of all that wildness.

Me: What?

Vince: Lol. Don't get scared. Just messing with u. I like hot, passionate sex with a hot, passionate woman.

I don't know what to say so I don't respond. A few minutes later, my phone rings. It's Vince. I hope he's not calling to continue our sex talk because, sincerely, I can hide behind the text and talk dirty, but that's where it ends. Beyond that, I'm freaking out.

I answer the call. "Hi, Vince."

"Ice, I'm sorry to bother you with this, but I have no one else to call."

"Tell me, Vince. Anything for you..."

"My little girl is coming back from boarding school today. The school is on midterm break. I planned to go pick her up, but something very urgent came up with a client. The bus will be dropping her off, and I need someone to be in the house for me to receive her. I'm in the middle of a very important business..."

Trouble is brewing in paradise. I have no idea how to relate to kids. How am I supposed to behave around her? *But this is your chance, Miki,* I tell myself. I've been worried that Vince has everything to offer me and I have nothing to offer him. Maybe this is it. It's not easy to be a single dad. I can be of help; the problem is I don't know how to.

"Miki..." Vince calls.

His voice breaks through my thinking. "What?"

"You know what? Never mind."

"Yes, Vince. I will be at your house to receive your daughter."

"You will?"

"Yes, I will."

"Thank you. All you have to do is receive her. I've called the agency, and they've agreed to send in a nanny that will watch her till I get back from work."

"Okay. Not a problem."

And then I hang up.

Breathe in. Breathe out.

All I have to do is receive her from the bus driver and hand her over to the nanny. It's simple.

I head to Vince's house. I have his spare key, but I've never been at his house without him. I wonder why he gave me the key anyway. Guess spare key is another way guys let ladies know they mean business.

When I get to the house, the bus hasn't arrived. Vince's house is huge—fancier and bigger than my apartment. I understand his need for a big house, though. Kids need space.

I let myself in and relax on the couch. I don't know what I'm supposed to be doing. I'm a woman who can't have a child, and I'm already resigned to my fate.

Maybe I should clean the house before she gets back, or maybe prepare her some food. Oh, I should have bought her something. Everybody likes a gift.

I'm about to rush back and buy her something when I hear the school bus honk its horn. I hurry out of the house to the gate. The bus driver hands me a paper which I sign before he releases the girl to me.

As soon as the bus leaves, she turns to me.

"Who are you?" she asks in a very sweet, little voice.

God, she's so adorable. Beautiful, and in more ways than one, she looks like her dad. Her hair is neatly braided in corn rows. She has beautiful dark skin, just like her dad. Big brown beautiful eyes, just like her dad. Perfectly formed eyebrows, maybe not exactly like Vince's. I'm guessing like her mom.

"I'm a friend of your dad's."

"Okay. We haven't met before. I'm my dad's daughter. My name is Tiwa."

Introducing herself as her dad's daughter just get a smile out of me. "My name is Miki."

Her cute face lights up. "Are you my dad's girlfriend?"

My eyes go wide in surprise, and it takes me more than a second before I can respond. "How old are you again?"

"I'm seven years old," she replies with an 'I'm-proud-to-be-seven' kind of attitude.

I nod and smile. "Alright, Tiwa, let's get you inside the house."

"Okay."

We start to walk into the house. I watch her struggle with her big backpack, but me being me, I don't offer to help.

"So what do you know about boyfriends and girl-friends?" I ask.

"My daddy can't know I know anything about boy-friends." She glances up at me with those eyes. "Please don't tell him."

How can I say no when she's looking at me like that? "Okay, I won't tell. It's our little secret."

She holds out her little finger. "Promise?"

I twine my little finger in hers. "Promise."

She smiles, and we resume walking.

"The last time I was home, I heard my dad say your name in his sleep."

I don't know if my reaction should be 'eeew' or 'wow'.

"Really? He did?"

"Yes. At first I thought he was saying milk. But it makes more sense when you told me your name."

I nod and smile. "So my name sounds like milk."

"Yes. What does your name mean?" she asks.

"I don't know. My dad's name is Mike. My mom's name is Kiki. The first two letters of their name is my name."

"Oh. That makes sense now."

I glance at her. "How about you? You like your name?"

She nods. "Yes."

It's not as awkward as I thought it would be. She's easy to have a conversation with. Maybe she talks too much, but I talked far more than that when I was seven.

I open the door, and we step inside the house.

"Alright, Tiwa, take your backpack upstairs and change your clothes."

"Okay."

She hasn't taken more than two steps when my phone rings.

"It's your dad. You want to talk to him?"

"Yes."

I press the green button and give her the phone.

"Hi, Daddy. Where are you? I've missed you... Aww... okay. Buy biscuits and chocolates for me when you're coming home. Okay, Daddy... And Daddy, I..."

Her voice fades as she climbs the stairs to her room.

A few seconds later, I hear the doorbell ring. Opening the door, I see a young boy of about nineteen or twenty years old standing at the door.

"What? How may I help you?"

"You ask for a nanny? The agency sent me."

"I wasn't expecting a boy nanny."

He smiles. "I know, but I do my job okay. I'm certified in CPR, qualified in First Aid, extensive training in child development and..."

I cut him off. "Okay. Come on in."

He smiles, bows slightly, and gently steps in.

The moment passes until Tiwa comes back to the living room.

"Thanks," she says as she hands me my phone.

"You're welcome." I take the phone from her and then grab my handbag. "Tiwa, this is..." I turn to the boy nanny.

"My name is Afam."

"Tiwa, meet Afam. He's going to watch you till your daddy gets back."

Disappointment crawls across her face. "You're not staying?"

"No, baby. I have work in the office."

She looks so sad. "Alright. 'Bye."

She walks over to me and gives me a quick hug.

"Bye, and enjoy your midterm break."

I walk out of the house and straight to my car. I've only drive for about two minutes when it hits me. How can I leave that boy nanny alone with that little girl? What if...? My God, I was about her age, 8 years old to be exact, when my troubles started.

I run my fingers through my hair, frustration and regrets eating me deep on the inside. That girl is too adorable to go through all that. *Miki, you have to save her. This is your chance to make sure it doesn't happen again*, I tell myself.

I turn back and head back to the house. When I open the door, the boy nanny is sitting on the floor in front of the television playing video games.

"Really?" I say. "You are CPR certified and trained in child development, and yet you're playing video games instead of actually doing your job?"

He jumps to his feet and bows. "I'm sorry, ma'am."

I drop my purse on the couch. "You're fired."

"Please, ma'am. I promise I'll do my job right."

"I'm not firing you because you're playing video game. I would have fired you even if you did your job right." I grab my handbag and take out two hundred naira. "Take this as a payment for your trouble. I'm grateful that you watched her for few seconds. And I hope to never see you again."

Gently, he carries his bag and walks out of the house.

Immediately after he left, Tiwa rushes up to me. "You rock." She gives me a high-five. "I like you."

I roll my eyes at her. "What? Why?"

"I like the way you sent him away. You did it like a boss."

I smile.

"I didn't like him anyway, I think he's weird," she says.

"Who? Boy-nanny?"

She nods, laughing at the name I called him.

"Yes, he's weird," I say in agreement.

And then I grab my cell phone and make a quick call.

"Hey, Sade, go ahead and cancel my 3:00 clock. Reschedule to tomorrow."

I hang up and then glance at Tiwa. "It's you and I till your dad gets back."

"Yay!" she says in excitement.

I smile back. "So what are you up to?"

"I'm hungry. I was about to prepare food..."

I look at her and raise a brow. "You cook?"

"Not really..." Squeezing her face together like she had done something horrible, she gently covers her face with her palm.

I hope it's not what I think it is.

I rush to the kitchen. And there it is, an empty pot on a stove.

Very quickly, I turn off the stove, take a napkin and move the hot pot.

I turn over to her, scowling. "Are you trying to burn down the house?" I yell.

I'm not asking her a question. I'm angry as hell.

She shudders. "I forgot I had a pot on the stove," she says quietly as tears fill her eyes. "I'm so sorry."

Her tears cut through my heart and my anger disappears as fast as it appeared. Walking over to her, I hold her in my arms, squeeze her tight, and smile sadly. "It's okay."

When I release her from the hug, I crouch; look into her dark chocolate eyes, and smile. "Now tell me what you want to eat."

"Noodles."

"I'll cook noodles for you if you promise to wash the dishes."

She nods.

I hold out my little finger for her. "Promise?"

She smiles and twines her little finger in mine. "Promise."

I smile back, stand, and walk back to the stove. "Go to the living room. I'll let you know when it's ready."

"But I want to help."

"Okay. Open the fridge and give me a tomato, hot pepper, egg, and onion."

She runs to the fridge. And then she gives me each of them, one after the other. "You're going to put all these in the noodles?" she asks.

"Yes."

"It's going to be yummy."

Chapter Eleven

Miki

"Yummy," Tiwa says at the very first taste of her noodles.

I sit opposite her, watching as she devours her food.

"Are you going to teach me your recipe?" she asks.

I give a sarcastic smile. "Maybe. When I decide you're old enough to cook without burning down the whole house."

She gives me a sideways glance.

"What?" I say. "You almost set fire to the house today."

She smiles, and I give her a smile, too.

I don't know why, but I'm so happy that she likes my food. I'm not looking for her approval, but somehow I'm proud of myself. For once in my life, I've sincerely done something for someone not because I'm trying to push them away, but from the bottom of my heart.

I watch her finish her lunch, and then we go to the kitchen to do the dishes together. After that, I walk back to the living room and relax on the couch.

Tiwa joins me in the living room with two cups of orange juice in her hands. She hands me one.

"Thanks, princess," I say as I take the cup from her. I drink about half the juice and place the cup on the table.

I pat the couch beside as a gesture for her to sit. "So what activities do you have planned for your midterm break?"

She sits beside me. "We have a midterm party in school tomorrow."

"Midterm party?"

"Yes. It's like a big party. Daddies and mummies come with their kids, and we kind of have fun together."

She's all excited talking about it, but I still don't get it. Why does a school send the kids home for midterm break and expect them to come back the next day for a party?

She probably notices I'm not at all in on the party.

"I brought my photo album from school. I'll show you pictures of the last party we had."

She didn't wait for my response before running upstairs. And in a split second, she's back with her backpack.

Unzipping the backpack, she brings out her photobook and sits on the floor close to my leg, placing the book on my laps.

She opens it, and when I see the first picture, I understand why the party is such a big deal. It's a really extravagant party.

Pointing to herself in the picture, she says, "That's me, and that's my daddy, and that's my teacher, Miss Bello, standing next to Daddy."

"Aww... cute, you." I smile and pull her cheek. "You look so beautiful."

"I am?"

I nod. "Yes. You're perfect."

She flashes me a cute, small smile. "Thanks."

We continue to look at the pictures while she keeps showing me her friends. And then at a point, I kind of pick up a trend in the pictures.

"Tiwa, why are you wearing jeans and a T-shirt when all your friends are wearing dresses?"

She didn't look at me. "My daddy is not good with dresses. He can pick out the best jeans in a store, but I'm not sure he knows what the best dress looks like. He thinks it's better I wear the best jeans and stand out from my friends than wear a bad dress."

I don't know what it is, but something pulls at the strings of my heart when she says that. "Your daddy could have asked one of his female staff to help pick a dress for you."

She gives me a small smile, devoid of joy. "My daddy doesn't like asking for help. He is a proud man."

"No, he is not," I say as I caress her shoulder. "I guess he loves you so much. He's doing his best for you, but he's so afraid that his best is not going to be enough. He thinks if he asks a stranger for help, they might think he's incapable of taking care of you. That doesn't make him a proud man."

She nods in understanding.

"How about you and I go out to the boutique tomorrow morning and get you a beautiful dress?"

Her eyes flash with surprise and excitement. "Really? I can have a dress?"

"Yes. I'll ask your dad as soon as he gets here."

She makes an exciting squeal and hugs me.

I'm not expecting it, and I hesitate for a second, frozen. When I snap out of it, I slowly wrap my arms around her and hold her in warm embrace.

The moment passes, and she release herself from the hug. "Can I have your kind of hairstyle, too?"

I shake my head. "Absolutely not. My hairstyle is for adults. But I can fix you a hairstyle that will be perfect for you."

"Okay. Do I get makeup, too?"

Again, I shake my head. "No, makeup is for adults. But that doesn't stop me from letting you try on lipstick."

"Really?"

"Yes, go ahead." I point to my handbag, which is sitting on the couch next to us.

She rushes over and after a vigorous search, finds the lipstick. In a split second, she's upstairs, in front of a mirror.

"Be careful," I say, raising my voice to make sure she hears me.

As I sit there on the couch waiting for her, I smile to myself. When I was her age, I'd steal my mom's lipstick and try it on in the bathroom. When I heard her footsteps, I'd quickly wipe it off with a towel. Of course, I never wiped it all off, so she always found out in the end.

Tiwa reminds me of me. Girls will always be girls.

"How do I look?" she asks when she comes back to the couch beside me.

Drawing her face closer, I clean off a smear of the matte red on her lips. "Now you look perfect," I say, smiling, almost as excited as she is. "Let's take a picture and send it to your dad."

"Is he going to be mad I'm wearing lipstick?"

"No, he's not going to be mad."

She put her face next to mine. We both make duck lips for the camera and *click!* Our first selfie together.

Leaning closer, she takes a look at the picture. "It's so cute."

"Yes. Let's see what your dad thinks."

I send the picture to Vince and in a few minutes, he texts me back.

Vince: Cute. U ladies are having fun without me, huh?

Smiling, I show the text to Tiwa.

She reads it and smiles. "He likes it, and he's jealous."

I wink at her. "Yes, he is."

The hours pass by quickly, and it's almost 9:00pm. Tiwa takes her shower and changes into her nightie. After a long day, I'm tired, too. I take a shower and change into one of Vince's T-shirts. Tiwa won't stop laughing at how big her dad's T-shirt looks on me.

"Can I watch *Binta and Friends* before I go to bed? It's my favorite TV show."

"Of course."

We walk back downstairs to the living room, where I turn on the TV. I sit on the couch as she cuddles against my side.

A few minutes later, she yawns and places her head on my lap. Fondling her hair, I stare at her. I can see her eyes are heavy. Reminiscing on all the wonderful moments we've had today, I never thought being a mother was a huge deal. The sweet moment I had with Tiwa told me how wrong I was. Being with this little girl feels so right.

Tears fill my eyes.

It hurts that I can't have my own child.

It's in this moment that I understand the gravity of what Jaye Jamal took from me; how much harm he did to me.

****

Vince

"Miki."

My voice is slightly above a whisper as I pat Miki's arm, trying to wake her up.

Opening her heavily lidded eyes, she blinks a few times before getting a focus. "Vince, you're back."

"I'm sorry. Work was hectic today."

"Shhh..." she says, trying to make me keep my voice low as she glance at Tiwa. I nod to let her know I understand. Very gently, I put my arm around Tiwa and let her slightly remove hers and maneuver herself from behind Tiwa.

I lift my baby in my arms and take her upstairs. Getting to the bedroom, I lay her gently on the bed. Sadly, she's too asleep to notice I've changed her blanket as she required. Last time she was home, we had a whole argument about it. She was angry I bought her a blue blanket. She says girls love pink. I made sure to change the blanket before she got back this time.

"Daddy..." she calls, her voice very soft and almost in whisper.

Kneeling beside her bed, I lean in and place a kiss on her forehead, my fingers tracing the lines of her corn rows. "I've missed you. How is school?"

"Fine. I've missed you, too."

I want to say more to her, but her eyes close a bit. She must be falling back to sleep. I'm trying to stand when she grabs my arm, gently.

"I like her."

"Who?" I ask. "Miki?"

"Yes. Are you going to marry her? Is she going to be my new mommy?"

Her question shocks me to the bone. Things kids know, you never can tell they know it. Besides, I'm not expecting her to fall in love with Miki just in one day. Miki has her own issues. I guess she's changing fast. I don't give her enough credit.

"When the time is right, you and I will ask her if she would like to be your mom."

She falls back to sleep again.

Placing a kiss on her forehead, I say, "Good night, Tiwa."

And I can hear her tiny voice in my imagination saying *Night-night, Daddy.*

I walk out of her room and meet Miki standing in the hallway. Holding her waist, we walk in to the master bedroom.

Let me say this is the first time Miki is sleeping over. Tiwa made the magic happen.

I lead her into the room and she flies to the bed immediately. She's wearing my t-shirt. It looks big on her, but it looks good, too, exposing those beautiful, smooth thighs of hers. I can't help imagining how nice it would be to rip that shirt off and...

"You came back late."

Her voice breaks through my thoughts. "I'm sorry. I'm going to attend Tiwa's midterm party tomorrow, so I tried to clear the workload on my desk."

"Is it okay if Tiwa and I go shopping tomorrow? She wants a dress for the party."

"Sure." I unbutton my shirt and throw it in the laundry basket. "I'll let you have some cash tomorrow morning."

"Don't worry about it. I got it."

I remove my pants and boxers and throw them in the basket. Almost immediately, I notice Miki averts her gaze. She reaches for a magazine on the side of the bed, opens it, and pretends she's actually reading it.

But I swear I can feel her gaze all over me.

"Any tip on what Tiwa likes?" she asks, her voice suddenly breathy like something had gathered up in her throat. I can see her swallowing hard, stealing a glance at me at every opportune second.

"She's going through a pink phase right now, so pink is her color." With that, I grab a towel and walk into the bathroom.

My water bill is probably going to shoot up because of all the cold showers I've been taking recently. Miki has a way of exciting your sexuality and ditching you when you're sexually high. Damn, merely looking at her gets me high, let alone when she makes those sexual gestures of hers.

Nevertheless, I take a quick shower and crawl back to bed. She's sleeping at the far edge of the bed, so I close in the gap by pulling her protectively against my warm chest. For a moment, there's only the sound of our breathing.

"How did you get all the way here?" I ask.

I can feel her smiling as she playfully smacks my chest, and then her hand takes a permanent position right there. Arms around her, I draw her close to me, her face so close to mine I can feel her breath awakening the nerves in me, my hard dick pressing against her belly as my hands roam across her back.

When I can no longer resist the urge, I lean in and kiss her. My tongue flicks against the softness of her lower lip, luring her to accept me. As if she has been waiting for me to make the move, she responds, kisses me back with so much tenderness that my blood boils and I can't resist my hand going beneath her shirt to her ass, up to her back, and to...

Before I can go any further, she breaks away. "Miki, I need you..." I say huskily in a deep baritone voice.

"No. No more."

She's shaking now and worry takes over my sexual animalistic instinct.

"Come here." I pull her in again and she rests her head on my chest. My dick still hard, I caress her back and before I know it she bursts into tears, crying as if she's in pain. As if there's a part of her she wants to share with me, but keeps holding back.

"I can't give you what you want," she says between sobs.

Wrapping her in my arms, I keep caressing her and speaking in a soothing voice. "You know what I want? I want to enjoy you, Miki. I want to enjoy everything about you. I want to be your best friend, your lover, your confidant, your everything. I'll worship you, protect you, fight for you till the end, and not even the secret that you carry can come between us."

Chapter Twelve

Vince

I'm still for respecting Miki's secret. I'm not going to force her to tell me anything she doesn't want to, but that doesn't mean I can't find out by myself. Earlier this morning, I called Wale, my doctor friend, who said he'd be here any minute. Now I just want the ladies to go out shopping before he gets here.

Standing in the living room with a cup of tea, I raise my voice. "Ladies, you have to hurry. You should leave early so you can be back to prepare for the party."

"We're almost ready."

That is Tiwa's voice.

Women—funny how they spend long hours dressing up and even more shopping so they can dress up.

Finally, few minutes later, the two most important ladies in my life walk down the stairs to join me in the living room.

I drop my cup of tea on the table as Tiwa runs into my arms.

"You ladies ready?" I ask.

Tiwa nods.

"Yes, we are," Miki says.

I crouch, holding Tiwa in my arms and passing my hand through her hair. "Have fun, okay?"

"Okay, Daddy. And can I buy two dresses?"

"Sure. Daddy doesn't mind if you decide to buy the whole boutique."

She laughs. "Aww, thanks, Daddy."

Arms around my neck, she hugs me.

"So Daddy will be home all day and will prepare you lunch before you get back. What do you want for lunch?"

"Fried plantain and fried egg."

"Okay. Lunch will be ready by the time you get back."

Placing a quick kiss on her cheek, I release her from my hold.

"Bye, Daddy," she says as she walks to the door.

"Bye, sweetheart."

As soon as she walks out of the door, I put my hand in the pocket of my shorts, bring out some money, and hand it to Miki.

"I told you I got it."

I nod. "Yes, but I want you to have this. I can take care of you, and I can take care of my little girl."

"It's not a question of whether or not you can take care of us. God, I have an idea of how much you're worth. But I just want to buy this dress for Tiwa as a gift, you know, if that's okay with you."

I smile. "Of course it's okay with me. You can buy her anything you want to. But take this, in case Tiwa actually tries to buy the whole boutique."

Miki laughs and takes the money. And then I pull her in against my chest and place a hot, wet kiss on her lips.

"Do you want fried plantain and fried egg, too?" I ask.

She smiles. "Hell, yeah."

And then she kisses me back, a very short kiss. "I have to run. Tiwa is waiting."

"Okay, baby."

Before she takes more than two steps away, I reach out and give her a gentle pat on her ass. I love that ass; can't take my eyes off it.

She glances back, smiles, and blows me a kiss.

As soon as she leaves, I go back to waiting for Wale to get here.

After few minutes of waiting, the doorbell rings and I rush to open it.

Immediately he steps into my house. He shoots me a scrutinizing look. "God, Vincent, you look depressed? Are you sex-starved?"

I arch a brow. "What?"

"You know, you stopped coming to the club because of this chick and I thought you could be tired of fucking the same pussy every day."

"Fuck you, Wale."

Wale has been my friend since childhood. He's a medical doctor, but he knows how to go back to the level when he's with his homie.

I wasn't always rich, and neither was Wale. We grew up on the streets of Lagos and struggled for survival, hawking pure water on the highways. And even though our hard work paid off and we've evolved into better people, we still kept our street language for when we see each other. Once the street is in you, you never really get it all out no matter how many expensive suits you wear.

Wale is almost as tall as me, about six feet one inch. He's dark in complexion and has a charm on women like I do. But while I'm a man that can be committed to one woman, Wale is far from that. Don't get me wrong, I love all varieties of women, but once I fall in love with one woman, there can be no one else.

Wale shoots me a cocky grin as he drops onto my couch. "No need to get vexed, bro. I always know you're a one-pussy man."

I throw him a punch on his shoulder.

He laughs.

I wait, watching my friend relax back and throw his feet on my table. The bastard. Raising my leg, I sweep his feet off my table. "Take your damn feet off my table."

His feet find balance on the floor and he glares at me. "Was that really necessary?"

Now, it's my turn to grin my evil smile. "Yeah, it was."

His face turns serious. "By the way, there's this girl, Jessie. She comes to the club every night asking if anyone knows a Vincent. She won't have any other man except Vincent. Of course, I didn't mention I know a Vincent, but you must have really hit her hard to make her keep wanting more..."

"Whatever, Wale. I don't remember fucking any Jessie at that club."

He holds out his hand for me. "Too many girls to remember one?"

I take his hand in a street-style handshake and laugh. "Yeah, bro."

The moment passes, and Wale finishes the drink I offer him. "So, bro, you said you wanted to see me."

"Yeah."

"Make it quick. I have to rush to work. I'm on call."

I sit up and lean forward, resting my elbow on my knee. "My sister, she told me about this issue going on with her and I said I'd ask you."

"What's that?"

"Um... she has this problem. A problem with sex-related issues."

"What do you mean 'sex-related issues'?"

"You know, she panics. Gets all worked up. Sometimes she cries."

He lowers his head and when he raises it, his face is serious. "Don't lie to me, Vincent. I've known you since childhood. You don't have any sister. No siblings at all."

"Not my sister; sister like that. She's like a distant cousin," I answer, maybe *too* quickly.

He gives me a sarcastic nod. "And that's coming from a guy who has no relatives I've ever met and she just opens up to you. I'm your only living relative, Vincent, just like you're mine. You forget? We met on the streets of Lagos and survived together."

I let out a sigh. "You caught me. It's the lady I'm with now."

"Dammit, bro. If she's got probs with sex-related issues, dump her ass."

"I can't."

"Why not? The Vincent I know would have dumped her ass and moved on to the next available ass..."

"Fuck!" I slam my fist on the table. "She makes me crazy. One minute I'm sane and the next I'm totally losing it. I think she's so beautiful that I can sit and look at her for hours. And looking at her, just looking at her, makes me happy. She can be stubborn and as cold as ice, but I even like her that way because she's strong. She knows exactly what she wants. She's determined. Smart. Considerate. The way she looks at me makes me feel like I'm everything, like I'm ten feet tall. She sees me not as the owner of the most successful law firm in the country, but as a man, and she accepts me as I am. She cares for my daughter like it's her child."

Breathless from my rant, I relax on the couch and suck in a breath of air. The room is quiet for a long minute.

A hint of emotion spreads across my friend's face. "I understand, bro. Trust me, I do. You love her. You can't leave her because of this little setback. If you do, you will regret it for the rest of your life."

Love. Pain. For one moment, I can see all that emotion on Wale's face. My friend is just not sharing my pain. Only someone who has known those feelings personally can show that much empathy. So my friend once fell in love, after all. By the time I open my mouth to ask him about it, his face has gone expressionless.

"Did you talk to her about it?" he asks me.

"At the start. She said she wasn't ready for sex just yet, and I agreed to it."

"Maybe   she's   the   I-don't-wanna-have-sex-until-marriage kind of girl."

I shake my head. "No."

"Are you sure?"

"I'm sure. She would have told me that if that's the problem, and I sure as hell wouldn't have a problem with that. Hell, I would have married her immediately."

I can see Wale stifling a grin. My frustration is just funny to him. The table is bound to turn one day, and I'll be the one laughing at his problems.

"She initiates sex sometimes. She talks dirty. You know, when we text, she can fuck me on text, but not in person. She's a very good kisser, but she just stops in the middle sometimes. She panics. I just know there's a part of her that's striving to explore her sexuality, and then there's something like a strong force holding her back."

"That strong force... could you describe it as fear?"

I hesitates a while, my mind going back to our every attempt at sex. The one time she panicked and threw me out of the house. Other times, she's shaking and can barely look at me. Another instance, she just burst into tears. "Fear doesn't quite cut it, but it fits."

Wale let out a deep breath. "Now I'm not sure this is what it is, but there's a medical condition called genophobia."

"Genophobia?"

He nods. "It's not exactly a medical condition. Genophobia is the physical or psychological fear of having sexual intercourse. I'm saying it's not exactly a medical condition because most people who haven't actually explored their sexuality have it. Some people have it because of a moral teaching that sex is wrong. Others have it because of insecurities—you know, they're not sure if they are sexually appealing enough. For example, a 14-year-old virgin boy may have fear before his first sexual attempt, but most people, if not all, finally get through this. While this phobia can be minor in some people, it can be a major big problem in a few people's lives. These few people are extremely genophobic as a result of a mental health condition that may arise if a patient has been sexually abused."

I keep staring at him. I'm at a loss for words.

"I'm not giving a diagnosis here. I'm not saying for sure that's the problem your girl has, but that's the only thing I can think of for now. And if that's the case, I'm afraid I'm not going to be in the position to help because it's not my field, but I know a very good psychiatrist I can recommend."

I let out a deep breath. "Thanks, bro. but... you know... you said you're not sure that's the problem. So there's no need to be ahead of ourselves yet."

"Okay," he says and takes a quick look at his watch. "Bro, I have to run. I'm late for work."

He stands abruptly and buttons his suit jacket. "But if you decide that you need a hole to pour those milk seeds into..."

"Don't even start!" I growl with no malice in my voice. If there's anything I've learned today, it's that my friend has had his own fair share of the painful side of love. I suspect that that's the reason he's going through women so fast. He's trying to let go of the feelings of the past, shutting off to emotion. But what he doesn't know is once you let a woman in, she stays there. Miki is my whole world now, and no matter what—come rain, come sunshine—there can be no one else. Not even genophobia can come between us.

Wale's charming smile is back. "You love me, bro. You know you do."

"Yeah, like a toothache."

Wale walks smoothly to the door, his suit and tie undisturbed. He places his hand on the knob, but before he can open I call him in a husky voice. "Wale."

He turns back with a questioning look. "Yeah?"

"Thanks for listening."

The look that sparks between us speaks a lot more than we could put in words. Wale is more than a friend—he's a brother. Besides my daughter, he's all the family I've got. He's had my back through it all. When I lost my wife, he was there for me.

"You've been through a lot, bro. I really hope you and your chick gets through this," Wale answers, his voice full of support as he exits without another word.

Blowing out hot air, I stand there for a while, and then rush to the kitchen to prepare lunch before the ladies gets back.

****

Miki

Tiwa makes me feel compassion.

She makes me feel love in a different way than what I feel for Vince.

She makes me feel the need to be caring and nice and kind and all the things I'm not. And even though it's scary, it's the sweetest feeling I've ever felt.

That child affects me.

Needless to say, we enjoy our day out together. I try to restrain her from buying everything in the boutique, but I still let her buy as much as she needs.

We buy a lot of matching dresses. Seriously, in the next few days, we will probably be stepping out in the same style.

We stop by the salon to have her hair styled in preparation for her party this evening.

By the time we got back home, we are tired. And fortunately for us, we came back to a delicious lunch prepared by the love of my life.

After lunch, Vince leaves for the bedroom. I spend some more time with Tiwa, and then tell her to go to her room and rest a little before I start to style her for the party.

Finally, I open the door to the bedroom. Vince sits on the far corner of the bed busy on his laptop. I let out a deep breath and collapse beside him on the bed. "It's been a tiring day. My bones ache."

He didn't take his eyes off the laptop. "You need a massage?"

He looks busy, so I'd rather not disturb him. "No, I need a shower."

I manage to push myself up from the bed. I walk to the bathroom and take my clothes off.

"Hey, baby," Vince calls.

"Yes?" I reply, trying to raise my voice so he can hear me.

"I called the child care agency today. I wanted to pay the balance and was told I didn't have to pay because you sent back the nanny."

Taking the towel, I wear it around me before I walk back into the bedroom. "The nanny is a boy," I say.

Vince is no longer sitting on the bed. I glance around and see him standing by the window. Hands in the pocket of his short, he lifts both his shoulders in a shrug. "He's a boy. So?"

His face is blank, totally expressionless.

"So I sent him back."

"I don't understand why you sent him back. Did you send him back because you wanted to spend time with Tiwa? That I'd understand, but because... he's a boy..."

I cut him off. "Yes, because he's a boy. I can't trust him alone with Tiwa. You'd be surprise what those boys are capable of. When I made that call, I did it because I thought that's the best thing for Tiwa. I was protecting her."

Gently, he moves away from the window and sits back on the bed. "Why would you think the boy would hurt Tiwa?"

I hesitates a moment and let out a deep breath.

Feelings of the past come rushing back and before I know it, lumps have built up in my throat. I have to swallow hard before I can speak. "I just know," I'm trying very hard to hide the tears in my voice right now. "I can just feel it."

He lowers his head for a while. And when he looks back at me, he says, "Miki, I'm sorry."

Confused, I ask; "For what?"

"For everything. For every time you had to worry about me when you have your hands full already. And mostly for all the drama I caused after you threw me out of your house that night. I've never really apologized for that."

"Vince..."

I couldn't say more. My heart is reaching for him. What's happening? Where's all this coming from? I don't know what to say. I don't understand anything that is going on here right now.

I'm quiet, and so is he.

He's staring at me, and every second he holds me in his gaze makes my heart flutter.

His eyes moves up and down my body, darting quickly from my breasts to my legs and then back at my face.

"Come here," he says gently, but with a very hoarse and thick voice.

I hesitate a while... but that's because I'm self-conscious. I'm wearing only a towel, my underpants and bra lying in the bathroom.

I walk over slowly. He takes my hands, and I can see the bulge in his pants. It makes me excited knowing that merely looking at me can do this to him.

"Sit here," he says and pulls me down to his lap.

Gently, I sit on his lap, until he lifts one of my legs over him so that I'm straddling him. Now I'm on his lap facing him, his eyes completely locked with mine. I raise my arms up hesitantly and wrap them around his neck. And then I feel strong, powerful hand move gently to the knot of my towel.

"Vincent..." I say his name, my voice almost a whisper.

"Miki," he calls and gazes deep into my eyes. "I will never hurt you. All I want to do is give you pleasure. Do you trust me?"

I manage a weak nod.

And in one slight move, he undoes the knot and my towel drops.

My breath catches in my throat.

For one long second, he's staring at my breasts like they're the most beautiful things he has ever seen.

He swallows hard. "They're beautiful," he says, his voice hoarse with longing.

A slight moan escapes my lips as his fingers touch my bare skin. His touch sends a little spark through me and I shudder.

"Are you okay?" he asks in a whisper.

"Yeah. Just..." I pause and swallow. "I'm loving this."

He grins, and I feel his mouth close hot and wet on my right nipple, sucking at it, fondling it with his tongue. I want him to move to the other breast, but he keeps teasing this one, making the other yearn for his touch. Finally, his other hand, strong and powerful cups my left breast, caressing it, squeezing it.

I moan louder than before.

To enjoy every bit of this moment, I do what Dr. Lara told me. Eyes shut, I tell myself you're at the beach and the sand is soft. The ocean waves are small and make little noise...

I arch my back, leaning forward and offering him more. He moves from one breast to the other, sucking it, stroking it, squeezing and pressing them together, licking my nipples with his tongue and fondling it.

My entire body quivers.

I don't know where my mind is right now. I'm thinking of nothing. Only that I'm desperate to be closer to him. I yearn for him. For more of him.

My hand moves swiftly from around him down to his pants. As my fingers close in to the massive shape beneath his trousers he shut his eyes and groans.

His hands placed over mine, he tries to stop me. "No, baby. This is only for you."

Only for me.

He's going to deny himself pleasure just to make me feel good.

Ohhhh... dozens of emotions build up inside me right now, and I'm about to explode.

By now my nipples are rock hard. He lets one hand continue the caressing on my nipple while the other hand moves slightly down between my legs.

I lean back into his body. His fingers brush across the inside of my thigh and wander until they find my lips. He begins to tease my lips, his touch like liquid fire.

And then his fingers move to the most sensitive part of my body, circling it, stroking it. So soft... so slow... then gradually harder...

GOD... it feels so good.

The electric touch of his skin on my clit sets my blood on fire and makes my arms around his neck shake. I whimper and shudder over and over again. I'm so overcome with need and desire, my eyes flutter. I close my eyes against the rush and surge of desires coursing through me.

And then I open them again and stare at him. I feel alive as I gaze into those lustful, beautiful, brown eyes.

At that moment, he owns me.

And this is where I belong. I try to push every other memory back.

My mouth opens slightly for air as I feel his fingertip rubbing my clit, his other set of fingers teasing my nipples. He begins to massage me ever so softly... so slowly...

His other hand leaves my breast and circles around me, forcing my body closer to him.

Fear shoots through me.

At that moment, a part of me wants to stop.

"You still trust me, Miki?" he asks.

I remind myself that he's Vince. I trust him. He could never hurt me. And then I let go.

His face buries into my cleavage, his breath on the skin of my breasts so sensual. And then, ever so slowly, his fingers glide into my hole. My wetness makes his fingers glide in easily. The desire is overwhelming; the heat intense.

I haven't had anything like this in my life. I feel like my body is starving. Starving for passion. Intensity. For someone like Vince.

I gasp as his tongue comes back for my nipples and his fingers move back, pressing amazingly on my clit, stroking it faster, harder and faster, and sending me into insane contractions of pleasure, pushing wave after wave of bliss into me...

I let out a loud moan as his thumb swirl around me, pressing, massaging me up and down. Long, slow, overwhelming waves of intense pleasure surge through me from between my thighs and through my belly. I hang on to dear life as I cum, digging my fingers into his body.

My body jerks and shudders as I scream, then reduces into tiny, soft moans... and then I collapse on him, trembling.

He kisses my lips and neck and strokes my hair. He let his hands move gently down my bare back, sending more shivers through my spine.

When I'm finally calm, I look him in the face and smile shyly.

I feel high. I feel on top of the world. I feel like I'd rather be in this moment. I want to be able to playback that moment and live it all over again.

GOD, it's the sweetest moment of my life.

My smile grows into a laugh. I'm laughing, and it may seem that I'm crazy, but it's all the sweet emotions that are driving me to insanity.

"See?" he grins. "I told you I can give you pleasure."

I nod in agreement, smiling. I don't know how to respond, so I just lean in and give him a long, sincere kiss on the lips. A kiss of gratitude from deep within my heart. When I break the kiss, I stare at his face.

"I love you, Miki," he says quietly.

I look into his eyes. His eyes are full of so much love that at that moment I'm certain all the love in his eyes is for me.

He smiles at me genuinely, and then helps me to my feet. "Come on, go take your shower."

I'm wobbling to the bathroom on weak knees when I feel a gentle tap on my butt. I turn and glance at him.

"Sexy ass..." he says.

I wink at him, and bite my lip, trying my best to be seductive. I guess it worked, because he's now grinning like a madman.

And then I walk into the bathroom.

Chapter Thirteen

Miki

I finish taking my shower and as I stand in front of the mirror, my mind goes back to the last few minutes, I have a deep urge to live the moment again.

"Something tells me you're going to be smiling to yourself a lot for the rest of this week." Vince's voice breaks through my reverie.

I had no idea I have been smiling.

He hugs me from the back and places a kiss on my neck.

"Keep this up and I'm going to be smiling forever," I say.

He smiles and kisses me again.

Is it me or Vince who seems different? I don't know. I can't just place my hands on it yet, but he seems different.

There is just something about him...

"Vince..."

He cuts me off with a kiss on my lips, and then he says; "I have to shower. It's almost time for Tiwa's party."

He rushes into the bath while I try to look for something to wear. I should go home and bring more clothes for myself.

I slip into another of his T-shirts and then walk to Tiwa's room. When I open the door, she's already wearing her long, pink dress.

She rushed over to me. "How do I look?"

A sweet smile spreads across my face. "Wow. You look gorgeous."

She smiles and claps her hands softly in excitement.

Holding her by the waist, I move her back to the mirror. She sits on the dressing chair, facing the mirror as I place my hands gently on her shoulder. "Now let's touch up your hair, shall we?"

She nods.

I spray her hair with hair oil and then brush it out. After a few minutes of brushing, we are both satisfied with the look. And then I place a pink rose hair clip on the side.

She smiles and nods to let me know she likes it.

As soon as I finish, she can't wait to show herself to her dad. She slips into her shoes and rushes to the door.

Fortunately, as soon as she opens the door, she runs into her dad.

Vince is wearing a black suit, white shirt and a pink tie. I want to tell him how amazing he looks in that outfit.

"Tiwa is wearing a dress, so I figure maybe this instead of doing casual. What do you think?"

"You look good, Dad," Tiwa says.

He stares at Tiwa and then back at me. "You've turned my girl into a grown lady. Now I'm going to be watching the boys in the room to make sure they're not staring."

Tiwa stifles a grin.

Walking closer to Vince, I lean in and adjust his pocket square. "You both look gorgeous," I say. "And you both are running late."

"Oh... we should be on our way."

Tiwa glances at me. "You're not coming?"

I can see the excitement on her face rushing away.

"Yes, Tiwa, I'm not coming."

Her face is covered with disappointment and sadness. "Why?"

God, I hate to break this little girl's heart.

Vince steps in. "Tiwa," he calls gently. "Only parents or guardians acknowledged by your school can come to the party. Now everything happens so fast and there was no time to add Miki to the list. I'm so sorry. I will make sure to add her today."

It took more than a second before she's actually able to process the explanation. Gently, she nods her head in understanding.

Vince holds out his hand for her, and she takes it. As they walk toward the door, she looks back and glances at me. Her almost wet eyes break my heart, and slowly my hand finds a resting place on my chest as if that will comfort me.

Before I know what's going on, Tiwa releases her father's hand and stands right in front of me, looking reassuringly into my eyes. "Don't worry," she says, "you will go with me next time. Okay?"

God, so sweet of her to try and comfort me.

It brings tears to my eyes, and before the tears can actually flow, I say, "Come here." Squatting, I pull her into my arms and hold her tightly for only God knows how long, allowing some sweet instinct to take over.

"Have fun, princess." I instinctively kiss her forehead.

She smiles, places a short kiss on my cheek, and then runs back to her dad.

As soon as they leave the house, I change into my own clothes and head back to my place. I've been away from home for almost two days now, but it doesn't feel like it. With Vince, I feel at home, as if that's where I really belong, and I sure as hell haven't felt that since I was eight years old.

Needless to say, my house feels boring. It feels cold, like there's no love in the air blowing through my house.

I pack a few things that I need and head back to Vince's.

After a one-hour wait, Vince and Tiwa walk through the door. Tiwa won't stop talking about the delicious meals, the games she played with her dad at the party, her friends... I think I know all her friends by name already and could describe each of them if asked to.

After another hour of unending, never-boring chats between Tiwa and me, I tell her to go shower and get ready for bed. As she leaves, I stay back to make a quick nighttime snack—a protein shake.

It takes me a total of fifteen minutes to get it ready. Serving it in a cup, I head to Tiwa's room. When I open the door, I find Tiwa sitting at her reading desk, her reading lamp turned on.

"Someone is reading..." I say as I set the cup on the table. Stumbling on a rumpled paper on the floor, I crouch and pick it up.

All work and no play make Jack a dull boy.

I read the content out loud.

"And what's this?" I ask.

Her eyes fix on her books; she barely looks at me. "I forgot I have this homework assignment from school. And school starts tomorrow."

Walking closer to her side, I caress her hair. "Can I help?"

"Maybe. The assignment is from my art class. We're supposed to come up with a quote, write it on a drawing paper, and make a design, sort of."

Now I understand the crayons and colored pencils lying on her desks.

"How is your teacher going to grade it? Is she grading the quote or the design?"

"25 points for quotes, 30 for design."

I nod. "So they're both important, huh?"

"Yes. And it's not just about the quotes and the design. She's actually going to make us stand in front of the class and explain them."

I frown. "That class is too hard. How old are you? Seven? You're supposed to be drawing and painting apples. Not something this complicated. Do you even know how to write a complete sentence?"

"Yes. I'm turning eight soon, and next year I start secondary school. If I can't write a sentence, how am I going to pass my entrance examination?"

I give a small smile. "My God, you're too smart. I was say nine years old before I took my entrance examination into secondary school."

"Nine is good." She tries to keep her voice low. "My dad was thirteen when he took the entrance examination."

"Yeah. Your dad didn't have it easy like you and me. You know he had to work the street to pay for his tuition, so studying might be hard on him."

"Yes. But my dad is a lawyer now. He is very intelligent," she smiles proudly.

"Yes, your dad is very intelligent."

The moment passes and I stare at all the scrap papers on the table. She's struggling with this assignment. "Do you really have to take this art class?"

"Yes. I want to be the best artist in the world when I grow up."

Patting her shoulder, I smile at her. "Well, that's good.

When I was your age, I wanted to be the best doctor in the world. And then one year later, I wanted to be the best singer in the world, and then the best lawyer, and then the best engineer."

She laughs. "You never really could make up your mind."

"Yes."

"So everything you ever wanted to be, you never became any of them."

Her words hit me and for than a second, my voice caught in my throat. Goosebumps runs over my body. This little girl couldn't be more right. Everything I would have become, I never became. Something was taken from me.

Finally, I find my voice back. "Why don't you drink up your shake, and we can talk and maybe I can help you come up with a nice quote?"

She didn't disagree, so I push the cup closer to her. She picks it up as I pull up a second chair and sit.

"A bad day, a bad year or years does not equal a bad life."

She almost chokes on her drink. "I like that. Can I use it?"

"No, you can't. You have to come up with your own quote."

She raises a brow. "Why?"

"Because you won't be able to explain it when you stand in front of your classmates."

"Oh," she says and releases her brow.

"But I'll teach you how I came up with that, and then you can do yours."

"Okay."

I let out a breath before I begin. "A long time ago, bad things happened to me." I pause for a second. This adorable little kid is the only person that has come close to hearing my story. "Really bad things. People I trusted, people I believed in, hurt me. Really bad. I hated my life..."

"Um... is that why you don't like people?" she asks, her eyes filled with kindness and pity.

I didn't know how to respond. My brows pulled together, I give her a sideways glance.

"I hear my daddy call you Ice," she tries to explain. "I ask why and he says you don't like too many people. That you can be mean sometimes."

"Why did he tell you that? I don't want you to see me like that."

"It's okay," she answers sincerely. "Besides, I like a badass. I like a tough mommy."

That moment, my heart feels something it has never felt before. She called me mommy. She wants me to be her mommy even with all of my flaws and imperfections.

"You don't want me to call you mommy?" she asks.

Far from that. I want her to call me mommy everyday till I enter the grave, but it's too much emotion for me right now. I can't put it into words.

"Daddy says we'd ask you at the right time, but I'm going back to school tomorrow... and... and I just want... to know you'll be here when I get back. I want to know you're not going anywhere, that you'll be here... like forever."

I can't say I understand, but I know what she's feeling. She lost her mommy to death at an age when she doesn't even understand what death means.

Looking reassuringly into her eyes, I swallow hard. "I'm going to be here. I'm not going anywhere, princess."

She nods, and we both fall quiet for a while.

"Drink up your shake," I say, trying to take tension off the moment, "and I'll finish my story."

Lifting the cup to her mouth, she empties it in one gulp.

"So, really bad things happened to me. I thought I'd never make it through those bad days. I had no one to hold on to. I thought it would be the end of my life. I hated my life. Fast forward to now, somehow, my life turns better. I own Daniels Group, one of the greatest business corporations in the country."

She nods and gives me that I'm-proud-of-you look. "True, a bad day doesn't mean a bad life."

"Okay. Now think of the best moment of your life and write something about it."

She grabs a pen and a paper.

"Let me see how smart you are. How about you do it in three minutes? Do it in three minutes, and you can ask me anything you want."

She gives me a sideway glance. "Anything?"

"Anything."

Sharply, she focuses on her paper, and then she's biting her finger. About two minutes later, she's writing on her paper.

"Done! I did it, right?" she asks, giving me the paper.

I smile and take the paper from her. "Yes, you did it."

After d dark, there's always light.

I read it out loud.

"Hmm...That is wise. Can you explain how you come up with this?"

Her excitement leaves her for a second, and she averts her gaze from me. "When my daddy told me my mommy was gone and that I might never see her again, it felt like I was in the dark. Like I'm in a hole. My daddy is a great dad and in a way, I know he feels what I feel. But the last few days, it's been like... as if nighttime is over, and I woke up to a beautiful morning."

The last few days? Am I responsible for the light that came after her darkness?

"Okay. Can I ask for anything now?" She says, all her excitement back again.

"Yes, but please don't ask me to bring the moon down to you."

She grins and shakes her head. "I'm not going to ask you to bring down the moon. I want it to be you and daddy that drives me to school tomorrow morning."

"No. No. Absolutely not. I've got work tomorrow. My work is important. Daniels Group is the best thing that ever happened to me."

Yep, yep, I shouldn't have said that. Maybe that was too much. But I'm just being me. You know, honest and all. Maybe I'm changing, but you know what they say about old habits dying hard.

"Anything," she says in a pleading whisper.

"Holding me to my promise, huh?"

"Please..." she pleads, batting her eyelashes.

"I can't," I insist. "I have to go to work."

Her face falls and she gives a slow nod while frowning. "Now, back to my homework."

"About that," I cut in, glancing at the paper on which she wrote her quote. "The is spelled t-h-e. You can't write it as just 'd'."

"I know. But my daddy writes it like that."

"Your daddy is not a student." I can barely finish the sentence before a big yawn escapes my mouth.

"You know it's okay if you go to bed."

"Really?" I ask.

"Yes. I got it from here. And thanks for helping with my homework."

"Anything for you."

Standing, I put the chair back in its place. I grab her empty cup in one hand and use the other to fondle her hair. "Good night, princess."

"Night night."

"Don't stay up too late," I say as I walk to the door.

"Okay, Mommy."

Chapter Fourteen

Miki

I reflect on it overnight and realize the pain I caused Tiwa by refusing to drive her to school. And then I decide to give her a surprise in the morning by going.

"Hurry up, ladies," That's Vince's voice. "Don't spend two hours dressing up today."

With that, I hear the slamming of the front door. He's going to his car already.

"C'mon, princess, hurry up. Your dad seems in a hurry."

She nods, and I check her luggage again. I want her to have everything—everything she wants. I want school to feel like home for her, except that there won't be home-cooked meals.

Canned milk, biscuit, cereals, canned juice, chocolate, everything is all in place. I know kids love sugar, so I didn't forget to get her dozens of candy bars.

I wish she could have more, but the school has some regulations in place to limit what the kids bring to school. Still, I want her to have everything, enjoy her childhood. Which brought up the subject that had been lurking in my mind for days.

"You know what? Can you finish up for me? I've got to talk to your dad real quick."

"Sure."

"Thanks."

The next second, I'm charging from the room down the stairs and then outside to the garage, barefoot.

Vince is clearing out the trunk for Tiwa's luggage. He lifts his head out of the trunk and smiles as he sees me. "Babe, what's so urgent you have to run out here without your shoes?"

He's smiling, but I cut to the chase. "Does Tiwa like going to boarding school?"

"No. Why?"

Reading his expression, I can tell he's confused. "If she doesn't like boarding school, maybe we could let her go from home, you know what I mean?"

"No, I don't," he snaps. "And don't tell me how to raise my kid."

I don't know why, but I feel the need to press further, for Tiwa's sake. I don't want her to feel she's growing up without parents. Because that's how I felt throughout my childhood. My parents are alive and well, but I grew up an orphan.

"I'm not trying to teach you how to raise your child, but..."

"Drop it, Miki," he cuts me off and starts to walk away. "That school is only a boarding school. They don't let kids come to school from home."

Following him as he walks off, I say, "Her father is Vince Ali & Associates. I am Daniels Group. I'm sure together we can pull a force that can change the mind of the school. Or maybe we can change schools for her."

"We're not changing schools. That school is the best in the country. It's the best for her. I'm paying a fortune for her to be there. Children of the most powerful people in this country go to that school, and she belongs there. I'm giving the best to my daughter."

"But still..."

He stops walking and turns around to glare at me. "Stop it, Miki!"

I shiver. "I'm only trying to help."

"What gives you the right to even talk about this? Because she calls you 'mommy' now, is that it? You come into her life like a glorified savior when you know she's vulnerable. You're not even sure if you want to spend the rest of your life with me, and yet you let my daughter call you mommy. You're confusing her. And now you think that gives you the right to make decisions in her life. I am her father, Miki. And I decide what is best for her. Not you, not anyone else. And my decision is that boarding school is the best for her."

His rage is spent already, but he's still glaring at me.

His words cut through me like an ice-dagger.

God, I wish it was not the man I love who just yelled at me now. I wish it was some random person who I didn't give a rat's ass about. Because I will never take this from anyone. Anyone. I would flex my muscles and yell back. But this is Vince.

His words hurt me deeply, and he reminds me that Tiwa isn't mine. It hurts even more because I know I can't have my own baby. But no matter how upset and sad I am right now, I won't give up on Tiwa. After all the happiness and love she's made me feel, I owe her.

"Are you sure that's best for her? Because I'm guessing you sent her off to boarding school so you could have it easy, you know, go about your life while she's not here."

His glare deepens. "Don't you dare accuse..."

I cut him off. "No, no, if that's the reason you sent her off to boarding school, I'll understand. You're buying the best care for her while giving her a good education. But you don't have to do that anymore, because I'm here now. You don't have to care for her all alone. Let me help. I can help. We both have busy schedules, but I'm sure we will work it out."

He's quiet now. I'm guessing he's at a loss for words, but he's still wearing his glare.

"You know, when I was about Tiwa's age, my parents were running around trying to gather so much money, trying to send me to the best school... the best this... the best that. To give me all that, they had to kiss rich people's asses, and I suffered so much for it. The best they wanted to give me became the worst; the beautiful dream they wanted me to have became a nightmare. What I'm trying to say is, it's not only about what you think is best for your child. The reasonable things that the child wants should be respected, too. If my parents had done that, my life would have turned out better."

Almost when I finish my long speech, Tiwa rushes out of the house carrying her backpack. "I'm ready. Can we go now?"

"Sure," Vince replies, the glare on his face suddenly disappearing. "I'll grab your bag."

"And I'll grab my purse and put on some shoes."

Vince and I walk back into the house, but we don't say anything to each other. And in the car, as we drive Tiwa to school, we both communicate to Tiwa, but not to each other.

Getting to school, Vince carries the luggage bag and hands it to her teacher. The teacher reminds us we can't accompany her beyond that point before disappearing with the bags. Standing in front of her hostel, he says, "So this is it. I'm not seeing you for the next month and a half."

She nods. "I'll miss you."

Arms widespread, he gestures for her to come to him, and she walks happily into his arms. "I'll miss you, too, my baby." After a few seconds of heartbreakingly sweet embrace, he releases her and looks into her eyes. "Be a good girl..."

She cuts him off. "Be a good girl, respect your teachers, and be nice to your friends. Yeah, yeah, I remember all of it."

He flashes her a cute smile. "And don't forget I love you."

"I love you too, Daddy."

She's about to glance at me when the bell rings.

"Ugh! It's time to leave," she says, glancing at me and then back at her dad. "I'm not stupid. Both of you are fighting. You're not speaking to each other."

"Tiwa Ali!" Her teacher calls.

"I have to go," she says. "The person who is wrong should just apologize to the other. Both of you forgive each other already." She runs into my arms. "Bye, Mommy."

I hold her tight in an embrace and she whispers in my ear. "Two weeks from today is visitor's day. Come and visit me, okay?"

I can only manage a nod.

"I..." I want to say that I love her, but I hold it back.

"Bye, Daddy. Bye, Mommy!" she says as she runs into her hostel.

After a few seconds of staring into nothingness, Vince gives me a tap on the shoulder. "Time to go."

I don't respond. We get into the car and take another quiet drive back. He drops me off at my work and before he can say anything, I get out of the car.

When I walk into my office, Sade is surprise to see me.

It's been a few days and I've been totally absent from work. She had called me a thousand times and left me a bazillion messages. And guess what? I never replied to any of them. Because me being me, I don't have to explain myself to anyone.

"Good morning, ma'am," she says, immediately rising to her feet as I walk in.

"Good morning," I reply. "You drive, huh?" I cut to the chase.

Confused, she answers anyway. "Yes, ma'am."

"Pen and paper please."

Searching through the stacks on her desk, she pulls out a paper and a pen and hands them to me. Very quickly, I write on the paper and give it back to her. "Go to that address and bring my car," I say, throwing my car keys at her.

She catches it, but I can see that her jaw is almost dropping. Searching through my purse, I find her a few notes and give them to her for taxi fare.

"Don't worry, Sade. You'll be alright." I feel the need to reassure her. "If anyone questions you about the car, tell them I sent you. Or you can call me on the phone, and I can speak to the person."

"Okay, ma'am."

"You've got thirty minutes."

"Yes, ma'am."

As soon as she leaves, I walk straight into my office. Sweet Lord, I can't believe how much work is waiting for me. There's this big, tall stack of paper on my desk. If I'm lucky, they will just be things I have to sign.

Taking off my heels, I sit back in my luxurious armchair which I've missed more than anything. I grab my phone and plug my earpiece in my ear. Music makes my work easier.

As Asa's *Be My Man* blasts at full volume, I immerse myself into my work. I don't keep track of the time, but I know about an hour later Sade comes in to give back my car key and give me the rundown of what I've missed.

I keep working, trying to clear my desk of all that paper. After several hours, my phone rings. I'm absolutely more than eager to pick it up. But seeing who is calling, I'm more than disappointed.

"Lola! Stop calling my phone," I yell immediately after pressing the green button.

"I'm sorry, Ice, but..."

I cut her off. "What can I do you for?"

"See, the thing is, I didn't realize the TV station employed me because of you. It's not because I'm good or anything. They want me to be able to convince you to invest in the TV station and sponsor some shows. They say they're willing to work out some partnership deal with you, and you can even buy the station if you want. All I have to do is convince you to do this, and I'll have my job."

"NO."

"Ice?"

"I mean no. I won't do this."

"Ice..."

"Hold on, Lola. Now I understand how you played this game all the while. You apply for a job with this TV Station, then at the interview, you boast that you know me, and they say prove that by inviting me impromptu to your talk show, which I was too stupid to see at the time. I will not do this for you, Lola. Friends are friends. You do not use friendship for personal gain. You don't play games with friendship. If there's one thing you're good at, it is failing. Go back to your boss and tell him you do not have access to me. Screw up. Fail. Get fired. Go back to being jobless on the street and start whoring yourself like Jessie." And then I press the red button.

It's like I've suddenly grown a conscience. I realize that that was way too harsh. I shouldn't have said that. But it's true. I've said it and can't take it back. With a quick glance at my watch, I know it's time to go home. I just have to decide which home I want to go to: mine or Vince's.

****

Vince

As I drive home, I imagine how lonely the house is going to be. Tiwa just left for school and she won't be back until six weeks from now. And Miki hasn't even called me today. She's probably still upset with me for every dumb thing I said this morning. But I've spent the whole of today trying to right my wrong.

I'm not expecting her to come to my place tonight. She's probably packed the few things she has and moved back home. This man is going to be alone tonight.

Driving into my garage, I see Miki's car still parked in there.

She's here!

Words can't begin to explain how I feel.

Smiling like an idiot, I walk into the house. She's not in the living room, not in the kitchen.

Bedroom.

I run upstairs and open the door to my bedroom and there she is sitting on the bed, laptop on her legs. She's wearing that silky, transparent nightie she always wears.

"Hey, baby," I say as I open the door, giving her a happy smile.

She glances at me, but doesn't respond.

"I'm sorry I didn't call you today. I was so busy with..."

She doesn't respond.

All women are not the same, but there's only a little difference between them. She's giving me the silent treatment. I understand this attitude very well.

Taking off my suit jacket, I give the same fate to my tie and shirt. "I started a petition against Tiwa's school today, you know, how the school shouldn't be only a boarding school. Students should be allowed to come to school from home."

Wide eyes glance at me. "Really?"

Yeah, she's broken her silent treatment.

"Yes, really. The school says they'd consider it if I can get fifty parents to sign it. And guess what? I got forty-five parents already. I'm sure I'll be able to get five more tomorrow. And next term, our baby won't have to live in the boarding house."

Jumping out of bed, she runs into my arms in a rush. "Thank you, Vince."

I hold her tightly against my chest, warmly and protectively. "I'm so sorry for all the things I said. It was stupid. And dumb, and I am so sorry. And you're right. I wasn't entirely honest with myself. Sending her to that school is so she can have the best and I can have it easy."

Taking her head off my chest, she glances up into my eyes. "It's okay."

"Really? You forgive me?"

"Yes."

And then she places a kiss on my lips.

"I'll take a quick shower," I say.

"Okay. Have you had something to eat?"

"Yes. You?"

"Yes. But I'm in the mood for a fruit. I'll grab some oranges in the fridge. You want some?"

"Sure."

She walks out of the room while I take off the rest of my clothes and head for the bathroom.

****

Miki

I just finish my orange when Vince walks out of the bathroom with only a towel around his waist. No matter how many times I've seen him like that, I just want to keep staring.

GOD, his body is heavenly. His skin, so flawless and perfect, like that of a Greek god or something. His body is athletic, his muscles well-sculpted; a six pack on a washboard stomach. He's not too hairy. Just the right amount of hair on his chest.

Swallowing hard, I try to relax my sexual desires sizzling between my legs. "Orange?"

"Sure," he says, crawling into the bed and sitting next to me.

He smells so good, mostly of lemon soap, but delicious to me.

I grab the last of the orange, take a bite, and fluidly put the orange in his mouth and hold it there as he takes a wet bite.

I want it to be his lips on mine in a hot, wet kiss like that.

I want to feel the full pleasure of a man inside me. For real, this time.

Pushing the orange harder into his mouth, I watch his

eyes. I love this man so much. Why should I let a fear of something that happened long ago disturb me from feeling some intimacy with him? Will I grow into old age without knowing what it means to be loved in this way, to feel like a real woman?

I want him so desperately in a way I have never wanted anything in my entire life. I can feel my need for him crushing the troubled part of me into submission.

Teasing him, I take the orange from his mouth and place it back on the plate sitting on a stool beside the bed. Juice runs down his chin. Gently, slowly, I lean over and lick the sweet juice away. He doesn't move. I keep watching his eyes, so alive yet so dreamy. Our faces are so close that I share his breath as he shares mine: quick and warm.

I shudder as a soft moan escape my lips. My chest is heaving heavily; my heart pounding loudly into my ears. I run my wet fingers down his chin, his neck, and chest, gliding them over the hard muscles under his beautiful skin.

Ever so gently, I move over and sit on his lap so that I'm straddling him, facing him. Firmly caressing his chest, I let my hands glide slowly to the hardness of one his nipples. I fondle it, play with it, and squeeze it as I let my eyes close for a moment while sucking in much-needed air. Gently but forcefully, I push him down on his back. He goes straight down to the bed without protest.

I lean over him with my hands on his chest for support, enjoying the rigid firmness of his muscles, and the heat radiating from my skin, setting me on fire. He's breathing heavily, his chest rising and falling with the very life in him.

Slowly, I lean in, bringing my face closer to his, my long, thick hair cascading around his face as my lips brush his.

His thigh muscles flex between my legs, sending shivers through me. I gasp, opening my mouth to get my breath. I lose myself in his gaze, in those eyes that feel as if they are evaporating all my bad memories, replacing them with gripping desires.

A strong, powerful hand slides under my nightie, caressing my back and slowly tracing the line of my spine. I grind my hips on the bulge under his towel, gyrating around it. I want to feel it everywhere. More than that, I want it inside me.

When the grinding is no longer enough, my hands move slightly down to pull it out, remove the piece of towel that is between us, little sounds escape with some of my breaths as I did.

Before I can remove the towel, I feel his hands over mine.

I lean closer, my lips brushing his at the same time, watching his eyes. "I want you," I say in a breathless whisper.

Pain lurks behind the passion in his eyes. "Only if you tell me the secret you've been hiding."

I'm not hearing anything he's talking about. I just want him so desperately in a way that I've never wanted anything before. I begin to kiss his neck, then lick slowly down to his chest where my tongue finds one of his nipples.

His hand collects a fistful of my hair and gently pulls my head up to meet his gaze. "I mean it. You have to tell me first."

His words cut through me, and I can feel the seriousness in his voice.

Unable to look at him, I sit back on the bed. How can I tell him? He won't want me anymore. He will hate me.

Tears fill my eyes and I let my palm cover my mouth before any sob can be heard, trying desperately to stop the tears from flowing. How can he know I'm a piece of semen trash and still want me? Half the men in the country have...

God, how can I tell him all of that?

A sick feeling crawls in the pit of my stomach.

He sits up on the bed, closer to me, hands over my shoulders. "You don't have to tell me if you don't want to."

Still trying to hold the tears back, my eyes can hardly focus on him. "Vince...please." Tears can be heard in my voice already.

Pulling me tenderly against himself, he holds my head to his chest while wrapping his other hand protectively around me, rocking me and occasionally kissing the top of my head.

"I promise you, Vince, I'll tell you everything, but not tonight. Maybe in the morning. But just hold me this night..." *because it might be the last time.*

I don't say it out loud, but I can swear he hears it in my heart.

He slowly lies back down, embracing me tightly with his strong, powerful arms. "And I promise you, Miki, no matter what you tell me, I'll always hold you like this every night."

His words give me a little relief until morning, when all the secrets will be spilled. I shudder with the chill of it.

Chapter Fifteen

Miki

I wasn't born genophobic. Dr. Lara says it's my brain or my mind trying to react to the horrors of my past. You cannot understand that until you know what exactly happened in my past.

It all started when I was about eight years old. I was a bright, smart, and funny kid. Everybody I've ever met loved me. When visitors came to our house, they never had one second of rest because I'd chat them up, telling stories and jokes, and they'd have no choice but to fall in love with me. And when my parents came back to the living room, the visitors would say nice things about me. Things like, "Your little girl is so smart," and "She is made for great things."

And though my parents would usually say, "She will be great if she learns to shut up because she talks too much," I could see the look in their eyes that they were proud of me. More and more, they felt the need to give me the best; to actually see their little daughter become as great as predicted.

I attended the best school in the country, with the children of kings and top politicians and rich businessmen. But my father wasn't any of those. He was a normal man, a middle-class businessman who wanted to provide for his family the things that only rich men can provide.

To attain that, he kept only rich friends. One I particularly remember is Jamal of Jamal Corporations. My father was friend with this man. Well, not really friends—more like my dad sucked up to him, wanting to be his friend whether or not that man wanted the friendship. My mom was always sucking up to his wife, too, and they forced me to be friends with their daughter, Jessie, even though I didn't really like being friends with her.

But there was one person in the Jamal family who seemed to have no place in my family: Jaye Jamal, the heir of Jamal Corporation. He had no one his age to be friends with in our family because I'm an only child. Jaye Jamal is exactly ten years older than me, so I always called him big brother. He was the only thing close to a brother I ever had.

Now Jaye had failed his entrance examinations to the university. He failed WAEC, failed JAMB, failed SAT, and so he lost any chance to go to a university that year both at home and abroad. His parents had no other choice but to enroll him back in secondary school so he could take the examinations again.

The thing is, the school he enrolled at was closer to our house than the Jamal house. Mr. Jamal suggested that Jaye should stay with us until he finished the examinations, not only because of the distance, but because Jaye was used to having everything. They thought if he stayed at our house where he couldn't get everything he wanted, he would learn a few responsibilities and thus be able to study well and pass his examinations.

But they were wrong. My father knew Jaye was the heir to Jamal Corporations, and found it important to be in his good graces. My father gave him everything he asked for. My father sucked up to him like he did Mr. Jaye.

Our little service to the Jamals paid off. Mr. Jamal promised to give my father big money to start his own business. And Mrs. Jamal gave my mother a lot of money, too. I was a kid then, so I don't know how much, but I know it was a lot—enough for my mother to start her own jewelry business.

With that money, my mother travelled to Dubai to purchase some jewelry for sale. She was supposed to be away for one week, leaving me, my dad, and Jaye in the house.

That fateful day, my dad went out, meaning it was only Jaye and me in the house. I was in my room, studying for my exam when all of a sudden my door flew open.

"Big brother, are you okay?" I asked, glancing up at him. For one second he stood there and said nothing. His eyes were red and scary. He looked wild and different. He was probably high on something—alcohol, drugs, something. Of course, I didn't know it at the time, but came to understand it much better when I grew up.

So I stood up from my reading table and took a few steps toward him. "Big brother..."

"Stop right there!" he yelled, and pointed a knife at me. A big knife, the one my dad used to cut the chicken's neck at Christmas.

My little brain couldn't understand what was going on. Slowly, he took one step after the other until he was only a few inches from me and I could feel the knife, icy cold, on my neck. "If you move, I'll cut your neck. If you scream, I will cut your neck open and you're dead."

Pushing the knife a little more into me, he glared into my eyes. "Do you understand?" he asked, his voice sounding dangerous.

I nodded, tears running down my neck as the knife cut into my flesh. It was painful, yet I was so afraid I couldn't make a noise.

"Sit down."

I sat down slowly on the bed without protest. And then gently he dropped the knife on the floor and removed his belt. Very slowly, he pushed down his pants. Putting his hands into his boxers, he brought out his... penis.

I had seen the penis of little kids—you know, babies when their mothers were changing their diapers or something. But I had never seen any that was that big or long. The sight of it was scary.

Reflexively, I used my hands to cover my eyes. I sat frozen for more than a few seconds and I didn't hear any sound of movement or anything except for groans coming from him. Taking my hands off my eyes, I saw him stroking his penis. He seemed to be enjoying it. He seemed preoccupied with it, and I thought why not make use of the opportunity and run for the door.

Before I knew it, strong hands pulled me back.

"I told you not to move!" he yelled as he pulled me and threw me several feet across the room. My head hit the wall before I landed on the floor. I don't know for sure, but I think I passed out.

All that I know is that when I opened my eyes, I was brought back by a severe, sharp pain in my privates. It was so painful that I screamed so much I felt my lungs ruptured.

"Fuck! Your pussy is so tight... so sweet."

He forced himself into me in one motion. Blood rushed out in brooks.

All that I felt was pain. It felt like I was going to die.

For several minutes, I didn't know what was going on around me. I passed out, I think. The next thing I knew was that I found myself lying on the hospital bed. When I opened my eyes, my father was the first person I saw.

"Daddy," I called, my voice weak. The screams must have put a strain on my voice.

Sitting beside me on the bed, he held my hand. "Miki, who did this to you?"

My memory returned to me slowly, bit by bit.

I glanced around until my eyes fell on the devil. Slowly I raised my hands and pointed my fingers at him. "Him," I said. "Big brother..."

I saw my father's gaze turn into a vicious glare. He shook with a kind of rage that I had never seen before.

"Calm down, man," Jaye said. "I didn't do it. I told you I walked in, the door was open, and I her saw her laying in blood on the floor. It could have been anyone. I didn't do it."

"Are you saying Miki doesn't know you? She's too young, she doesn't know the face of who violated her?"

"I don't..."

Before he could make a complete statement, my father threw a punch at his face. Blood rushed from Jaye's nostrils. Using his palm to collect the blood, he glared at my father. "Do we have a problem here? I guess I should call my dad."

That was it. My father's fist withdrew itself and for one long second, he shook with impotent anger. And then he glanced at me with that look that told me he was between the devil and the deep blue sea.

I get it. Jaye's father was our ticket to a good life, and the relationship with him was almost as important to my father as his relationship with me.

For the next few days, I went in and out of sleep. I didn't see big brother at all, and I didn't really see much of my father.

On what seemed like the third day, I saw my father again. His eyes were puffy, red, like he had been crying. Walking slowly to my bedside, a sad smile sat plastered on his face. "Hey, angel."

I managed to sit up on the bed. "Daddy."

"The doctors have done everything necessary. All the test results are out and you're okay. The doctor said you are good to go home today."

I feigned a smile, too, the same sad smile my father had. "I feel fine."

He nodded and sat on the bed close to me. Grabbing my hand, he looked calmly into my eyes. "Angel, I'd like to talk to you about what happened."

I nodded for him to continue.

"What happened a few days ago wasn't your fault. You didn't ask for it, and you didn't deserve it," he paused for a while before he continued. "I know you might not understand everything that's happening, but Miki, whether you ask for it or not, you're an adult now. This incident has made you into an adult. And if there is one thing adults know for certain is that life isn't fair." He swallowed hard. "Life is tough, Miki, and you have to be tough to live through this. You have to be tough, Miki. And that's why you're going to put this behind you. You're going to forget that this ever happened. You're going to forget, okay, Miki?" He squeezed my hand to make sure I understood.

I nodded in agreement.

"You're not going to tell anyone. Most importantly, you're not going to tell your mother. Okay?"

I nodded again.

"If you are ever confused about what happened, if you ever needed any explanation, if you ever want to talk about it, I'm here for you. This is going to be our little secret."

I didn't respond.

"You have to promise me, angel. Promise me you won't tell anyone."

"I promise, Daddy. I won't tell anyone."

He pulled me in and held me in his arms. For a long time.

By the time we got back home that day, my body felt better. I mean my privates still felt kind of sore, but I feel okay physically.

My father opened the front door and I walked in, only to see big brother sitting on the couch and watching TV. He was still sitting on our couch! I felt a kind of anger that I've never felt before in my life.

"Daddy, he hurt me. Why is he still here?"

My father dropped the bags we brought from the hospital and shut the door. "You know it's words like that I told you not to say to anyone. Things like 'he hurt me'—you're not supposed to say that."

I scowled. "But it's true. He hurt me."

"You remember when I told you to be tough? Well, part of being tough is respecting people in the place of power. Jaye's family they are not just in the place of power, they are power! And you have to respect that."

My scowl deepened. "He should be punished for what he did to me. He shouldn't get away with it."

"You think I don't know?" he yelled at me. "You think this is easy for me? I'm doing this for you, Miki. I'm trying very hard to secure your future, to give you the best future. If you want me to go to the police, yes, I'll go. We will fight the Jamals and try to get justice for my girl, but you know what will happen—we will lose. The Jamals will make sure of that. We won't only lose the fight for justice, we'll lose our ticket to a better life, too. And after all of that, your name is going to be in the news forever; your face will be everywhere. Your friends in school are going to remember that you were sexually violated. The world is going to remember that little girl that was violated forever. You will never be able to separate yourself from the scandal. The story is going to follow you to the end of your life. When they mention your name ten years from today, or maybe fifty years, it's going to be the first thing that will pop up. You will never be able to live free and forget the horror of what happened. I have to save you from all of that. But don't you dare think for one second that this is easy for me."

I didn't really understand everything he was talking about, but I got the picture. I glanced at Jaye as he broke into a victorious smile. It's pretty much impossible to describe the flood of emotions I felt at that moment.

Rage.

Hatred.

Hurt.

Shame.

Tears filled my eyes, and I ran up to my room to cry alone. That day was the beginning of the rest of my dark life. It was the last day anyone ever saw that smart, kind, and funny Miki who was full of life.

Chapter Sixteen

Miki

When my mother came back from her business trip, I was awfully quiet, but she didn't even notice. She had the business to occupy her mind. It was about her customers, how much money she was making, and her business trip. That was all that mattered to her. I wanted her to see me; to be worried about me. The only thing she noticed was that I started avoiding my father.

She asked me about that, but what can I say? I promised Father that I'd never tell my mother, and he had been holding me to that promise at every opportunity.

The Jamals fulfilled their promise. They gave my father a lot of money to start the bottled water business. The business was called Jamal Bottled Water. You know, it's easier to break into the market if you are with a trusted brand. Being under the Jamal Corporation, a certain percentage of profit went to the Jamals, which means, in some, way we were still servants to the Jamal family.

We had a financial breakthrough. Things got a little better for my family. And time passed by. Time heals everything. That's what people say. But time didn't heal me. I had a lot of unresolved anger, and I had to keep to myself to keep a lid on it. My childhood was lonely. I had my parents, but I felt like an orphan.

Like I said, time passed by. Big brother finished his examinations and left. But the scars he left me remained.

Eight years later, I turned sixteen. I had written my entrance examinations for the university and was waiting to be admitted. I counted each day until I'd finally get to leave home and live by myself at school. I was counting the days to my freedom.

During this waiting period, something else happened. Mr. Jamal told my father he'd liked his son to stay with us for about a month. Brother Jaye was about 26 years old, graduating straight from college. Mr. Jamal was preparing him to take over the Jamal Corporation, and he wanted him to learn how to grow a small business—and he couldn't think of anyone who had a small business other than my father, the one person he trusted to really mentor his son. In exchange for that, he'd make sure my father kept all the profits from the bottled water business. And he could change the name of the business and create his own brand.

Of course the offer was too sweet for my father to turn down. Finally, he was going to stand on his own two feet. I bet he'd dreamed of the day that the business would become Daniels Bottled Water.

Without anyone caring about my opinion, Jaye moved in with us again. I tried as much as possible to ignore him. I didn't talk to him in the least. If it so happen I was home alone with him, I'd stay in my room with the door locked. I didn't care if I was hungry, even to the point of death. I wasn't getting out of the room until there was a third person in the house.

I remember the one time my mother came into my room to talk to me.

Opening my door slightly, she peeped in. "Hi, Miki. You awake?"

"Yes," I replied as I sat up on my bed.

"May I come in? I'd like to talk to you."

"Sure."

Walking in, she sat opposite me on the bed. "You're okay?"

"Get straight to the point, Mom."

She shot me a chastising look. "You know, it's this type of attitude that I'm here to talk about. What is wrong with you? What is your problem? You don't talk to anybody in this house. You don't talk to your father. You don't talk to Jaye. You don't even talk to me."

I glanced away, letting her know I wasn't interested.

She scowled. "Look at me, Miki. You want to be an island? Good for you! But there's only one thing I'm certain of. You cannot go through life by yourself. Nobody can. Nobody can be an island. You need people. You need your parents. We want the best for you."

I didn't respond or even look at her.

"Are you even listening to anything I'm saying?" She was quiet for a while, and the next time she said something, her voice betrayed that she had been crying on the inside. "God, what is happening to my baby?" She touched my lap until I just had to look at her. "What happened to you, Miki? You used to be this adorable girl. What happened to you? Where did I go wrong? I don't even know who you are anymore. Miki..."

Her voice broke away. I could see she was trying hard not to cry and my heart went out to her. "Brother Jaye, does he have to live with us?"

All the emotion disappeared from my mother, replaced by a kind of anger that I can't explain. "Is that the reason you've been acting up? Let me make this clear—Jaye stays for as long as he wants. God, how can you be so ungrateful?

We owe his family. Everything we are today we owe to his family. The good life that you have is because of..."

I cut her off. "Yeah, yeah, yeah. I get it. We're alive because of his family. Can you leave now? I want to sleep."

She rose angrily from the bed. "Suit yourself."

I broke into tears as soon as she left. I expected her to ask why I wanted Brother Jaye to leave the house. But she got angry just because I mentioned it. I've always had some questions in the back of my mind. Would things have been different if it was my mother who found me in blood eight years ago? I just got my answer. She would have done the same thing my father did.

The next day was a Sunday. I got up early to prepare for church. My father and mother said they couldn't go because they had some business to handle. They promised they would be back home before I get back.

I returned from church a few hours later and I noticed my parents' car was not in the garage. They were definitely not back. I was just going to go in and lock myself in my room as usual. I couldn't trust that devil.

I walked into the house. The devil was sitting on the couch playing a video game with a friend. He brought a friend over to the house. Without saying a word to either of them, I walked toward my room. Before I could get there, I heard footsteps behind me. Soon, Jaye caught up with me and threw himself in front of me.

"What?" I asked, trying to build up some courage.

He laughed a laugh without humor. "Paul, she's asking me a question."

"So, answer the question," his friend replied, raising his voice so he could be heard over the distance.

Jaye walked two steps closer to me. He was now six feet tall, muscular, and handsome enough to get any girl he chose. Looks apart, the fact that he was a Jamal could get him any girl he wanted. I just didn't understand why he was so obsessed with me.

I took two steps backward. "Please, let me go into my room. I don't want any trouble."

"Paul," he called again, "she says she doesn't want any trouble."

"Tell her you don't want any trouble, too."

He walked closer to me again. "You hear that, huh? I don't want any trouble, too."

He was in my way. I knew there was no way he would let me into my room. I decided to just leave the house and come back when my parents were back. As I reached the living room, Jaye's friend threw himself in front of me, too, standing in my way.

"Please, let me leave. You two can have the house to yourselves."

By now, Jaye had joined us in the living room. "Thanks, friendie," he said to his friend. "I'm willing to share if you want some."

They both gave a wicked laugh.

What happened next, I don't think I can go into the details.

It was...

I felt...

I try to fight them off. I tried. It only got me into more trouble. They beat the living daylights out of me. Their fists became the expression of their love for me—a way to let me know they want me. After using all my strength, I knew fighting two men was futile.

So I just let go.

I stared up at the ceiling as Jaye pounded into me. Tightening my lips together, I tried not to scream. I knew nothing would please them more than to hear me scream for help. I bit down hard on my lip, so hard that I could taste my own blood. He slammed in one more time and groaned before rolling off me.

And then it was his friend's turn.

I just lay there, never taking my eyes off the ceiling. One sheep. Two sheep. Three sheep. Four sheep. Five sheep. I made it to around fifty sheep when he pounded deeply into me, grunted into my ear, and collapsed beside me, breathing hard.

Slowly I got up from the couch and grabbed my skirt and underpants. With Jaye living in our house, a part of me knew this was bound to happen. Yet that didn't make it easy for me to bear. I wanted to feel rage toward him, but it felt like all of my anger had been used up over the last eight years.

Instead of anger, I felt tired. Tired of life. Tired of fighting. Tired of being tough. Tired of everything. I didn't even have the strength for words. Still, I summoned all of my strength and tried to look at him. "You will pay for this. You will..."

He gave another of his wicked laughs devoid of humor. "What are you going to do? Tell daddy? You know daddy isn't going to do nothing."

He was right. My parents wouldn't do anything. They wouldn't fight for me; they wouldn't protect me. He was right.

Walking into my room, I slammed the door shut and kept it locked. I cried for days. It got to the point that I was drained of tears but I kept crying on the inside.

I was tired of my life. I just wanted to die.

I hated myself. I hated Jaye. I hated God for allowing me to be born to my parents. And most of all, I hated my parents for making me the price that was paid for our better life.

For two days I didn't eat, I didn't drink. My parents tried to get me to open the door, but I refused. I thought that if I could just hold on, I'd die of hunger and sadness.

On the third day, my mother knocked on my door. She told me that my admission letter came and that I had been admitted into the university.

Finally, I opened the door. I was happy that I was free. I thought that once I escaped from under the roof of my parents, nothing bad could happen to me anymore. I didn't know that the things that awaited me were much more than anything I'd been through.

Chapter Seventeen

Miki

I had an excellent college life. I attended one of the best private universities in the country and graduated as the best student in business administration. My parents paid a fortune for me to be there, but who cares? It was my ass that had to be banged before we could get the money.

I graduated from college, returned home and waited to be chosen for the NYSC program, or the National Youth Service Corps. It's a program where college graduates work for a lower wage for one year in a government or business organization. It's like service to your country, a way to contribute your own quota to move the country forward. After completion, you get a certificate that states you've successfully served your country. Most jobs nowadays require applicants to be NYSC certified before they can be employed, so it's a really important program.

I didn't want to be idle while I waited for my NYSC letter so I started running Daniels Bottled Water alongside my father. After six to seven months of waiting, I finally received my NYSC posting. You can easily guess what business organization I'd been posted to.

Jamal Corporation.

I need not be told that my father had used the little power he had to influence my posting. I raged into his office and threw the letter at him.

"What is this?"

Confused, he pulled his brow together. "What is what?"

"That." I yelled, pointing to the letter I threw on his desk.

Putting on his reading glasses, he opened the letter and read it. "The letter says you've been posted to the branch of Jamal Corporation in Lagos state."

"And you didn't have anything to do with that?"

He threw the letter back at me. "Would you believe me if I said no?"

"Dad, how could you?"

"Jamal Corporation is the controlling power in the business world. It's going to be a nice experience for you, and it will look good on your resume. Jamal Corporation is the best for you. End of discussion!"

I kept ranting, but my father said nothing else. He was done talking—that's what he meant by end of discussion.

I moved to Lagos and started working for the Jamal Corporation. The pay was good and it would have been a good environment to work if Jaye wasn't my boss. Six years passed since our last encounter. I was twenty-two years old now, and he was thirty-two. He seemed to have outgrown every one of his old ways. He was responsible, hardworking, and every other employee had only good stuff to say about him. Most of the female employees were fan-girling all over him. And to my surprise, he didn't seem to care for any of them. He was nice, respectful, and pro-fessional. He was far from the Jaye Jamal I had ever known. In fact, if I were to come forward with my experiences with him, no one would believe me. He was an angel in the eyes of everyone—and he seemed to have really changed for the better.

Lest I forget, I wasn't the only one who did my NYSC

service at Jamal Corporation. My friend, Lola, did, too. We rented an apartment together on Victoria Island in Lagos. We were roommates, even though I made all the payment and she didn't pay a dime.

For the first few months at Jamal Corporation, I avoided the boss as much as I could. If I had to turn something in to him, I let Lola do the job. If I had to receive any specific orders from him, I made Lola do it for me. I tried everything that I can to avoid him. It was a big organization, so it worked.

At least until he ran into me one evening in the parking lot.

"Hi, Sis," he said as he suddenly appeared behind me in the parking lot.

Hearing that devilish voice, I was more than a little jumpy. Something seemed to crawl through me, and bumps ran through my arm. I recognized that voice. It haunted my childhood in the form of nightmares. "What? What can I do you for?"

"Ahem..." He seemed at a loss for words. "I know you work with us now, but it's surprising we haven't run into each other."

"Is it?" I said and began to walk straight to my car, ignoring him.

"Miki," he called as he ran after me. Soon he caught up with me and held me by the shoulder.

Glaring at him, I jerked my shoulder free of his hold.

"I'm sorry," he apologized. "Look, Miki, I've been trying to appear before you, but I'm so ashamed of myself. I know sorry don't quite cut it. But I am so very sorry for everything that happened between us. I am so sorry, and I deeply regret it. I hope you can find a place in your heart to forgive me."

Forgive? What planet was this guy living in? Forgive him? That's like saying, "Hey, I raped you when you were eight. I took your innocence when you were a child. I violated you and did it again and again. Please forgive me."

Forgiveness, my black ass!

"You're right, Jaye. Sorry doesn't cut it."

Opening the door of my car, I cranked the key in the ignition and drove off, tires squealing in anger.

I didn't run into him for the next month, until one day he sent me a folder through his executive assistant. In the folder was a letter that said I was supposed to represent the company to negotiate a multi-million dollar deal.

It was beyond me. I was low on the chain at Jamal Corporation, and that kind of business was way out of my league. I wasn't stupid. I knew my boss was trying to get my attention. Did he think I'd come running to his office and ask him why I was chosen for this assignment? Well, he thought wrong.

I went on the assignment, but I didn't bother to put in my best. Whatever came out of the negotiation, profit or loss, I didn't care. I was counting my days till I finished this program, and then I would be free from the Jamals forever, never to see them again.

About two weeks later, my boss called a meeting and I had no choice but to attend. At the meeting, he announced that I was employee of the month, given my ability to pull off a deal that landed the company a 2% increase in profit.

I received congratulations from everyone. And then the meeting was brought to a close with a cup of champagne served to everybody present. I had just finished my drink when Jaye walked up to me.

"Miss Daniels, do you have a minute?"

I had to play along or else everybody would begin to be

suspicious of our history. "Sure, boss. What can I do for you?"

He started talking on and on about business until everyone left. I remembered I felt dizzy. And that was all I remembered.

My drink had been laced with some kind of numbing or sleeping pills.

When I opened my eyes, I was cuffed to a pole in the basement of a house I guessed belonged to Jaye. The floor was made with black marble, and the room was painted a cream color. There were two set of old chairs in the center of the room. It was dirty and dusty, as if no one had lived here for years.

My mind did a quick rundown of what kind of fate awaited me in this dungeon. The thought of it made me icy cold. I shook at the chill of it.

Struggling with the cuffs, I tried to release myself. I had to escape. After several hours of struggling, I realized it was impossible to break free. Glancing around, I saw what might be the key to the cuff sitting on the chair.

I stretched my legs, trying to pull the chair closer. Try as I might, the task seemed impossible. I fought against my helplessness with everything I had—every energy, every strength. It wasn't enough. I felt tears run down my cheeks as I broke out into a loud sob, screaming for help.

I screamed morning and night on the first day.

Everything repeated itself on the second day.

It was on the third day that I finally saw the face of my captor.

Jaye Jamal.

He came into the basement, where he had kept me for three days with no food or water. I had lost track of time, but I could tell it was evening. He had on one of his many expensive suits, and his face looked tired. He just got back from work, so it's definitely evening. He came in with nothing but two slices of bread and a cup of water.

I need not be told. He didn't intend to feed me to be strong. He was just keeping me alive.

Then and there, I knew Jaye was my nemesis. There would be no escaping him.

Still, I tried to summon enough courage, even though my body was weak. "It's a terrible mistake to think you can get away with this. Someone will notice I'm gone. My parents will look for me."

He didn't seem to care one bit about anything I was saying. He slowly removed his suit jacket. "Your parents called. I texted them back simply with 'I'm fine. Don't worry about me.' And guess what, they fell for it because that's what you would have done, right? You don't really get along with them."

He was damn right. My parents wouldn't suspect anything. I'd gone a whole year without talking to them, and only communicated through text messages. He was right, but I wasn't ready to let him think he won.

"Lola will notice I'm gone."

By now he had already removed his shirt and tie. "You mean your roommate? I saw her at work today. She seemed fine. She seems happy that you left the house to her."

He removed his belt, threw it on the chair and gave the same fate to his pants and boxers, standing before me as naked as the day he was born.

I averted my gaze. "Why are you doing this?"

"I have a sexual fantasy in my head that I have to live through. And you, Miki, you fit into my fantasy."

Tears betrayed my false courage and rolled down my

cheeks. "But why me? You're rich and handsome. You can get any woman out there to live your fantasy."

Now, he's towering over me, pulling his brow together in irritation and covering his nose.

Apparently, I stink.

I had to pee on myself.

He got used to the smell and returned to our conversation. "Because you're easy, Miki. And I like easy."

"Easy?"

"You cry yourself to sleep every night. *Daddy didn't fight for me. Mommy didn't protect me.* You could never make a stand and fight. It's not in you, Miki." He crouched before me and caressed my face with his thumb. "Just imagine for a second that a man dare to lay a finger on my sister Jessie and my parents turned a blind eye like your parents did. You know what Jessie would do? Do you? Can you guess?" Using his thumb to caress my awfully dry lips, he licked his own lips. "Jessie would put a bullet in the man's head and save two other bullets. One for Daddy with a shot to his head, and one for Mommy, too."

I shook my head to force away his dirty finger. His words cut through me like a dagger to the heart. The truth of his words weakened me.

In a split second, he tore open my shirt and the buttons flew several feet away. He watched my breasts cupped in a push-up bra. He kept watching, like he was fascinated by them.

"Do you know you have the sexiest boobs I've ever seen?"

I shook my head.

"Well, now you know. They look almost the same as when you were sixteen."

For a moment, I thought he was going to tear open my

bra, but he didn't. He just pushed me over to lie on my back. One of my hands had been cuffed to the pole, leaving me with only one hand to defend myself. When I had both of my hands free as a teenager I couldn't stop him. Now that my body was weaker than an old woman nearing her grave, I didn't stand a chance.

Separating my legs with his thigh, he pushed my panties to the side and guided himself into me in one smooth motion, opening his mouth in pleasure to breathe in much-needed air.

I didn't give him much of a fight. All I could do was cry that he was right about me. I am easy and weak and not capable of doing anything for myself.

When he was done, he cleaned his penis with the tip of my skirt and then he left my side. I watched him put on his clothes and walk back to my side to release me from my prison.

Using my other hand, I massaged my wrist as I glanced at him, confused.

"You earned it because you didn't fight me." He slid the two slice of bread and the cup of water toward me. "You've earned that, too." And then he pointed his hand to the right. "There's a bathroom over there. You stink. Take a shower."

He turned to leave, but then he stopped abruptly when he reached the door. "Keep in mind, this is the only door that leads out of this basement, and I'll make sure to keep it locked." Opening the door, he shut it after him and I ran to the door as quickly as I could. My effort was futile. It was locked. And for the first time I wished I knew how to pick a lock.

I ate the bread hungrily, even though I felt a sharp pain at the tip of my stomach right under my breast.

If Jaye didn't kill me, hunger might.

I went straight to the bathroom and spent hours in the shower. I thought if I could wash myself enough, maybe I'd wash bad luck away from my life. I cried until I had no more tears.

Chapter Eighteen

Miki

I was lying on the couch when I heard the door open. I thought it was the next day, but I'm not sure. I stopped keeping track of time.

Jaye came in with two slices of bread and another cup of water. Only this time, he wasn't alone. He came in with another guy. He was almost as tall as Jaye, but he was young, probably in his early twenties.

I thought Jaye was going to share me with him.

I was wrong.

Jaye sat on the couch and gestured the guy to go ahead. I screamed when the guy came over to me. Grabbing both my hands, he held them together above my head. I used my legs to kick his balls. He groaned in pain for a second before he angrily slapped me hard across my face, his five fingers printed on my cheeks. And then his fist landed on my face. My nose began to bleed.

Hot tears filled my eyes.

He held my hands together above my head and used his other hand to unbuckle his own belt.

I spat in his face and cursed at him.

He laughed as he pulled my skirt up and worked down my panties.

He unfastened his pants with the other hand, and then

leaned in and covered my mouth with his; suffocating my screams as his hand went between my legs.

His pants dropped, and his thigh forced my legs open. I grumbled against his mouth while trying to scream, hoping to prevent what he was doing to me, but I couldn't. I felt him as he pushed into me.

My eyes turned red with tears and impotent rage. My chest heaved. Trying not to look at the man who was pounding heavily into me, I glanced away—only to have my gaze capture Jaye sitting in the chair, pleasuring himself as the man violated me.

God, this man is sick. He needs help.

At that moment, I understood.

Jaye said he had a fantasy, and that fantasy was to derive pleasure as he watched helpless women been violated. He took sadistic pleasure in tormenting me.

A loud groan escaped from the guy's lips before he collapsed by my side. Jaye seemed to cum at the same time as the guy. I heard him moan, too.

"Clean yourselves up," Jaye said as he stood from the chair and walked out of the room without locking the doors, probably waiting for this guy to leave before he sealed me in again.

The guy sat beside me on the couch, watching my face as I cried uncontrollably and tried to wipe his semen off my privates. Pulling a white handkerchief from the pocket of his pants, he tried to wipe the blood dripping from my nose.

I kicked his hand off. "I don't need your help."

He kept his hands to himself for a long time. "I'm sorry," he finally said.

"I don't need your apology."

"I know, but I have to say it," he said, his voice shaky as

if lumps had built up in his throat. "I'm a college student and my mother is dying on a hospital bed. He said he'd give me 300,000 naira if I did this. I need the money, so I agreed, but I didn't think about the person I'd be destroying."

I glanced at him and could see in his eyes that he meant it. I can't say that I forgave him, but I understood him. The only reason I was in that dungeon was because my parents were willing to do anything to get money, and I was that price. Same as he had to do whatever it took to get money for his family.

I only gave a small nod. I didn't give a response.

"If there's anything I can do..."

I cut him off. "Get me out of here."

I could see the fear in his eyes. "No, he'll kill me."

Holding his arms, I pleaded with him. "Please, I'm begging you in the name of God, please help me."

He looked confused, like a part of him wanted to help and the other part didn't want to take that risk.

I held him tightly, my fingers almost digging into his skin as I looked pitifully into his eyes, tears running down my cheeks non-stop. "Please."

"Alright," he said.

"Thank you," I said, shaking and waiting for him to put on his clothes. When he was done, he walked to the door and told me to wait for him in the basement and be ready. Gently, he climbed the stairs.

I waited for him, praying that he didn't change his mind and leave me down there.

In a minute, he was back. "No one is there. I think he's in the bathroom. This is your chance," he said, his voice slightly above a whisper.

He led the way, and I followed. We took the stairs and

reached Jaye's magnificent living room. I was scared and had no backbone to look around, but I knew it was large with a high-ceiling, neat and glittering, as if everything in there were made of pure gold.

We ran across the living room toward the front door. Seemingly from out of nowhere, I heard a deafening sound and the guy dropped on the floor, blood oozing out of his head. Keeping my eyes shut from the horror, a loud scream escaped my mouth. I screamed until it felt as if my lungs were shutting down.

Jaye dropped his gun and dashed toward me, pushing me to the ground. I hit the floor with terrible force, but I was too overwhelmed to feel any pain. Pinning me to the ground, he removed the towel wrapped around his waist.

"You love his dick, huh?" He tore open my skirt. "You're going with him because you love his dick."

His strong thigh forced my legs open. "Here it is! Love mine too."

He pushed his penis hard into me, pounding into me deeper and deeper. But I felt nothing. I was glancing at the dead guy lying next to me as his eyes stared lifelessly at me. I shook with fear. He's dead because of me.

When Jaye was done with me, he threw me back into the basement. I hit the floor so hard; I thought my bones would break.

It wasn't only me he threw in the basement. The dead guy, too. He locked me up with a corpse. He cuffed me back to the pole, the corpse lying next to me, his eyes open and staring at me, icy cold with the horror of death.

I don't know for how many days he locked me in there, but I will remember that smell—the smell of death—for the rest of my life.

He was a good guy. He did bad things, but he felt remorse, and he lost his life trying to right the wrong. He was a good guy who was nothing more than a smelly, rotten corpse now.

The corpse was bloating, smelly water dripping from the body. The smell filled my nostrils, then filled my stomach until I threw up more than a dozen times every day. There was no food in my stomach, but water spewed out of my throat. I hadn't had much to eat and my body was kind of shutting down, so I blacked out every now and then. I kept losing bits and bits of time.

For days, I sat in my vomit and in the smelly water of death. I would have guessed the smell should cover the whole of the house, and Jaye shouldn't be able to stand it. But when I didn't see him in days, I guess he left the house so I could suffer the odor alone.

After a few days, he returned. His nostrils and hands covered, he moved the corpse to I don't know where, but when he returned, his shoe stained the floor with a dark soil. He must have dropped the body in the nearest river.

He handed me cleaning gadgets and ordered me to clean the floor. I did as I was told. I was weak and spent several hours doing something that shouldn't take an hour. I removed my clothes and put them in the trash and then I sprayed the house with a sweet-smelling fragrance.

After that, I scrubbed myself clean.

By the time I finished my shower, I refused to go back into my dirty clothes. I stood before Jaye completely naked.

"If there's anything I've learned since I got here, it is that there's no getting out of here. I know that now," I began.

My body was weak, but I had never felt stronger in my entire life. I had no other choice than to be strong. For myself, and for the dead guy so his death wouldn't be for nothing.

"But there's also something I've learned: your fantasy is to derive pleasure from men violating a helpless girl. It is insane, but I understand." I walked closer to him, our gazes locked together. "Here's what I propose. I'll put on a show for you. Bring all your guys. I can take them all. I'll fight and try to be helpless and you get all your pleasure from watching them fuck the hell out of me. In exchange, you will treat me okay. Good food, good clothes, and you can have me. I won't try to run."

I saw the surprise on his face. I thought he wouldn't agree to it, but he leaned closer and placed a short kiss on my lips. "I love you, Miki," he said, smiling.

Hell, yeah, Love my black ass!

Well, it looked like he accepted my proposal.

From that day onward, everything changed. Every other night, Jaye brought guys in threes. One hitting up my asshole, another in my mouth. Some of them would shove their penis into my throat and I would gag and gag and gag until I couldn't breathe and I'd pass out. Of course, they'd pour a bucket of cold water on me to wake me up to continue their act while Jaye sat in his chair and watched, pleasuring himself. Different guys every other night. I saw the different varieties of penis; short, long, thick, small. I saw it all.

Jaye never thrust his penis into me anymore.

Semen trash can.

That's what he used to call me. He said he couldn't dip his penis into me anymore because I was nothing but a semen trash can. He had my ass way before anyone ever did. And when everyone had, I became less attractive to him.

He made sure I had good clothes, good food at the right

time, but the one thing I didn't have was good medical attention. So many times the guys would fight over who wanted to have my asshole or who wanted the blowjob, and they'd begin to get violent, and I was always at the receiving end of it. I got plenty scars, and I always had to take care of them myself.

I thought I was getting Jaye to trust me enough to leave the door open and believe I wouldn't run. It was working. More and more every day, I earned his trust. He stopped cuffing me to the pole. He let me sit in the living room with him once in a while. It was all falling into place, and I was planning my grand escape. I had it all under control

But then something happened that I couldn't control.

I fell sick.

Fever, nausea with vomiting, loss of appetite, fatigue.

Jaye wasn't having it. He told me he was feeding me with good food, and I should have a strong enough immunity to fight any strange diseases.

For one week, I didn't get better no matter what.

I didn't know what was making me sick until one day Jaye came into the basement with a pregnancy test kit and handed it to me.

And then it occurred to me that I could actually be pregnant. My menstruation date was the last thing on my mind, so I didn't even know if I had missed a period. I was so consumed with my plan to escape that I stopped paying attention to me.

Jaye stood by me in the bathroom as I took the test. I peed and put a drop on the test strip. Pink single line means negative. Pink double line means positive.

We waited one minute to get a result. One minute seemed like one year. My heart was racing, my blood rushing, my cheat heaving. I was sweating in all part of my body—my palms, my feet. I had never been that anxious in my life.

And when I saw the double pink line, my butt went straight to the floor. I just wanted to die. My life couldn't get more ruined. I was pregnant with a baby who had no father.

Before I could really process anything, a hot slap landed on my cheek.

"How could you?" he roared.

For a second, my vision was blurry, and I was deafened.

"How can you get pregnant?" he barked again, kicking my butt on the floor where I lay. And then he changed his mind and started kicking my stomach.

"I'm going to kick the baby out of you."

And suddenly he stopped. Face in his palm, he screamed out loud, shaking in anger or regret. I don't know.

"I didn't intend for it happen. I didn't..." And then he ran out of the basement.

I crawled out of the bathroom to lay on the couch. I held my stomach, but it didn't ease the pain.

Later in the evening, Jaye came back with food. Rice and stew and a cup of orange juice.

"Sit up and eat," he said as he dropped it in front of me.

"I don't have an appetite."

"C'mon," he said, helping me to sit up. "You have to eat. If not for your sake, for the baby's sake." He took a spoonful of rice and fed it to me.

Tears filled my eyes as I chewed on the food.

He tried to feed me again.

"No. No more," I said, shaking my head.

"If not food, then take a drink." He gave me the cup of

orange juice. "You need your strength."

I took the cup from him and drank it all in one gulp.

"Good. Rest for a little bit. Okay?"

I nodded.

"When I get back, we will discuss what you want to do with the baby."

He left the room, and I lay back on the couch. I had roughly about two hours of sleep. When I woke up, the couch I slept on was soaked with blood. I had some kind of heavy vaginal bleeding. I stood up and ran to the bathroom. I could barely move, I was dizzy.

Getting to the bathroom, I removed my skirt and my panties. It was soaked with blood. The floor was also wet with my blood. I came out of the bathroom only to see Jaye waiting for me.

"What's happening to me?" I asked.

He didn't respond. Instead, he gave me some new panties and a maternity pad, the kind used by women after giving birth. "You will need it."

I gazed at him in confusion as I took the pad from him.

"Miki, you can't have the baby. I thought you wouldn't want the baby either. So I laced your drink with some pills."

"You did what?"

"You will bleed for one or two days, and the baby will be gone. I know you might not appreciate me now, but you will later."

Anger took over my sense of self. Putting all my strength into it, I slapped him hard across his cheek.

"It was my decision to make."

Summoning the strength I didn't know I still had, I slapped him again. "It should have been my choice. Not yours."

I was aiming for the third one when he caught hold of my arm.

"Enough!" he yelled and shoved my arm away. "Clean yourself up before you soak the floor with blood."

Anger still boiling in my blood, I went back to the bathroom to clean myself up. When I came back to the room, Jaye was cleaning up the blood on the floor and couch. I let him do it all by himself as I sat on the chair and watched.

I bled for the next twenty-four hours. Jaye kept bringing me different kinds of herbal medicine meant to replenish blood in case I lost too much.

On the second day, he brought me another herbal medication and swore that it would stop the bleeding.

About an hour later, the bleeding doubled, the flow unstoppable. No amount of sanitary pads could contain it.

Jaye held me in his arms as my very life bled away. I knew for sure that death was imminent.

He was crying, sobbing so loudly as he held my head against his chest.

"I'm going to die, aren't I?" I could barely get the words out. It took all my energy to say those few words.

He didn't answer my question.

"I didn't mean for this to happen," was all he kept saying.

Apparently the last herbal concoction he gave me wasn't to stop the bleeding. It was to play a trick on my ovary and prevent me from getting pregnant again. He could have gone to the pharmacy store to get the medications, but he didn't want to get caught. It might raise suspicions, so he settled for the local herbal medicine.

"I..." I wanted to say something, but there was blood rushing out of my mouth instead. My body was finally shutting down, but I never felt more at peace. I continued to stare on as everything before me disappeared into a dark nothingness.

When I opened my eyes, I was laying on a hospital bed. Jaye took me and dropped me in front of my house at Victoria Island, where Lola found me in time to get me to the hospital.

The doctors and nurses tried hard to stabilize me and save my life.

When I was finally stabilized, the doctor told me that the abortion I attempted wasn't done right and he had to perform a dilation and curettage to clear my uterine lining and stop the bleeding.

For the next few days, they performed so many tests on me. I tested positive for three sexually transmitted diseases, but fortunately for me, nothing untreatable.

But the worst thing was that the herbal medication Jaye gave me caused an infection in my ovaries and fallopian tubes. The tissue developed an abnormality and so much big medical jargon that I didn't understand. All I knew was that I was in so much pain. To save my life, the doctors had to shut down my ovaries and stop them from making estrogen, which eventually would stop the tissue abnormality. At twenty-two years old I was forced into menopause, which meant I could never have my own child.

I had been gone for four months. Jaye held me hostage for four months. When I finally reappeared, everybody wanted to know where I'd been. Journalists from every media house, the minister of women's affairs, celebrities fighting against sexual abuse, and human rights activists all came together in my hospital room promising to bring down heaven and earth if I talked to them.

It wasn't long before I found out that one of the doctors had received money to leak out that he'd examined my privates and found so many bruises that was likely I had been sexually violated over the last four months.

If there was one thing I've learned, it is that no one can be trusted. I kept my story to myself. It was an election year, and I knew that the minister of women's affairs only wanted to champion my fight just to gain more votes for her political party. I knew all those celebrities and human rights activists were pretending to care just to build and promote their brands. And the journalists just wanted to be the one to break the story.

No one really cared. I'm wiser now, I'm no longer the stupid girl waiting for her parents to be her superhero and save her. I can save myself now. I can fight for myself.

I knew the only way to avoid this kind of tragedy in my future life was to succeed, give my greedy parents more than they needed. My only option was to succeed or succeed. I had no other option.

I kept my story to myself, got well, and left the hospital before returning to Abuja and taking over my father's business. And then I singlehandedly molded Daniels Bottled Water into Daniels Group. I lost all compassion, but I felt alive. Being successful gave me power, and I loved it. But no matter how successful I had become, my mind could never forget the horror of what happened to me. It could never forget the face of the man who took everything from me. When I think of sex, I remember pain. I remember horror. I remember death. And I remember Jaye Jamal.

Chapter Nineteen

Vince

Hell!

That was intense. I suspected she's had it difficult, but I never imagined she went through something this terrible. No one should have to go through that much. It is too much for just one person.

How is she still sane?

How did she have the courage, the strength to pick herself back up?

I've never met a woman as strong as Miki. She's like a raw gold that has to pass through a fiery furnace before it comes out shinning.

Hearing her story, I don't know what I'm feeling; I don't even know what to feel. Imagine all these intense, heartbreakingly emotional stories thrown at you all at once. I don't know what your response would be, but right now I feel... I feel...

Rage.

Pure anger.

Without saying a word, I stand up from the bed where we had been sitting as she told her story.

She follows me. "Vince, say something please."

I slip into my sport wear and shoes. I need to get out of the house. I need fresh air. I need to think about what happens next after everything I've just heard.

"Vince?"

I glance at her and try to say something, but I don't have any words. I don't even want to see her right now.

I walk away from her. And she knows better than to follow me. She needs to let me be for now.

Putting my tennis ball and bat into my backpack, I storm out of the house to go to the tennis court.

I play tennis with Wale for one hour straight. I can't stop. I don't want to stop. But soon my friend is tired. He has to leave. He only came out here because I asked him to. He knows something is going wrong with me, but I'm not up for discussion right now.

Soon Wale leaves, and it's just me. I sit on the grass, my head buried between my knees, trying hard to sort out my feelings.

I feel rage.

But not at Miki.

At the man who did this to her and got away with it.

At the parents who didn't deserve to have a child.

I feel compassion.

Sympathy.

For the woman who had to endure all of this.

Most of all, I feel love.

I love her even more. I feel connected to her. I see her. I feel like I know her now, like her very soul has been stripped bare for me to understand.

Tears fill my eyes for her, and I have to man up and try not to cry. I've always thought I had it hard, that no one could suffer more than I did. My parents died when I was really young. I grew up alone without their love and support on the streets of Lagos. My home was under a bridge. I know what it means to eat breakfast and have nothing to eat for lunch and dinner. I've cleaned people's toilets, scrubbed people's floors, collected trash from people's homes, and sometimes even stole a few notes just to survive. I know poverty, and poverty knows me. For a while, I envied those who had parents. I thought if my parents were alive, I would have it easy, but I was wrong. Very wrong.

I stand up and rush home. I need to get to Miki very quickly.

I drive home as fast as I can. When I get there, I rush to the bedroom where I'm certain she will be.

As soon as I open the door, she raises her head and glances up at me. Her eyes are red and puffy and her face wet with tears. Hell, she has been crying. Did she think that I left her?

Closing the door, I sit beside her on the bed. "Hey..."

"Hey..." she replies in between sobs.

I try to wipe her tears, but I don't say anything. I know there's nothing I can say that can take away all that pain.

And she doesn't say anything either.

She's quiet, her beautiful face watching mine with a sadness that hurts.

"I hate that," I finally say. "I hate that all those bad things happened to you. I'm angry. Angry at the guy that got away with this, and I'm angry at your parents for doing nothing. But mostly I'm angry at myself because I wasn't there for you. I wish I could go back in time and save you, protect you, and make you feel better."

"You do that every day." A sad smile spreads across her face. "You make me feel better every day."

Silence settles around us again. "Thank you, Miki."

She gives me a puzzled look.

"For telling me everything."

"Thank you for being the person I can tell it to."

Slowly, she places her head on my chest, and I hold her in there protectively for so long. Finally, she releases herself from my hold. Pulling her dress over her head, she leans back into me.

"I'm ready, Vince," she whispers. "I can feel it. You've loved me to readiness, and now I'm certain that I am."

She's naked and my body responds to her nakedness. Just watching her has me going hard. Instinctively, my hand begins to caress her. "Only one condition, Miki."

"What?"

I kiss her softly on the lips as I take off my t-shirt. "I want you to look at me. Don't close your eyes. I want you to see me. I don't want you to remember that monster ever again. I want it to be my face you remember every time you think about pleasure."

She nods.

****

Miki

With those words, his lips seal against mine.

He kisses me so soft and tender. A wet, short kiss on my lips...then my cheek and down to the hollow of my neck... and then back to my lips.

My eyes closed, a small sound escapes from my lips and he takes my mouth with his. His tongue gently parts my lips, then caresses me as he kisses me gently.

I can't help but respond as feelings and sensations stir up inside of me. I lift myself to bring one hand up so I can stroke his face, loving the feel of the heat radiating from his body. Leaning closer, I open my mouth to feel him more deeply, to breathe him in like pure air as I rub my breasts against his chest.

His hand moves to my shoulder, tracing one finger along my arm and stroking me in little circles. He slowly caresses my breasts, light like a feather tickling against it. He brushes his fingertip slightly over my nipple, and I feel it stir into hardness beneath his touch. I moan slightly and lose myself in the kiss as he kisses me harder. Pressing close against him, I curl my arms around his neck and pull him into me. His touch on my skin feels so very good that I can feel all the nerve endings in my body coming alive.

He makes a low grunt in his throat, and then breaks our kiss to bury his face in my neck, the feel of his breath arousing me more. "Miki," he calls out, kissing the hollow of my neck, "you can still stop this, even now..."

Vince is the only thing that I want, and nothing will ever get in the way of that. Not the fear of not being wanted; not anything in my past. I want Vince more than I want anything else.

My hand floats from around his neck to his chest. His heart beats fast and firm under my hand; my own pulse is pounding so hard I can hear it in my ears. "I'm not going to stop."

My hand moves to pull his shorts slowly down. Tracing my fingers lightly across his skin through a thatch of hair, I find what I've been looking for.

Wow.

To my surprise, it's so massive and thick that I doubt I can get my hands around it. I open my eyes slightly to take a look. It's the most gorgeous one I have ever seen. Uncontrollable desire surges through me.

I gently take him in my hand, caressing him, stroking him, gently and softly.

It jumps in my hand, expanding as contraction make him longer and thicker.

He groans in response.

I'm pleased with his reaction. I'm not very good with this, but I try to take note of what he seems to like most—what makes him groan or jerk.

I squeeze him again and start to stroke him.

Just holding him and feeling him expand in my hand is turning me on, making me so wet, making me need him even more.

I moan into his mouth when his fingers explore between my legs, slipping one finger inside. It feels so good I move my hips, shamelessly wanting more.

"Are you ready?" he asks in a thick voice, placing a soft kiss on my lips as he watches my eyes.

"Yes, please."

I can't believe I'm begging for it. The thing that caused me so much pain in the past is now bringing me pleasure. I'm going to lose it any moment if he doesn't give me the real deal.

Ever so gently, he lowers me onto my back. His body shifts as he positions himself on top of me, slightly pushing my legs apart.

He leans over and kisses me deeply, gently and slowly, as his finger guides the tip of his shaft inside me. I feel him nudging at my entrance and I cum immediately, crying out as currents of pleasure spark through my entire body.

Maybe it's a little more than a cry. I might have screamed, probably more like a really loud moan, occasionally opening my mouth, gasping and breathing in air. It feels so... I lack the words for it. It's like an overwhelming tingling throughout my body. You know, my whole body shudders as if a wave of sensual electricity sparked through me.

I'm a girl who has never orgasmed before. Well, maybe the one time that Vince pleasured me by playing with my clitoris, but other than that, I've never orgasmed before in my life. And I've had uncountable sexual encounters and multiple partners. But I felt nothing. I was beginning to agree with people who think that the female orgasm is false—until now.

My vision is blurry for a little while. After it's all over, I open my eyes only to meet his gaze, staring down at me with a proud smile.

"Can you go on?" he asks gently, his eyes dropping into a worried expression.

I nod. "Just... be gentle," I say in a whisper.

"Okay," he whispers back.

My body shivers in anticipation. He leans over and kisses me as I feel his full length enter me.

Overcome by pleasure, I try to close my eyes, but then I remember my promise to look at him and remember him as the face of my pleasure for the rest of my life. Opening my eyes, I find him staring at me from just strides away. I lose myself in his beautiful brown eyes, eyes that feel as if they are probing my soul, stripping it bare.

I feel him penetrate me as his hips rock back and forth, not violently, not wild and not too fast, just with a smooth rhythmic pace. I move with him so passionately that time seems to stop. It feels like the whole world pauses just for the two of us.

Every once in a while, he'll lean over and kiss me like he can't help himself, just like me. Every part of my body is out of control. My heart is racing, my breathing is rapid and shallow, and my vision occasionally blurry as I try to keep staring into those beautiful eyes that watch me with so much passion.

I let my hands move gently over his back, then over his ass. I hold on to him tightly, my fingers almost dipping into his skin as I pull him into me, wanting more and more of him as he pushes into me.

Everything feels so right, so, sooo good, that I can't help but moan out loud.

"Oh... Vince..." I gasp, unable to hold in all the pleasure as he move deeper and deeper inside me, causing a knot to form in my stomach.

My dam is about to break.

"Miki..." he grunts my name in response as his thrust intensifies.

Just the way he calls to me, huffing out my name as if he needs me more than his breath, sends me over the cliff into ecstasy.

Wave after wave of pleasure spreads through me. I claw at the back of his shoulder as I feel my insides tighten with an amazing sense of fullness as his steady, powerful thrusting intensifies the heat between us and sends stronger vibrations through my entire body.

My moans and screams push him over the edge. I can feel every hard inch of him pulsing bigger, filling me, thrusting deeper and deeper. Pushing my boundaries. Deep into my own pleasure, I hear his final moan as he spasms inside me and his hot moisture explodes deep inside me. My body melts into him; my eyes drowsy with passion. We stare into each other's eyes, our gaze locking with such intensity and intimacy that I feel lost in them.

And then he leans over and kisses me on the corner of my mouth, my lips, my cheeks, my neck before collapsing beside me on the bed, holding me. I hug into him tightly, grateful to him for making me have this good feeling. I swell with pride for having giving him this. He has waited patiently for it.

"That was amazing," he says.

****

Vince

"Since you've been honest with me today, I guess I should be, too," I say, watching as Miki lays naked next to me. "I've known about your condition for a while now."

Her eyes open wide. "You knew? When? How?"

"I..." she cuts me off before I can respond.

"Wait... wait... Which one do you know about? That I was genophobic or my real *real* story."

She's freaking out right now. "Calm down, babe. One question at a time." I press a kiss on her lips. "I knew that you were genophobic. That's all I knew before you told me everything."

She let out a breath of relief. "Still... how did you know?"

"With the way you act up at every sexual attempt, it's not difficult to know."

"Was I that bad, or were you smart enough to know?"

I give a kind of cocky smile. "I'm smart."

She playfully smacks my shoulder and scuffs. "You wish."

I smile. "Well, I had my suspicions, so I had to talk to my friend, Wale. You know him, right?"

She nods.

"Yeah. So I had to talk to Wale to be sure. And he confirmed it."

"When was that?" she asks.

"The day you took Tiwa out shopping."

Her face lit up. "I knew it. The way you were acting that day, I knew something was up."

I move by body slightly over hers and she shifts gently under my weight, watching my face. "Is there anything else you have to be honest about?" she asks.

"Yeah." I lean in and place a kiss at the corner of her mouth, staring intently into her eyes. "You should really know that before today is over, I'm going to make love to you again."

"Just for today? I was thinking for the next three days." She winks at me. "Just you and I."

With those words, she crawls on top of me, straddling me, and before I know it, she's grinding her hips on my erection, her wetness against my hardness.

Overcome with emotion, she throws her head back and gasps. My whole body is on fire. My hand goes reflexively to her breasts, cupping them, squeezing them. Never in my life have I felt anything like I do when I'm with Miki. The feeling of her is intoxicating. I've known so many women and hell, I've had more than my fair share of great sex, but nothing has ever felt as amazing as it is with my girl.

After the second round, she collapses on the bed. Lying down on her belly, her eyes close as she drifts away into a deep sleep. But I'm not done yet. I feel amazing. I feel strong and could go all night. I lay there and watch her sleep, loving the peaceful look on her face. The more I watch her, the more every nerve ending in me comes alive, wanting more of her. I know I should let her sleep. She deserves it after her first attempt at sex in a long time, but I can't help it. She's really beautiful as I watch her sleep. Hell, she's sexy enough to make any man go crazy. I wonder how she was able to stay all these years with no man by her side. With her enchanting beauty and sexy body, it's enough to make any man fall at her feet and vow to be her slave for eternity.

"Wake up, beautiful," I demand as I position myself on top of her, my chest rubbing against her bare back, my erection on her gorgeous ass.

Shifting beneath my weight, her eyes open gently and she flashes me a cute smile. "Are you trying to have enough today because you're afraid I'll wake up genophobic tomorrow?"

"Of course not," I say as I move my fingers slowly, gently down her back.

"Good," she replies. "Because I plan on enjoying sex for the rest of my life. With you." She turns her head back to look at me and slowly licks her lips.

I take that as an invitation and slide a fistful of her hair gently to the side and kiss her hungrily. The sleep fades from her as she responds to my kiss. She moans into the kiss as her hand moves to my neck, pulls me in, and deepens the kiss, her other hand squeezing the sheet in pleasure.

My hand gently floats down between her legs. She's drenched. I must say, she's the most sensitive woman I've ever met. Her body is so responsive. I still can't forget how she came immediately after she felt me nudging at her entrance.

My fingers play between her legs for a while, gently pushing a finger in and out.

And then I use my fingertip to guide myself inside her wet hole. She moans as she feels my full length slip inside her, and she begins to rock her hips. Overcome with emotion, I'm out of control. I begin to thrust in and out of her. Faster. Deeper. Faster. Deeper... each stroke sending shockwave through me.

My need to be so connected with her grows with each thrust. I want her to be with me, to be a part of her. I lean in and kiss her with a passion I never knew I had inside of me.

I feel her moving close to orgasm as she quivers against my dick. I begin to pound into her hard, until the pleasure becomes unbearable, kissing her and breathing her name... staring into each other's eyes, overwhelmed by the outburst of emotion as I explode.

Collapsing beside her, I see her eyes grow watery. "Are you okay?" I ask, breathing hard as I try to catch my breath.

She blinks the tears back and gives me a smile. "I've never felt this good in my life."

I hold her, kiss her softly, caress her as I hold her protectively against my chest in a way that lets her know how precious she is to me. Come what may, I promised to hold her like this for the rest of my life. And I plan to keep that promise.

Chapter Twenty

Miki

"You should let me do something nice for you," Vince says after almost forty-eight hours of our sex marathon. He's sitting on the couch, and I'm all cuddled up against him.

Smiling at him, I say, "You've already done something nice for me." My hand moves slowly down to the massive bulge beneath his pants.

"I know," he responds amidst hitching breath. "I mean something nice besides orgasm."

My sex-drunk brain snaps back to reality. "Oh, that! I'm sorry I can't think of anything nice right now except the big O."

He smiles at me, caresses my face and kisses me. "That is good. But we can't stay indoors forever. Let's go out. Let me take you out. Let me take you shopping; buy you something nice. Let's go to the cinema. Anything that boyfriends do for their girlfriends besides the big O."

"Come to think of it, I've never had a guy buy me something before."

"I've bought you something before," he counters.

"I know, but I mean something like taking me shopping and paying for everything I buy. I always do that for people. No one ever does it for me."

"Is shopping what you want to do right now?"

I nod.

"We'll go shopping—and I will pay for everything."

Smiling, I look up at and kiss him. "Thanks!"

He doesn't respond. He just leans in and kisses me again. After a few seconds, he breaks the kiss and stares at me, brows pulled together. "How come none of your past boyfriends did that for you?"

A forced smile plasters itself on my face. "I didn't exactly put myself out there because of my condition, and even when I try to, they all left me a few days after they kind of suspected I might be genophobic. It never lasted beyond a week or two."

I might be smiling and pretending that remembering my past relations doesn't hurt, but I could never hide my true feelings from Vince. So I stop pretending and let my true feeling come out. "You're my only boyfriend ever, Vince. You stayed with me even when there was no hope I could be a better person. You are the first man I've ever willingly given myself to. You made it possible. You loved me into feeling something. You loved me into being a better person."

A look of pain seems to run across his face. Pulling me very close, he holds my head to his chest and hugs me tightly.

"Thank you, Miki."

Moving my head slightly, I look up at him. "For what?"

"You said I'm the first guy you willingly gave yourself to. I'm thanking you for that. You may not have had that little piece of skin on our first time, but to me, you are a virgin all the same. I'm thanking you for giving me that part of you." His fingers softly caress my face. "And just so you know, Miki. I love you. Deeply. From my soul."

From there, it happens naturally.

I reach up and kiss him, smiling into the kiss. I've never being happier in my life. Not even my success with Daniels Group made me this happy. What I share with Vince is beyond what I can explain, beyond what's possible in my own understanding.

I keep kissing him, my eyes closed, overcome with emotion. I let my hand wander out blindly, back to his erection. And before I can fondle it, he places his hand on mine to stop.

"I appreciate the gesture, but I'm taking you out of this house. We're going shopping."

"Yeah, yeah, I get it." I place a kiss on his cheek before managing to pull myself up. "I'm going to take a shower." Caressing my left breast, I stick out my tongue at him. "Of course, someone is invited."

His breathing becomes rapid. "Miki, you're going to kill me."

That's all it takes to make him grab me from behind and hug me tightly from the back, his palm over mine squeezing my breast, his breath on my neck sending waves of pleasure through me.

Putting his arms around me, he lifts me up, takes me upstairs into the bathroom and into the shower where we have an amazing shower filled with multiple orgasm.

Finally, we get out of the shower, get dressed, and head out. Vince is wearing a sky blue T-shirt over denim jeans. I'm wearing a white round-necked T-shirt over three-quartered faded Gucci jeans and a white, five-inch-heel sandal. Vince takes the driver's seat while I go for the passenger's seat. As we drive across town to the boutique, I stare out the window. It feels as if I see the world differently now. To me, the world used to be a boring place filled with so much pain and suffering no matter how wealthy you are. Now, I see the world as a very happy place, a place where our time is short and you have to live life to the fullest.

"Vince, how do you see the world?" I ask. I know it's an absurd question, but I have to ask.

He takes a quick glance at me before he concentrates back on the road. "Is that a trick question?"

"No."

Without taking his eyes off the road, he begins. "I see the world as a happy place. I think no matter what you're going through—the pain, the anger, the suffering—you can choose to be happy. Life is short, so I live on the edge. Live life to the fullest, I say." He takes another quick glance at me. "Does that answer your question?"

I nod and lean over, resting my head on his shoulder and staring up at him. "I think I'm seeing the world through your eyes now."

He looks at me. Our gaze meets and he places a kiss on my forehead before he concentrates back on the road. We don't say anything until we get to the boutique, but the silence between us speaks volume.

Getting to the shop, I look around trying to find anything I like. Shoes. Bag. As I look around the aisle, I see a purple Burberry tote bag I like. I take a keen look at it before showing it to Vince. "What do you think?"

Hands in his pocket, he keeps staring at the bag, his face expressionless.

"I like it," I continue. "Plus, I have these purple shoes, and I've been searching for a purple bag to go with them."

Holding the bag, I walk stylishly and parade myself in front of him. "What do you think? How do I look?"

"Perfect. It looks good on you."

I smile.

"You like it?" he asks.

"Yes. And that will be all I want to buy."

"Are you serious? Look around and see if you can find something else you like."

I shake my head. "No, that will be all. Let's go check out."

He bows his head and open one arm. "After you, my lady."

I smile and smack his shoulder, leading the way to the cashier.

Dropping the bag before her, I wait for her to do her thing.

"800,000 naira. Will that be all for you today?"

I nod. "Yes, ma'am."

And then she flashes this cute, sexy smile. She's smiling at Vince. "Blue looks good on you," she says. "I'm sure we have something that will look even better."

Is she really trying to sell her products, or is there something else she's trying to sell?

Looking at her, I notice the top three buttons of her shirt are loose, exposing her cleavage.

Vince smiles back at her. It's a warm smile, one that should be for me alone. "Thanks, but no. That'll be all for us."

I hate to admit it, but I feel a stab of jealousy. I feel the need to show her who's the queen around here, you know. So I lean in and rest my head on his shoulder. And trust my man, he responds with a passionate kiss on top of my head.

I know, I know, it's petty and it makes me seem insecure, but I love the look on her face after that. The smile disappears, and she shoots me a look of hatred as though she would stab me if she had the opportunity.

Seeing her face like that just makes me happy, you know.

"800,000 naira," she says.

I watch Vince as he reaches into his pocket and pays for my bag.

Don't forget, I'm the girl who has enough money to last me for at least two generations. But seeing Vince pay for me makes me feel good. I've been taking care of myself since I was eight. I've been responsible for myself, responsible for other people, taking care of others. It's nice to actually see someone take care of me for once.

The girl puts the bag in a plastic bag and hands it to Vince.

As Vince and I walk hand in hand out of the store, I tease him. "You like that girl?"

"She likes me," he says.

I shrug. "It's the same."

"No, it's not. Are you jealous?"

"No. Actually, I like that other women likes my man. It makes me feel like I got the best man around."

"So, I'm the best?"

I kiss his cheek. "Yes, you are. The girls can like you, but you can't like them back. If you do, I'll kill you."

"Yes, ma'am. I thought we agreed you were going to stop using threatening words like that."

"Oops. My bad."

****

Miki

The next day I'm ready to go back to work. I'm wearing

a grey office dress slightly above my knee. When I get to my office, I see Sade's face buried in the printer trying to change the ink or something.

"Good morning, Sade," I say in greeting.

She leaves what she's doing and glances back at me. "Good..."

She stops talking as soon as she sees me. It's like something suddenly took her breath away.

"Are you okay?"

"Yes, ma'am. Good morning, ma'am."

"Morning, Sade," I greet her again. "Are you sure you're okay?"

"Yes. It's... just..." she stammers. "...you know, you said our dress or skirt has to be beyond our knee."

I smile. "Oh. I'm sure I'm allowed to break my own rules."

She nods and gives a weak smile.

"What do I have for today?"

"Um..." Grabbing a folder on her desk, she opens it and reads out. "You have a meeting with Production at 10:00am. A meeting with Management at 12:00pm. There's a full load of proposals on your desk that you have to read through and approve or disapprove."

"Any letters?"

"Yes, ma'am." She opens her drawer and brings out some envelopes. "This one is from Father Paul."

"To err is human, to forgive is divine. Is that not what the note says?"

She nods. "Yes. And a check for 200,000 naira."

I let out a breath. "You still need money for your tuition, right?"

"Yes, ma'am."

"Cash the check and keep the money."

Her face lights up. "Really? For me?"

I nod.

"Oh, my gosh, thank you, ma'am." She's so moved she wants to hug me, but she stops herself.

I open my arms slightly. "It's okay, Sade."

Slowly, she walks into my arms and gives me a quick hug. "Thank you."

I smile. "I think it's high time we took care of Father Paul for good. Give me a pen and a paper."

When she gives it to me, I consider for a while what my response should be. And then I bend slightly, resting on her desk to write something.

Father Paul,

I'm not sure I can ever forgive you or your friend, Jaye, for what you both did to me. But I'm happy right now. I'm finally in a happy place in my life. All I can say to you is be guilt-free and be happy.

Miki Daniels.

"Send it to Father Paul," I say, handing the note to her and then walking into my office. I'm reading through a proposal on my desk when my phone signals I have a text.

Vince: What color underpants are you wearing? I forgot to take a look this morning.

Me: I'm wearing the leave-me-alone-and-let-me-do-my-job color.

Vince: Ouch.

Me: How about I come to your office later and flash you my panties?

Vince: Deal.

Me: ok.

I read through the proposal, approving the ones I can. And at 10:00am, I meet with the Production Department, and then with the Management at 12:00pm. By the time the meeting is over, I'm more than anxious to see Vince. Grabbing my bag, I'm ready to hit the road.

"Sade," I call immediately after I step out of my office.

She rises to her feet. "Yes, ma'am?"

"I'm stepping out. I should be back in two hours, three maximum."

"Okay, ma'am."

Before I can move, I hear her stomach growl. She's hungry. Looking back sharply at her, she's bowing with her hands on her belly.

"I'm sorry, ma'am."

Her apologies sink my shoulder. "What are you apologizing for?"

Staring at the floor, she voids my gaze.

My God, was I this brutal? Why does she fear me this much? Maybe the old me would have lashed out at her for something reflexive like that, but this is the new me. If there's anything Vince has taught me, it's that life doesn't have to be hard. Life can be easy, and I can be easy, too.

"It's lunch time, Sade. You want to go out to lunch with me?"

"Thanks, but no, ma'am. I'll eat something when I get home."

"Lunch is on me, Sade. I'm going to make a stop at Mama Pot Restaurant..."

She cuts me off. "You go to Mama Pot Restaurant?"

I shrug. "Yes. Why are you so surprised?"

She's smiling and all excited. "Mama Pot's food is the

best. I didn't figure you to be someone who liked to go to her restaurant. Guess, I misjudged you."

True, I didn't figure myself as someone who would stoop so low as to eat at a lowly restaurant like that, but I've loved it ever since Vince took me there. I love the food, but mostly I love the memory of sharing something like that with Vince.

"So are you going to let me take you to lunch?"

She doesn't respond, so I take it for a yes. "You have thirty minutes for lunch."

Hurriedly, she grabs her handbag, and we head out. I buy a meal at Mama Pot Restaurant, but she'd rather take it with her than stay and eat. When I say she has only thirty minutes for lunch, I mean it. It doesn't matter if she's out with me.

I buy a bowl of pepper soup for Vince, too. I'm going to take it to his office. I'm sure he's going to like it.

I give Sade a few hundred naira to take a taxi back to work. It's just a few minutes' drive from Mama Pot back to our office, so she should be fine.

I drive to the office building of Vince Ali & Associates. I'm more than eager to see Vince. It's just been a few hours, but I miss him already, like it's been years since I've been away from him.

I say a greeting to his assistant and push open his office door. His face is buried in the documents on his desk and when he lifts up his eyes, I can tell he's having a rough day. His tie is loose, his suit jacket lying somewhere.

"Hey, baby," he says immediately after he sets eyes on me.

"Hey, are you okay? You look kind of stressed."

"I'm fine. Just been doing some serious thinking on how to help a client. He's been charged with murder.

There's a witness, evidence, all pointing at him. It looks like I'm going to lose this one. I have no other choice than to plead guilty to get a lesser sentence."

I place my handbag and the lunch bag on the floor and walk over to his side. Sitting on the arm of his chair, I put my arm around him. "I'm so sorry."

Gently, he rests his head on my breast. "Don't be. It's not your fault. I can't win all the time."

I nod and caress his hair. "But I want to make you feel better and I don't know how."

He smiles. "It's okay, Miki."

Standing up, I remember the lunch I bought for him. "Guess what, Vince? I got you Mama Pot's pepper soup for lunch."

That actually brings a real smile to his face. "Really?"

"Yes, really."

They say the way to a man's heart is through his stomach. They are right. But I also know another way to a man's heart.

Sitting on his desk, I'm facing him. Very gently I pull up my dress a little and open my legs for him.

"You wanted to know the color of my underpants."

"White lace," he replies. Bold eyes, hungrily, look between my legs.

Slowly I reach forward and grab his tie, pulling him into me. "Does it make you feel better?"

"Absolutely."

In a split second, he's on his feet, his arms around me and his lips on mine. It's a sweet kiss, rough, fast, and full of passion. It's so intense that every nerve in my body comes alive.

Arms around my waist, he pulls me close and I feel his erection. I feel a rush of happiness, a sense of pride that just kissing me is doing this to him. It makes me feel special, wanted by him.

My hands go speedily and pull at his belt. Then the button. And then the zip. And the rest is history. I pull down his pants and love what I see.

He breaks our kiss, the rush evident in his eyes. "You undress me faster than I can you."

The few seconds he stops kissing feels like years. "This babe is not patient."

A smirk covers his face. I reclaim his lips, grasping his neck and kissing him as if my life depends on it, as if the air in his mouth is what I need to survive. All the while, my other hand keeps stroking him, enjoying the feel of how he gets bigger and bigger in my hand.

He reaches under my dress and works down my panties in one swift motion.

He lied. He can undress me faster than I can him.

With a sense of urgency, he grabs me and leans me against the wall. He grabs the back of my thighs and holds them against his thigh, pushing my back into the wall for support, and then he starts thrusting into me. In and out, in and out. Deeper and deeper, making me moan his name.

The pleasure is incredible.

I wrap my arms and legs around him, wanting him even more, kissing him hard and almost sucking the air out of him.

The orgasm builds up very quickly, and I break the kiss as I gasp for air. My fingers dig into his shoulders as he increases his pace. A loud moan escapes my lips as I come close to the edge. I hear his final groan, and my body spasm as the wave of pleasure rushes through me.

Vince holds me tightly against him, our breaths coming in quick pants.

Chapter Twenty-One

Miki

I feel like a teenager. My inner sex goddess is scream-ing to be seen. I want to experiment with sex in every way possible and in every place possible. In the car, in the of-fice, on the beach, in a public toilet. Seeing Vince just ex-cites the sexual animal in me.

You will enjoy him. I tell myself. *Forever.*

I trust him that much to know he's going to be around me forever.

I finish touching up my makeup and then step out of Vince's private toilet.

"Your phone's been ringing," he says, holding out my phone for me.

He's neatly dressed again and has cleaned up the mess we made in his office.

"Who?" I ask.

"Lola…" he replies.

"Ignore her. She's not important."

Taking the phone from him, I drop it into my handbag.

"Who is she?"

"She's a leech who can't do anything for herself except exploit and rip off of everyone around her. And she's good at one thing: failing."

He stands up and holds both of my hands in his. "That's too harsh."

"I'm not saying it behind her back. I tell it to her face every time I get the chance."

"That's even worse. How can you tell someone to their face that they are good at failing? Do you even know how to encourage people? Do you have any idea what to say and not to say that hurts people?"

I raise my shoulder in a shrug. "Why should I encourage anyone? No one ever encouraged me. Besides, my words might be harsh, but they are true. I'm just being honest. Being honest makes me happy. It doesn't matter..."

"...if it hurts other people," he finishes my statement for me.

I hate to admit it, but he's right. I've been hurt so much that I see being hurt as something that's not a big deal. You get hurt. Get over it and move on.

But all that has changed now. I see things differently and I'm trying hard to change. I just need Vince to see that.

"Changes don't come overnight, Vince. I've been like this for almost half my life. I can't just change in one day. I'm trying. And I'm going to change. I promise."

Pulling me into his arms, he holds me tightly for a while. And then be breaks the silence. "Ice, I want to meet your friends."

I release myself from his hug. "Wow. Where's that coming from?"

"I just want to meet them and see if they are who you say they are, you know."

"No, I don't know. Vince, forget about my friends."

"You've met my daughter, Miki. You've met Wale, the only relative I have. At least let me meet your friends."

"Okay. I'll call them and set up a dinner or something."

He smiles and places a kiss on my lips.

"I have to go," I say. "I'm running late. I have an appointment with my psychiatrist."

He presses another kiss on my lips, holding me so tightly in his arms. "Do you really have to go? You can skip this one."

His hands move down to my ass, squeezing it as he moves me even closer to him and I feel his erection on my belly.

"I have to go, Vince," I say, smiling. I like how he's erect every time he sees me.

"Okay," he says and kisses me again. "I'll walk you."

"Okay."

He walks with me to my car. "I'll be home before dinner," he says.

"I'll see my psychiatrist and then go back to work. I should be home for dinner, too."

He nods. "Okay. Call me if plans change."

I nod.

When I get in the car, he leans in the driver's side window. "Thank you for the lunch, and thank you for coming over to show me your panties," he says, a grin plastered on his face. "Tomorrow, you can pretend as if you haven't seen my nakedness, and I can come show it to you in your office."

I start the car engine, giving him my cute smile. "Mr. Ali, I don't remember ever seeing your nakedness."

He smiles back. "Good observation, Miss Daniels. I'll come show it to you at your office tomorrow."

"Deal," I reply with a wink.

****

I'm running late for my therapy session, for the first time ever. And I missed my last session, too.

I know.

I'm not taking it seriously anymore, but that's only because I've gotten what I wanted.

Opening the door to Dr. Lara's office, I walk in. "I'm sorry I'm late."

"It's okay, Miki. Don't worry about it," she says and points her hand to the chair opposite her. "Take a seat, and let's begin."

As I take my seat, she takes a good look at me and I know something is surprising her. "Your dress is above your knee and you are not disguising yourself."

I smile. "It's a long story."

"And I want to hear everything, but fill out the questionnaire first."

I fill out the questionnaire quickly. I give it to her and she reads through it. Satisfied, she drops the paper and glance at me, smiling. "So what's this glow I'm seeing on your face?"

I smile, almost shyly. "I'm no longer genophobic."

"What do you mean? Did you..."

I cut her off. "Yes."

"Sweet Lord," she says, her face covered with excitement. I can tell she's genuinely happy for me. "Is that why you didn't show up for the last session?"

"Maybe. I kind of have what I wanted."

She rests her elbow on the desk. "Miki, just because you've had sex once doesn't mean you're okay already."

I shake my head. "It's not once. If I have to count, maybe between twenty and thirty."

She leans forward, her eyes wide. "I don't believe you."

I smile. "It's true."

She reaches over and holds my hand in hers. "Congratulations, Miki. That's a really good improvement. More than what I expected." She gives me a sideway glance. "Vincent must be doing something right."

"I guess."

The moment passes and she lets go of my hand.

"Still, Miki, I do not think you're okay yet." All the excitement has left her face. "I suppose you've told Vincent everything about your past. Correct?"

I nod.

"Good. Then I'm not going to ask you to tell me, too, unless you want to. It's enough you've told one person, the man you love. That's enough. But let me ask you this: do you think you've finally moved on from your past?"

"Yes, I've moved on. I see myself as someone new. I'm starting afresh like you advised and making things easier, Vince sees me as undamaged, a new person."

I can tell she isn't convinced by my response.

"Have you thought of what your reaction will be if you see that man from your past again?"

"Jaye Jamal?"

"Is that his name? Jaye Jamal?"

If I see Jaye Jamal again? That isn't happening.

Just hearing her say his name sends chills down my spine. It wakes up the rage and hatred I buried in the past few days. And much more than that, it wakes up the fear.

"I'm not going to see him again. If I see him again, I'll kill him."

She doesn't respond. She's quiet for a while, and then let out a deep breath. "Miki, you're almost there, but you are not there yet. I'm not discouraging you. In fact, I admire your strength. You're not genophobic anymore, but I think you still have unresolved issues that may cause you to relapse—for example, if Vincent broke things off with you."

I get her. I understand her. I'm not entirely over it yet. My improvement is based solely on Vincent. If he leaves me, I might relapse and find it difficult to ever trust again. And while I trust Vincent, I can never really count on forever. Humans will always be humans. Sometimes we hurt people even when we don't intend to.

She's right.

"What do you suggest I do to get better?"

"You are better, Miki. We just have to find a way to loosen that grip you have on your past. I'm going to help you get rid of all the hate and anger and fear that you've carried for so long."

I nod.

She relaxes her back on the chair. "So, tell me something about Jaye Jamal. Anything, nice or bad."

"Well. For one, he's a sadistic sociopath. An idiot. A crazy bastard who gets away with everything because he's born to a rich daddy." I pause for more than a second, swallowing hard and then continuing. "He's calm." The anger in my voice is no longer evident. "He appears to be gentle, so it's easy to trust him. When you see him, it's impossible to think anything bad about him. He's generous, nice, commands everybody's respect. He's smart and, of course, good–looking. If you had to judge him based on what he appears to be, you would say he's an angel sent from heaven. But he's a devil; a pure animal. He's..."

Chapter Twenty-Two

Miki

"Miki," Lola says in a loud whisper as soon as I step into the restaurant, raising her hand and waving at me to let me know where she's sitting.

It's a small but very fancy restaurant. They offer mostly local foods and any type of drinks you can think of, from expensive wines to cheap juice. It's a classy restaurant, one mostly reserved for the town's elite. Dinner tonight is on Vince because he wants to meet my friends. Not that I have any trouble paying. Anything for my man, you know. I'd even bring the moon to his feet if he wants it.

Anyway, I smile back and walk over to Lola. She is wearing a white, long-sleeved shirt over high-waisted baby pink jeans, while I'm wearing a yellow cowl-necked blouse over a black pencil skirt.

As soon as I get close to her table, she stands and opens her arms, holding me in a warm embrace.

"Sorry, I'm late," I say.

I know.

I'm breaking my own rules. I said I don't believe in apologizing when people wait for me, but I've been doing the opposite of that.

Lola pulls me down to the chair. "Sit," she says. "I want to hear all about this guy that you want us to meet. Is he cute?"

"Absolutely. And I'm going to tell you all about him. Where's Jessie?"

"She had to be somewhere." She takes a quick look at her wristwatch and glances back at me. "She should be here any minute."

I hear footsteps behind me and turn around reflexively. "Speak of the devil."

Lola and I stand and give Jessie a quick hug.

"Sorry I'm late, girls."

"That's okay," Lola replies, pulling out a chair for her. "Sit and let's get started. I can't wait to hear all about this guy."

"Me, too," Jessie says, raising her hands while Lola and I slap it in a high-five.

As soon as Jessie sits, I clear my throat. "Okay, so..."

Jessie cuts me off. "Is he cute?"

"He's tall, dark, and handsome, so I guess I'm saying he's cute."

They laugh, but the excitement is cut short as the waitress approaches us.

"Good evening and welcome to Three Gbosa Restaurant. May I take your order?"

"A cup of water each for now," I say. "We're waiting for someone. We'll order when he gets here."

She bows slightly and smiles. "Okay."

And then she's gone.

"So where is he now?" Lola asks.

"He should be here soon," I reply. "He's finishing up with a client."

"What does he do?" Jessie asks.

"He's a lawyer."

The waitress comes over with three cups of water, but

we're all too excited to even take a second to drink it.

Lola leans in and kind of lowers her voice. "Did you guys..." she winks at me, "...you know, do it?"

"Lola!" I can't help but laugh. It's my first time having a girls' talk about boys like this. I missed out on things like that while growing up. So it's going to take some getting used to. The upside is that I'm so into Vince I don't mind talking about him while the whole world is listening.

So, I laugh shyly and grab my water and drink half the cup. "Yes, we did. And it's amazing."

"Oh, my gosh, Ice, I'm so jealous!" she squeals, but I know she's happy for me. "I've been on a dry spell for months. I feel like the Sahara Desert right now."

"No need to be jealous," Jessie says. "Virgin Mary finally lost her V in the 21st century. It's like freaking two thousand years already."

They both break out into a loud laugh and exchange a high-five.

I give a sarcastic smile. "And Gomer makes fun of Virgin Mary."

Lola rolls her eyes, and we all go silent.

"Who is Gomer?" Jessie asks.

Lola glances at me and then back at Jessie. "Gomer is the whore in the Bible... the one..."

Jessie scowls at me and folds her arms. "Ice, you need to stop calling me a whore at every opportunity. I sleep with different men at the club because that is what I want. That's what makes me happy. And it sure as hell is not any of your damn business."

"Hey... hey... Jessie, that's enough," Lola tries to calm her. "We're here for Ice. You girls don't have to pick a fight today. It's her happy day. We're meeting her boyfriend. For the first time. Ever."

When Jessie finally withdraws her frown, I begin, "Okay, so he's going to be here any minute. Please, please and please, I want you girls to behave." I glance at Jessie. "Jessie, please, I'd appreciate it if you don't mention anything about what you do. I didn't tell him I have an escort as a friend. My past is heavy enough to bear as it is, I don't want to add having a whore friend to it."

"Ice!" Jessie yells. "Stop calling me a whore!"

"Sorry," I apologize.

But she can tell from my voice that I don't mean it.

And then I glance at Lola. "Please, try not to ask him for anything—money, gifts, and all. Okay?"

She nods, the excitement gone from her face.

Hearing the front door open, I glance back. "He's here!"

Lola and Jessie manage to feign a smile.

Vince walks boldly over to our table. Standing up, I welcome him with a warm embrace. "Hey."

"Hey." He places a kiss on my lips. "Sorry, I'm late. Had to finish up with a client."

"It's okay." And then I glance at my friends. "Vince, meet Lola."

Lola gets up and gives him a side hug. "Nice to meet you, Vincent."

"Vince, meet Jessie."

Vince extends a hand in greeting. As Jessie tries to take his hand, a scrutinizing look covers her face. "Vincent?"

I look at Vince. He looks as confused as me. And then I glance back at Jessie. "You know him?"

She doesn't respond. She's looking at Vince, forgetting I even exist.

"Jessie. We met at the night club on Crescent Road," she says, trying to jog his memory. "You remember me?"

Vince shakes his head gently. "No, I'm sorry. I met a lot

of ladies at that club."

"Well, well," I say, trying to ease the tension that's already building up. "Let's have a seat and eat. Isn't that what we're here for?"

Before Vince can sit, Jessie stands up and leans forward, her hands resting on the table. "You don't remember me?" She looks him in the eye, almost wearing a glare. "Hello? I've had nothing as amazing as what you gave me. I don't want to lose you. I want to do this again with you. Again and again." Her glare deepens. "Those were your words."

Vince stares wide-eyed, like the memories are coming back to him.

"Jessica, is that you? You look so different."

Hell, no.

My throat feels like a desert, and I have no choice but to finish my cup of water.

Jessie smiles. "Yeah, I look different. Club look is different from my everyday look."

Vince nods, smiling. "It's nice to see you again."

Walking over to his side, she throws herself in his arm. "Nice to see you again, Vincent."

"The reunion can wait till later," Lola says. "Can we eat now?"

Jessie looks at Lola then at me, her face glowing with an evil grin. "So, Vincent," she says, playfully smacking his chest. "Where have you been? I've looked everywhere for you. I thought you said our one time was amazing."

She's doing this to spite me. I know.

"It was amazing," Vince replies.

Jessie smiles. "So why didn't you come back?"

"I met Miki. I found love."

Jessie stands frozen. I'm certain her breath caught for a

moment. For more than a second, she's at a loss for words.

Vince's response gives me the courage to speak up.

"Jessie, sit and join us if you want. If not, you're free to leave." I hold Vince's wrist. "But I'm sure my man wants to sit and eat."

Vince is about to take a seat beside me when Jessie pulls his other wrist. "Vincent!"

All of our gazes move to her.

She's quiet for a while, staring at Vince. "So it's Miki, huh?"

Vince doesn't respond. He slowly releases his wrist from her hold, unbuttons his suit jacket and takes a seat beside me. "Why don't you sit, Jessie, and we'll clear up this misunderstanding over dinner?"

Tapping her artificial nails on her thigh, she scoffs and grabs her handbag and walks away from the table.

"Jessie!" Lola calls. "Jessie!"

"Enjoy your dinner," she says as she opens the door and walks out of the restaurant.

Lola turns her attention back to me. Pity is written all over her face, but I can't tell if it's for Jessie or me. "So my Vince is the Vincent Jessie had been searching for."

She lets out a deep sigh. "It really is a small world."

"Yes, it is."

With a sense of urgency, Lola lifts her handbag and stands. "I have to go. You know, check on her to make she doesn't do anything stupid."

I nod gently.

"I'm sorry, Ice."

"It's okay. Run and catch up with her. Make sure she's alright."

"Okay." She glances at Vince. "It's nice to meet you, Vincent."

"It's nice to meet you, too. Sad we couldn't get to know each other more."

"I'm sure we will do this again."

"Sure."

"Enjoy your dinner."

And just like that, she's gone.

Vince takes off his suit jacket and hangs it on the arm of the chair. "So it's just you and me."

"Yes, it is."

"Look, about..."

"Hey," I call on the waitress and gesture for her to come over. As she's nearing our table, I stare down at the menu.

"What can I get you?" she asks.

"I want pounded yam with vegetable soup, goat meat, and beef."

She takes notes, writing as fast as she can. "What do you want to drink?"

"Orange juice."

"Your order, sir?" she says, turning to Vince.

"Same as her, but I'll have a cup of water instead of juice."

"Ok, sir. Your order should be ready in less than five minutes."

As soon as she leaves, Vince's hand reaches across the table and grabs mine. "Miki, I have to explain what happened between me and Jessie."

"You don't have to. I know what happened."

"Are you angry? It's really not what you think."

"I'm not angry." I manage a smile. "I know what happened and I understand. You've told me about how you were lost when you lost your wife, going from one club to the other until you met me. Jessie was one of the girls you met at the club."

His face studies mine for any hint of anger. "And you're not angry?"

"No." I let my voice sound reassuring. "I am not angry. When a woman has gone through as much as me, petty things like this don't get me worked up. You met her, it was fun, maybe you even felt something for her, but you chose me. That's all that matters. I believe so much in the love you have for me."

He caresses the hand he is holding in his. "Thank you for having so much trust in me."

The waitress returns and he lets go of my hand. She serves our meal and as soon as she leaves, I continue our conversation. "There's something I have to ask you, though."

"What? Ask me anything. I'll answer truthfully."

I look into his eyes. "Do you know Jessica's full name?"

My question confuses him, but he answers anyway. "No. We met at a club. People never give their full names in such places. Just the first name, or nickname. Some people even use false names. So what's her last name?"

I sigh. "Jessica Jamal. Her brother is... Jaye Jamal."

Vince freezes with a jolt. And then he slowly sinks back into himself.

****

Vince

Jessica is Jaye's sister.

I haven't been myself ever since Miki told me last night.

I have to stay clear of Jessie by every means necessary. And from what I've noticed about Jessie, she is relentless.

She's not the type that easily gives up. Something tells me she's still coming back for me.

As I park my Rolls Royce in front of my office building, I notice a silver-colored Ferrari with a customize plate number JJ4.

A client must be waiting for me. I don't like keeping my client's waiting.

Hurriedly, I walk into the building, and I'm totally surprised at who I see in the waiting area.

"Jessica?"

She stands up, sashaying toward me with her arms open in a red dress that's so sexy it's only meant for dancing in the club. "Good morning, Vincent."

I know her evil ploy.

It's not going to work.

I try to be courteous, so I return the hug. "How did you know where I work?"

"Your name is Vincent. Miki mentioned yesterday that you're a lawyer. It's easy to find a lawyer whose name is Vincent. Everybody knows you. Your law firm is the best in town."

"Thanks for the compliment, but..." I pause for a second. "...I don't remember giving you an appointment to see me today."

Jessie takes one step back. Her eyes go wide. She understands. "You don't want me here."

Glancing around, I notice my assistant and some other staff staring at us. In order not to wash my dirty linen in public, I try to feign a smile. "I'm happy to have you here. Let's go into my office."

I lead the way while she follows. I say a greeting to two staff members as we walk to my office. Unlocking the door, I hold it open and gesture for her to come in. As soon as I slam the door shut, my smile disappears. "You can't be here," I say firmly but gently.

She gives me puppy dog eyes. "But why?"

Before I can get the next word out, she places her hands on my chest and pushes me. Slowly, my butt finds the desk without protest. Taking a few steps closer, she very gently raises her leg and places her thigh over mine. My eyes go straight to her thigh, neat, soft and...

Arms curl around my neck, and she leans into me, her breath steady and warm all over me. I can feel the man between my legs getting hard even though I don't want her touch. He has a mind of his own.

Brushing her lips gently over my chin, to my cheek, and softly over my lips, she breathes my name. "Vince..."

But all my life there's only one person who has ever called me Vince: Miki.

My mind goes to her, remembering the passionate but wild sex we had right here in this office. How I held her up against the wall and...

Quickly, I unwrap Jessie's arms around my neck. Grabbing both her upper arms, I hold her at arm's length, glaring at her. "Stop this madness, Jessie." I shake her to jolt her back to life in case she thinks she's dreaming. "Nothing can ever happen between us. Not anymore. I went to the club, I needed an escort and you were there when I needed you. And it was amazing. But that's where it ends. I'm going to let you go now." I release my hold on her upper arms. "I want you out of my office. Leave Miki and me alone. Get out of our lives—forever."

The sexual hunger in her eyes disappears, replaced by a sad, straight face. "I looked for you, Vincent," she says, trying hard to keep her voice low and steady. "I came back to that same club every night hoping I would see you again.

I know it's stupid, but..." She pauses for a while. A tear betrays her and runs down her cheek. "You said so many nice things to me, and you made me feel more than an escort. You told me to wait for you. I waited for you, Vincent. And... you never showed."

Taking one step closer to me, she tries to touch my chest.

I draw back slightly.

She nods gently and keeps her hands to herself.

"I'm sorry, Jessica, if I said something that made you think that night was more than just sex. Maybe it could have been more, but I'm with Miki now. I love her."

"And I don't mind. You can still have me," she says desperately, coming even closer and her hands moving slightly down to my dick. "You can have me anyway you want. We can have an agreement. I promise I won't tell Miki. I won't ruin what you have with her."

"You want to be a side chick?" I say with all the disgust I can build up.

She takes her hand off of me. "What's wrong with being a side chick? There are a lot of women out there who are."

"Yes, but most of them don't ask for it. They either fell in love with a man who is unavailable or the men lied to them. Most of them don't ask for it. Cheaply. Like you."

She lifts her shoulders in a shrug. "Does it matter?"

Looking at her with resentment, I let out a breath. "Miki was right about you."

"What do you mean Miki was right about me?"

"Get out," I say, ignoring her question. "And never come back."

"Vincent..."

I cut her off and scowl. "Get out."

"Please... Vincent."

"Out!" I hate to yell at a woman, but she's given me no other choice. And it seems to be the only language she understands because she runs out of my office the minute I raise my voice.

Chapter Twenty-Three

Jessie

I feel humiliated.

Vincent humiliated me just because I was honest about my intentions.

I have wanted him ever since our one night together. I want him even more now, despite all the humiliation he gave me today. And that makes me sad because I'm not this pathetic. I'm the girl who knows what she wants and never lets any man look down on me. I mean, I can get everything I want. I have all the money I need. I've had my share of great sex, even without having a steady relationship. Sometimes, I even pay men to have great sex with me. I never feel as if I needed a man for anything—until I met Vincent.

I wish I could stop wanting him. I wish all the attraction I feel toward him would just stop. I'm an escort, but I have my dignity. I'm an escort because I choose to. It's what I do for fun.

I just want to stop wanting him. You know what I mean?

All the cravings, the hunger for him... I want it to stop. I don't want to be this pathetic anymore.

Tears lace my eyes, but I don't shed them. I feel a depression crawling out from deep inside my mind and overwhelming me. I need not be told it's not healthy to be alone right now. I need to be around people.

Making a U-turn, I head to Lola's place.

As I enter her neighborhood, an irritating smell fills my nostrils. Quickly, I wind up the windows of my car.

Lola lives in the ghetto, and it smells like pee and shit.

I've only been to her apartment once, but I need her now. I don't exactly have many friends who understand me. She may not be going to clubs and calling herself an escort, but sometimes, when she's broke, she's had to sleep with men for money.

I think she understands me.

I park my car in front of Lola's house. As I step out of the car, I hold my breath to stop myself from inhaling the awful odor oozing out of the house. Slowly, watching the floor to make sure I don't step on any rotten shit, I walk to Lola's one-room apartment and knock loudly on her wooden door.

Opening the door, she frowns. "What?"

I feign a smile. "Hi. Can I come in?"

She shifts away from the door and gestures for me to walk in. "I told you not to come to my house. If you want to hang out, I can come to you."

I walk into the house, glancing around. It hasn't really changed since the last time I was here. Two wooden chairs at the corner of the room. One twin bed in another corner. A kerosene stove, cooking pots, plates and spoons in another corner. And then I notice her wooden wardrobe. Some designers in there: Gucci, Prada, Michael Kors. Calvin Klein.

Talk about someone with a misplaced priority. All the money she gets from me and Miki goes to buying expensive clothes, shoes, and handbags just to feel like she belongs.

"You know you can actually leave this neighborhood and rent a nice apartment instead of wasting your money on expensive designer wear just to show off?"

"Is that why you wanted to break down my cheap door?"

"I'm sorry for knocking too hard," I apologize. "It's the urgency of the moment."

She cleans up the chair so I can sit. "What's so urgent?" she asks, taking a good look at me. "And where are you coming from?" You're looking hot for a..." she takes a quick look at her old wall clock "...hot morning."

I smile, playing with my long braids. "Thanks."

She sits on the chair next to mine. "So where are you coming from?"

"Vincent's office."

"Which Vincent?" She's playing dumb.

"Same Vincent."

"Miki's Vincent?"

I nod.

"What? You went to Vincent's office looking this sexy, with your boobs and legs screaming like this? I'm sure he couldn't resist you."

I shake my head. "He yelled at me and walked me out of his office. He called me cheap, and humiliated me." Tears gather in my eyes as a lump forms in my throat.

"Oh, no," Lola says, pulling my shoulder and resting my head on her shoulder. "It's okay. You know you're not cheap, right? You're just a woman who knows what she wants and is not afraid to go after it."

Taking my head off her shoulder, I manage a weak smile. "Thank you."

She nods. "But Jessie, what did you expect going after Vincent like that? You know he and Miki has something strong for each other..."

I cut her off, frowning. "But he met me first. He wanted me first, and he wouldn't have stopped wanting me if not for Miki."

She nods. "I agree."

But I'm not finished with my rants. I feel an intense anger boiling within me, and I need to let it out. "It's always Miki, Miki, Miki. Why does she get to have everything? She has money, power, and a man who adores her. Why does she have it all? Why is she so damn lucky? Has she ever even felt any pain in her life?"

"Jessie, you're not thinking straight. Calm down."

My blood reaches a raging boil and I stand up from the chair. With clenched teeth, I spit out my hurtful words. "Don't tell me to calm down! You know I'm right! I mean, look at you. You sleep and wake up in abject poverty, and you're not even lucky enough to find a good man to take care of you. You have nothing. Look at me. I am unhappy. I can't make money on my own. I look up to my parents, and I can't even have the man I love. But Miki... Miki... she gets to have everything. Good parents, a good man, money, and power!"

"And she spites the rest of us who are not as lucky as she is with hurtful words."

Lola completes my statement.

Her support and understanding calm my nerves.

Gently my butt finds the chair, and I glance at Lola and give a gentle nod.

Both of us are quiet for the next two minutes or so. I don't know what she's thinking, but I know I'm thinking about how I hate wanting something and not getting it.

Ever since I was a child, I've always gotten everything I ever wanted. Except this time—Vincent.

You can say that my parents spoiled me rotten, but I don't think so. Everybody has it in them, I believe. To always want to have everything they want.

"If only Miki was not in the picture, I know Vincent would want me."

Lola doesn't respond. We are quiet again for another two minutes. Tired, I rest my back on the chair.

"Maybe I know a way to take Miki out of the picture so you can have Vincent." Lola says.

I sit up again, looking at her intensely. "What is it?"

She bites her lip and glances away. "I'm not sure. Don't worry."

I place my hand on hers. She looks at me, and I hold her gaze, studying her. "Please tell me. I promise I'll make sure you get everything you ever wanted."

She sighs. "I'm not sure..."

"Just tell me..."

She closes her eyes and suck in air. She opens them again and let out a deep breath. "Your license plate is customized as JJ4, correct?" she asks.

"Yes," I reply, wondering what that has got to do with anything.

"For how long?"

"Since I was 17 years old. My dad's plate is customized as JJ1, my mom as JJ2, my brother as JJ3. It's a family thing. What has that got to with this?"

She answers without hesitation. "Everything."

I wait, giving her my full attention.

"You remember eight years ago when Miki went missing for four months?"

I nod. "Yes. We looked for her. We thought she'd been

kidnapped, killed by ritualists. But you found her, brought her to the hospital and saved her."

"Yeah, that's what I told everybody, but that wasn't all of it."

"What else?" I hold her hand and shake it. I'm dying of curiosity. "Tell me."

"I didn't just find her, Jessie. Someone dropped her in front of the house. I didn't see a face, but I saw the car. The license plate was customized, JJ3."

It takes more than a second before I can exactly process what I just heard. I don't think I heard correctly.

I finally find my voice and "What?!" is all I can say.

"Jessie..."

"Do you know what you're saying? My brother might be the one who kidnapped Miki!"

"No, Jessie, you're getting it all wrong." She stares intently into my eyes. "When Miki and I did our program at Jamal Corp, I noticed a tension between Jaye and Miki." She hesitates a moment, perhaps trying to make sure I follow. "Jessie, what if Miki wasn't kidnapped? What if Jaye and Miki were lovers and she ran off with him, and Jaye only brought her back because she fell sick."

In deep thought, I sink in to myself. "You're right. But I don't understand—how does this help me get Vincent?"

"Jaye left for the United States almost immediately after that incident. He hasn't been home since."

Understanding her line of thought, I cut her off. "If I can convince my parents to ask Jaye to come back home, Miki and Jaye can continue where they left off. I just need Miki to mess up once with Jaye, and I'll let Vincent know."

She nods. "There are only a few men who can forgive their lovers for cheating, and I don't think Vincent is one of them."

"So when Miki is out of the picture, I can come in."

"And you can have Vincent..." Lola finishes the statement for me.

Just the mere thought of it excites me. I know it's weird and crazy, but I can imagine a future with Vincent, a future where he will hate Miki like shit and come running into my arms.

Throwing my slim arms around Lola, I hold her tightly. "Thank you so very much for helping me out."

"That's what friends are for."

Releasing her, I look sincerely into her eyes. "I don't know what I would have done without you."

"Aww." She gives me a kiss on the cheek. "Anything for you. Love you, Jessie."

"Love you too, girlfriend." Standing up, I put my arms around her waist and hurl her up. "Come with me, girlfriend. I have something for you."

She gives me a sideways glance. "What?"

"Just follow me."

Hand in hand, we walk out of her one-room apartment and head out.

"I hope it's not your used clothes."

"No, but you'd be lucky to have any of my used clothes."

She smacks my shoulder. "Jessie!"

"C'mon, it's just a joke."

"Oh, fuck you, Jessie."

Holding her upper arm, I pull her close to me. "I'm sorry. I didn't mean it like that."

She smiles. "It's okay."

Getting to my car, I take my handbag, pull out my checkbook, and write on it. And then I give it to Lola.

Looking at it with her eyes wide open, she opens her

mouth to say something. It takes more than a second for words to come out. "Three million naira!" she says and surprises me with a big hug. "Thank you so very much, Jessie."

"Anything for you, girlfriend. Get the money and get yourself out of this neighborhood."

She nods.

"Please, don't squander it on clothes and shoes and Brazilian weaves. If you do, I'll take all of it, sell it, and get my money back."

"Yes, ma'am."

We hug again, and I get into my car and drive off.

As I drive home, I think about the best way to convince my father to let my brother return home. I don't know why my father insisted Jaye stay in the United States, but I have to find a way to get him to reverse his decision.

When I see my father this evening, I'll say, '*Dad, this tenure might be the end of your political career. You're getting old. You can't return to business, and our family must continue its power and legacy. I am not very good with business. Why don't you let my brother return home so he can carry on the family legacy? And since Jamal Corporation has lost its relevance in the business world, we can partner with Daniels Group. Better still, we can merge it together if my brother and Miki Daniels get married. That is not strange. In the business world, people don't marry for love—they marry to gain more power and affluence. The same way, you and my mother married each other to maintain the power of Jamal Corp., Miki Daniels should marry Jaye. They were lovers once. And if she does have a problem with it, you can use her father to get to her. You've had a strange hold on him over the years.*

And if I know my father well, he will fall for this.

Chapter Twenty-Four

Miki

TWO WEEKS LATER

"Vince, I'm only having this dinner with my parents because you asked me to."

My dad called me two nights ago and asked me to join them for dinner. There's something important he wants to discuss with me. I didn't want to go, but Vince said I should, and to make it easier he said he'd go with me. He's been hell-bent on meeting the people in my life. First, it was my friends, and that didn't go well. Now something tells me that meeting my parents is going to be a disaster, too.

My nerves fray with anticipation, and unfortunately, anger at seeing both my parents again.

Vince takes his eyes off the road for a second, reaches an arm over the center console, and takes my hand in his. "Baby, our parents are our parents."

The warmth of his skin on mine melts away all the anger and tension in my body.

"We're biologically programmed to love them no matter what," he continues. "Now, I know what they did to you, but I'm sure you can tolerate them a little longer so I can get to know them. I'm a traditional guy. I'm still going to need their blessings before I can marry you."

I suppress a smile. "You're planning to marry me?"

"Pretend you didn't just hear me say that." He slows down a little and glances over at me, grinning. "I still want you to have that excitement when I propose."

I give a short laugh. "Trust me, I heard nothing."

"Thanks," he says and concentrates back on the road.

I keep staring at him; can't take my eyes off him. He's handsome. Strong. Masculine. Caring. And desirable. Looking at him—just looking at him—I feel lucky. I feel grateful to have a man like him. There are many good, perfect women out there, and he chose me. He chose the imperfect, flawed, damaged me.

"You're staring at me," he says. Immediately, I lean over and place a quick kiss on his lips. His mint-flavored mouth invites me in and I feel the warmth of the inside of his mouth. It was quick, but it's sweet and refreshing.

When we part, I smile at him. My hand still in his, he lifts it up close and kisses it.

Softly.

Sweetly.

And then he presses my palm against his strong chest, so close to his heart that I can feel every beat.

Getting to my parents' house, Vince parks the car, breathes out, and looks at me. "Are you going to be okay?"

I take a deep breath, too. "Yeah."

Climbing out of the car, we walk to the door and I press the doorbell. A few seconds later, the door opens and it's my mom.

"Miki," she says with a big smile as I walk into the welcoming embrace of my mother.

"Hello, Mom."

"How have you been?" she asks.

"Fine."

And then she releases me from her embrace and peeps at the man standing behind me. "Don't be rude, Miki. Introduce me to your guest."

I give a smile. "Mom, meet Vince, my..." I hesitates a second. "My boyfriend..."

My mom goes pale, like blood totally vanishing from her face.

"Mom?" I call her. "Are you okay?"

She blinks a few times before responding. "Yes, yes, I'm fine."

My mom is lying to me.

Something is wrong and she's not telling me.

"You don't look too well, Ma," Vince says. "Are you sure you're okay?"

She stares at Vince for a while, but doesn't give a response. Then she glances at me.

"Your father is waiting at..."

I cut her off. "Mom, you can't ignore..."

My voice is louder than I had intended, and I feel Vincent holding my wrist. I glance back at him and he gives me a face to keep me in check.

I respect him.

So I swallow back the rest of my words.

"Where is Dad?" I ask.

"He's waiting at the dining room table already. Come with me."

My black high-heeled shoes softly tread the marbled floor as we walk to the dining room. It takes a while because the house is very big, one of the biggest in the country. It cost me quite a fortune to build it. We walk past the rows of grinning moments of time, old and new pictures carefully hanging on the wall. I never look. I never pause to share in their memories. They are all pictures that capture the terrifying years of my life. They are all bad memories.

My mom pushes open the door to the dining. Hand in hand, I walk in with Vince.

"Hello, Da..." My gaze moves to the dining room table where my dad is sitting, but I can't believe who is sitting with him. My hand slowly slides out of Vince's.

I stand frozen.

My breath catches in my throat. Bumps run through my whole body.

I'm trembling. A dozen emotions run through me at once. I feel anger surge through me, and everything dead in me threatens to be awakened, to be let out.

"What is he doing here?" I ask, my voice hardened.

I feel my mom's arm over my shoulder. "Miki, you should sit..."

Shoving her arm away, I scowl over at my dad. "Sitting down is not happening! You better start telling me what Jaye Jamal is doing in MY house."

My dad clears his throat. "Miki, business is not strange to you anymore. In business, we always try to gain more ground and acquire more wealth. And one of the ways people do that is through marriage." He stalls a bit, and then continues. "Jamal Corporation needs Daniels Group to acquire more power. You need Jamal Corporation, too. To get it, you have to marry the heir of Jamal Corporation."

I feel the weight of his words, and my shoulders sink. I feel my breath catch in my throat. I feel surrounded by enemies. I feel suffocated.

I can't believe what I just heard. Gently, I walk over to my dad and stand beside him. "Dad?" I call gently.

He doesn't respond.

"Dad," I call again, trying to keep my voice steady.

He can't even look at me.

"Dad!"

Raising his face, he looks at me—not straight in the eyes, but at my face.

Just looking at him has my eyes filled with tears. "Dad, I can't believe you're doing this yourself. Your friend, Hon. Jamal is making you do this. Tell me, what does he have on you?" Lips quivering, I'm trying so hard not to cry. I just want to believe there's still good left in him. "Anything he has on you, I can save you. You don't have to be afraid of him anymore. Is it money? I have plenty. Is he blackmailing you? Do you want Jamal Corporation? I can get it for you without marrying a monster, but you have to be honest with me. I can help you. Let me help you."

"I'm doing this for you, Miki."

That's it. I've had enough. In a blink of an eye, I have my father's shirt in my fists. "You're not doing this for me. You do everything for yourself. You are nothing but a coward. A greedy coward who doesn't see anything wrong in destroying his child to get some cash." His eyes are wide as he struggles to back away from me. I tighten my grip on his collar until he can hardly breathe. "You're a coward. You wanted to be in the big leagues, and I made it happen. You wanted money, I made it happen. But you can't stand on your feet and fight for your daughter. You are a pathetic disgrace to fatherhood."

"Stop this madness, Miki!" my mom yells. "You bring home a man. Vincent. Is that his name? Vincent son of who? Is his father the president? Is he a king? Is this Vincent worth anything? Does he command half the respect and power you command? I guess no. Jaye is the best for you. That's what we are trying to tell you. And everything your father has ever done is for you."

I scream, let go of my father's shirt, and push him

backward as hard as I can. He almost falls off his chair. Unable to keep a grip on my anger, I walk over to my mom, glaring at her. "Shut up, mom! If you don't know what to say, just shut up! Do you even know what happened to your daughter while she was under your care? Do you care? All you cared about is your stupid gold business that yielded no profit. After all of your hustles, you and your husband would have died in poverty if not for me."

"What kind of a child are you?" she asks, her voice cold. She's getting angry, too. "You dare stand there and disrespect your parents?"

"You lost every right to demand my respect a long time ago. You failed me. You and Dad. You failed me."

"After everything we did for you, Miki. After all the sacrifices I and your father made, this is how you repay us?" She raises her hand and slaps me hard across my face. "You're such an ungrateful bastard!"

My eyes grow blurry from tears unshed and the anger flashing in them. "Don't you dare raise your hand to me ever again." I stand close to my mother, our eyes locked together as I shoot her a deadly glare. "Everything you and Dad ever gave to me, I paid for it. I bled for it. I'm still paying for it right now in ways none of you can understand." I lift my shaking hand to her neck, everything in me threatening to strangle her. "So next time when you want to call me ungrateful, you better know what..."

"Miki!" Vince's voice roars through the room, yelling my name to caution me.

Hearing his voice, I stop. Anger is still boiling in me, but I respect this man so much I cannot but heed his warning.

Swallowing hard, I close my eyes and suck in my breath trying to keep a lid on my anger as my hand slowly finds a resting place at my side.

The storm in me is about to be totally calm when I feel a touch on my left wrist.

"Miki," he calls.

I knew who that is. Just the sound of his voice makes me sick in the pit of my stomach, let alone his touch...

My palm folds into a fist. I turn around to punch his face when Vince's fist flies faster than mine and lands on Jaye's face. Blood gushes out of his nose.

Vincent holds me, his grip so tight it's almost hurting me. I can tell he's angry too, but he's doing a good job of controlling it.

Gently, he lets go of me. His expression still very dangerous, he glances at both of my parents. "I'm sorry we had to meet for the first time under these circumstances," he says gently, but with a hard edge to his voice. "Perhaps if I may introduce myself, my name is Vincent Ali. I'm the man who is going to be marrying your daughter. It's nice to meet you." He gives a gentle but obviously fake smile and bows slightly. Standing between Jaye and me, Vince next puts a finger under Jaye's chin and raises his face to meet his. "Know this, though, Mr. Jamal," he says, his voice is slightly above a whisper, "if you want Miki, you're going to have to go through me. Do you understand?"

He swallows hard and manages to give a weak nod.

"Good." The dark expression on his face is replaced by a calm stare. He removes his finger from under Jaye's chin, and then holds my arm in his. "If you don't mind, we'd like to leave now. Thank you very much."

Silence suffocates the room.

No one could say nothing. Not my dad, not my mom—not even the monster.

For the first time in a long time, I feel safe. I don't feel like the whole world is against me.

Resting my head on Vince's shoulder, we walk toward the door. At that moment, Vince is my everything. I need no one else.

Stopping abruptly, I turn back and glance at my parents. Something tells me it's going to be the last time I see their faces. "Dad... Mom," I call. The anger has left my voice, but it's still cold. "I want you to forget that you have a daughter, because as far as I'm concerned, I'm an orphan. My father is dead to me, and so is my mother." I pause and see the hurt on their faces, but me being me, I don't care. "Your bank accounts will be frozen. I'm taking my money back, and you have forty-eight hours to vacate this house. MY house," I say in a tone I use for people at work, people who are not family.

I don't wait to see the expression on their faces. I just turn back, hold Vince, place my head on his shoulder, and walk away with him. As far as I'm concerned, he's all the family I have. He's all the family I need.

We drive home in silence. More than once, Vince tries to talk about what just happened, but I'm not ready to talk. Not yet.

Chapter Twenty-Five

Miki

I'm sitting on my comfy leather chair, face immersed in my work when Sade pushes open my door.

"Ma'am, someone from the shipping department is here to see you."

"Is it important?" I ask, not at all interested in seeing anyone today. My personal life is too much weight as it is, let alone adding business to it.

"I don't know, but he's desperate to see you."

I let out a breath. "Send him in."

Relaxing my back on the chair, I wait for him. A few seconds later, the door opens and he walks in. From the look on his face, I can tell he didn't bring good news.

"Good day, ma'am."

"Good day, Mr... um..." Too bad for me, I have never bothered to learn any of my workers' names. "Please, take a seat," I say, pointing to a chair opposite me.

"It's not a sitting matter, ma'am. The deadline to ship our products to Ghana is this week. We have about fifty containers at sea right now that can't be shipped because the government put a ban on it on the grounds that we ship contraband."

A bucket of ice has been poured on me.

"What! But those products are not contraband."

It wasn't a question, but he answers anyway.

"They are not. They're just our regular product. The same products we've been shipping for years without a problem."

This isn't right. Something is wrong.

"Did you contact our guy in customs?"

"Yes, ma'am. He says there's nothing he can do."

Something is wrong, I know. As far as I'm concerned, no one would dare mess with me or my products. Not even the government. No one.

I've grown soft in the last few weeks and they think because of that they can mess with me. Well, the ice queen hasn't melted yet.

"Thank you. You can leave. I'll handle it."

He hesitates. "But ma'am..."

"I said I'll handle it. Get out!" I yell.

In a split second, he's out of my office. Grabbing my cell phone, I place a quick call to my guy at the customs office.

"Miki Daniels on the line. Why the hell is my product not allowed to ship?"

"I don't know, ma'am. The order came and..."

I cut him off. "Who gave the order?"

"I don't know."

"Give the phone to Agent Hassan."

"Ma'am?"

"I said give the phone to your boss!"

"Yes, ma'am."

For the next few seconds, silence roars in my ears. He's probably transferring my call to his boss. A little while later, a voice I recognized answers.

"Hi, Miss Daniels. You asked to speak with me?"

"I have more than fifty containers at sea right now waiting to be shipped. One of my workers just told me your office won't allow them to be shipped."

"Yes," he says, and then pauses for a while. "From my records here, your containers are not allowed to ship because they've been labeled as contraband."

"You and I both know I don't carry contraband. This is probably a ploy from my competitors. I need to make this go away. I need to know who gave you the order."

"I'm sorry, I can't release that information to you."

"Please." It takes me longer than normal to say the word.

"I'm sorry."

I ask him for a favor, and he turns me down. Vince says I should be nice. He says I should ask for a favor nicely. I have done it his way. It didn't work. Now, I'm going to do it my own way. Hesitating for a second, I swallow before I begin. "Mr. Hassan, your wife is a teacher at Maitama High School, correct?"

"Yes, why?"

"Sade!" I call out. In a split second, the door opens.

"Yes."

"Get the principal of Maitama High School on the phone for me. Now!"

"Yes, ma'am," she says, bowing slightly and leaving.

"What are you trying to the do?" Mr. Hassan says to me.

I shout into the phone. "Oh! I'm going to destroy your wife. I'm going to tell the principal that there's been a report that your wife has been sexually molesting the kids in her class. Let's see what the reaction of the principal and the parents is."

"You're bluffing. You don't have any evidence."

"I will manufacture one. I will pay students to come forward and accuse her. You will be surprised the extent people will go to for money. I will destroy every little bit of character your wife has left. She will lose her job and the only place she will be able to find another job is in my kitchen!"

"You can't do that."

"I think you have an idea of what I can and cannot do. I can and will do anything for my business. I don't care who gets hurt. They are acceptable sacrifices and..."

He cut me off. "Hon. Jamal."

"What?"

"The order came from the office of the senate president. From Hon. Jamal."

"Thank you," I say, and then press the red button.

My mouth opens slightly, and I find myself blowing out hot air. I'm not stupid. I understand what is happening. Jaye Jamal is coming for me. And he has the muscles of the office of the senate president behind him.

Without giving it much of a thought, I grab my handbag and hurry out of my office.

"Ma'am, the principal of Maitama High School is on phone for you," Sade says.

"I'll be back in fifteen." I walk past her without even giving her a glance.

About five minutes later, I park my car in front of Jamal Corp. and walk straight to the boss's office.

His executive assistant is sitting by the desk and without giving any greeting, I cut to the chase. "Is he in?"

"Yes, but..."

Walking past her, I head straight for the door.

"Excuse me, you can't just go in," she says, running after me.

Ignoring her, I push the door open and there sits the monster at the center of his large office on his comfy, leather chair.

Seeing me, he stands on his feet. "Miki," he calls, his voice very gentle, as if he can't hurt a fly.

"I'm sorry, sir. I tried to tell her she can't come in," the lady says.

"It's okay, Bose. You can go."

As soon as she leaves, I throw my handbag on the couch in his office and charge toward him. "I'm aware you tried to sabotage my business today."

Walking closer to me, he tries to calm me.

"Do not touch me!" I yell.

He shudders. "I'm sorry, Miki. I only did that to get your attention."

"Oh, you have my attention. But let me warn you. I am not the pathetic little girl you destroyed eight years ago..."

A small sigh escapes his lips. "Ah! Miki, give me just sixty seconds to explain myself."

Ignoring his plea, I rage on. "I wanted to pretend as if you didn't exist, like you didn't just crawl out of whatever hole you've been hiding in for the last eight years. But you can't just stay away from me—you had to come after me and sabotage my business, the thing that I value most in this world. Now you have my attention."

"Miki... please..."

"You may have the muscles of your father behind you, but I want you to know you just stepped on the wrong toes because I know all your secrets, your weaknesses, your crimes, and where every skeleton is buried. Literally. And if I were you, I would run away from that unstoppable woman called Miki Daniels. If I were you, I would be very afraid because you do not have the slightest idea of what I am capable of. If I were you, I would run. Run, Jaye! Run back to the hell you came out from because if you come near me my business one more time, I will kill you. I will cut your body to pieces and feed it to the dogs, and I will make sure nobody remembers your name or the name of any member your family."

He stands frozen.

I've made my point. I reach for my handbag and walk toward the door.

"Miki, sixty seconds to explain myself."

Placing my hand on the knob, I try to open the door.

"I beg you in the name of the things you love most. Sixty seconds."

In the name of the things I love most. I stop and glance back at him, wearing a look of disgust and anger.

He lets out a deep breath. "Miki," he begins gently, his voice even, "I did something terrible to you and I ran. I ran away. And you're right, I had my father to support me, and he helped me run even without knowing what I was running from. I ran to the United States. I thought I could get a clean slate. I wasn't for once sorry for what I did to you. I thought I could go on living like nothing happened." He stops for a moment and swallows hard. "One day, I was at the wrong place, with the wrong people, and I got arrested alongside some group of criminals. I spent seven years in jail for a crime I didn't commit. And..." his voice becomes shaky as tears collect at the corners of his eyes. "And then it hit me that I was being punished for what I did to you. I ran, but fate found a way to punish me. I spent seven years in jail, and I am corrected. I want to make everything right. I volunteer for community service at the National Hospital. I try to help people, but mostly I want to stand by you and make things right. I see things clearly now. I am corrected."

I stare at him for a moment. I'm not a fool. I can't believe his lies. "Tell that to the idiots who are dumb enough to believe you."

Opening the door, I walk out of his office and hurry to my car. As soon as I get in, I let out a deep breath. It's like I've been holding my breath ever since I walked into his den. I don't know if I put on a believable show, but I was scared to the bone. I was thinking the worst. Like what if he kidnapped me right there and then, and I had to relive my nightmare again.

Just the thought of it has my whole body shaking as the memory of it all returns to me. I can still see the eyes of that guy as he stares lifelessly at me. He lost his life trying to save me. I remember everything. And for a moment there, I can't breathe. I am being suffocated by my memories.

Opening the door of my car, I step out and try to breathe, try to forget. Then I try to remember something that makes me happy: Vince.

Finally feeling better, I get back in my car and return to my office. Throughout the rest of the day, I'm jumpy. I can't concentrate on anything without the fear of the past or fear of the future crawling back into my mind.

I manage to work till 10:00pm. I walk out of the building straight to my car when I notice a black SUV drive past me. A kind of cold air blows through me. Goosebumps run over my arm. I have a bad feeling, but I don't know why. I just keep having this feeling that something is wrong, but I don't know what. I can't just place my finger on it. I look at the car that's driving past me. The windows are tinted so I can't see who is on the inside. I make up my mind to dismiss the feelings until I see the license plate of the car: JJ3.

Jaye Jamal.

He's stalking me. Pain and suffering are stalking me as sure as a cat stalks a mouse to his death.

Pressing the remote control, I open the door of my car and get in very quickly, making sure to keep the door locked should someone try to open it from outside.

I crank the key in the ignition, turn on my headlights, and notice a sticky note on my windshield.

I want to get out of the car and check it out, but something tells me not to. I know it's fear that's warning me, and I hate it. I don't want to be that girl anymore.

Screw what may happen!

Getting out of the car, I grab the note and rush back into the car. I put on the light and read.

Everything you love shall be taken away from you.

I don't wait to think about anything. My heart beats fast as though it will jump out of my chest, I pull onto the street and head home. My hand is shaking, making the wheel swerve left and right. I clench my hands in an effort to still the tremor.

He's playing ruthless.

Was he not the same man who, just a few hours ago, told me he's corrected? He never changed. There's no way Jaye can be corrected. He's damned.

And if I know him well, he means everything he wrote in that note.

Everything you love shall be taken away from you.

My heart clenches with the thought of it.

There are only three things that I love in this world: Daniels Group, Vince, and Tiwa.

Chapter Twenty-Six

Miki

Twenty minutes later, I pull up to Vince's house. Glancing around, I don't see Vince's Bentley anywhere. As fast as I can, I open the front door and walk inside. The house is silent and dark. Turning on the light by the wall, I run upstairs straight to the bedroom.

Grabbing my luggage bag, I begin to pack everything that belongs to me. My clothes, shoes, underpants. I'm zipping up the bag when I remember I left a towel in the bathroom. I want to go for it, but then decide against it.

Carrying my luggage, I reach the living room downstairs when the front door opens and Vince walks in, closing the door behind him, his eyes glued to me.

Oh, no!

"Where are you going?" he asks, surprise written all over his face.

I stand tongue-tied for a second. Playing with the length of my hair, I avoid looking at him. "Home."

"I thought this is home for you."

"It was home for me."

"Was? What changed?" He walks closer to me. "Babe, did I do something wrong? Did I hurt you somehow? I swear I'll make it up to you, but do not leave me. Please, Miki."

I look at him, and he's staring at me with that look, a worried look that says he's blaming himself already.

"You didn't do anything wrong. You... Vince..." Slowly I raise my hand up and touch his face, sharing in his gaze.

"You are perfect. You're the best anyone could ever ask for." And then ever so slowly, I avert my gaze again. "But, me, I am full of flaws. I'm so imperfect that I'm afraid one day you're going to wake up and realize you shouldn't be with someone like me."

"I wake up every day grateful to be with someone like you." He places his hand over mine and caresses it, never breaking his gaze for a second. "But you know that. There's something else you're not telling me."

"Nothing," I reply, dropping my hand from his face and heading to the door. "I have to go. I'm sorry."

Before I can get to the door, he grabs my shoulders and pulls me back to stand in front of him. "You do not get to leave me without telling me why."

He's getting angry now, and I'm growing impatient.

"Okay. I'm going to keep it short. With the help of his father, Jaye tried to sabotage my business today, so I went to his office to warn him. He responded by sending me a note that says everything I love will be taken from me."

He cuts me off. "So you're leaving me because of Jaye?"

I shake my head. "I'm leaving you because I'm going after Jaye, and I want to have nothing to lose when I do."

He's quiet for more than a second, his face expressionless. Throwing his suit jacket and tie on the couch, he begins to unbutton his shirt. "I'm going to pretend I didn't hear you say that. We both had a long day. So, let's get in the shower, make love…"

The calmness in his voice infuriates me. Can't this man see that I'm doing him a favor by leaving him? I'm trying to save him.

"Vince!" I yell, my voice hardened.

Scowling, he narrows his gaze. "I thought you were a smart woman, but I doubt that now."

"What?"

"If you were smart, you'd know I'm not something you get rid of when you're going into battle. I am the weapon you take to the battle. I am your champion and your weapon, and you shouldn't even consider going into battle without me." He stops yelling, takes off his shirt, and throws it on the couch. And then he unzips his trousers and removes his belt. "And if I have to tie you down and tell you that every day before you know it, I will."

He takes my luggage from me and tosses it across the room. Grabbing my wrist, he drags me along.

"What are you doing, Vince?"

"Oh! We're going to take a shower together," he says happily as we climb the stairs.

Pushing me into the bedroom, he locks the door and keeps the key. He removes his pants and boxers and throws them into the laundry basket. Standing very naked before me, he stares at me, waiting for me to do the same.

I fold my arms across my chest and glance away, letting him know I have an attitude.

He shrugs. "Fine."

Grabbing my wrist again, he drags me into to the bathroom, making sure to lock the door so I don't run.

Still with my clothes on, he drags me with him into the shower. As the water starts rushing out, he splashes it in my face, smiling happily as he washes himself.

I try not to look at him because I'm not naïve. If he merely looks at me I will melt from the inside like wax near fire.

"Do you even remember what my cock looks like?"

I know his evil ploy. He's trying to make me look at him, but it won't work. I'm determined to end this, for both our sakes. If something happens to either him or Tiwa because of me, I won't be able to live. If he dies, I die.

His voice breaks through my reverie. "C'mon, you can take a look. I shaved this morning. I bet you haven't seen it yet without the hair."

Yes, I have. Or maybe not. As I stare away, I can't help imagining it. Just scanty hair, I tell myself, trying to re- member every other time I have seen it. Okay, maybe it's more than scanty when I saw it. Imagining the looks with or without the hair wakes something up between my legs.

Before I know it, I catch myself trying to steal a peep at him. He splashes water in my face before I can see.

He laughs. "I caught you."

I shut my eyes and swallows hard. For the next few seconds, all I can hear is the splashing of the water. I begin to wonder if he's still standing there.

Slowly, I open my eyes and glance at his face. He's watching me with a smile on his face. I begin to wonder why looking at me is amusing him.

I take a look at me. My hard nipples are screaming to be noticed under my wet dress.

MY GOD!

I'm soooo angry at my body for betraying me.

I watch his face. He's enjoying the betrayal. He knows my body responds to him. What's bad about that? No use hiding it.

I unzip my dress and raise it over my head, throwing it out of the shower. I give the same fate to my panties, and just when I'm about to start washing myself, he pulls me in and kisses me.

It's surprising, but inviting and needy.

Even though my mind is screaming against it, I enjoy it. It soothes me, calms me like it's exactly what I need at the moment.

When he breaks the kiss, he holds me close, protectively against himself under the shower. "Miki, why would you want to run away from this?" The flowing water disrupts his speech. He pauses a moment to catch his breath. "I love you, Miki. I can't live without you, nor you without me. Why would you want to run away from this?"

'This' is no use if he dies because of me. And he should not think for a moment that trying to leave him is not hurting me. It's the hardest thing I've ever done, and it's hurting me deeply.

I try to hold back the tears, but finally I let them flow with the waters as I cry quietly.

****

Vince

Taking the towel, I wipe the water off my body and then off hers, leaving the towel for her to tie across her chest like she always does after a shower. She ties the towel as predicted, and then ties her wet hair up in ponytail. Opening the door, I lead her out of the bathroom.

I walk over to the wardrobe, trying to figure out what to wear. Miki just stands there, arms folded across her chest. She still has that attitude.

I put on a white, round-necked T-shirt and shorts and try to look for Miki's nightie. It's gone. She's packed all her clothes into her suitcase. I grab one of my T-shirts and throw it to her. She doesn't catch it. She doesn't even try. She just lets it fall to the floor.

I stare at her, my anger about to burst, but I keep a lid on it. Walking slowly to her side, I grab the T-shirt and then remove the towel around her in one swift motion. She fights me, but there's little she can do. I help her into the shirt, almost like I forced her into it. Not that I wouldn't love to have her sit naked around the house.

"Have you had dinner?" I ask.

"Yes," she replies gently.

Leading her to bed, I help her sit. "I'll get some fruit from the fridge."

I know she likes eating fruit before going to bed. Anything to please her. I'll do anything for her. I'll die for her, if necessary, and I think that's the part that scares her. That's the reason she wants to leave me.

Pulling the blanket up to her knees, I leave her side and head out. I make sure to keep the door locked and have the keys with me. I can't trust her anymore. She has reduced herself to a prisoner in our home and reduced me to an unwilling jailer. All she wants now is to leave me. She's drifting farther and farther from me. I know I'm losing her, but I don't have the slightest idea what to do to prove to her that she doesn't have to run away from me.

I open the fridge and grab two apples. Washing them off, I set them on a plate and hurry back to the room.

"You know what?" I say as I open the door, keeping my voice cheerful in the hopes of cheering her up. "Since you want to leave here, I'm thinking we can plan a getaway. Like a vacation to actually take a break from this mess."

She doesn't respond. Instead she just glances away.

I sit by her side, placing the plate on a stool. I hold one of the apples up to her mouth. "Eat."

"No, thank you."

Struggling to keep my voice from betraying my anger, I smile. "C'mon, for me. You know you like your fruit before bed."

"What are you going to do? Hold me down and force it

into my mouth, the same way you force me to take a shower with you."

Her words cut through me, but I try not to let myself get angry with her. I drop the apple back on the plate and stare back at her. "For the vacation, I thought of London. Maybe Paris. Or Capetown. If you want, we can take Tiwa along. I know you like spending time with her."

She glares at me with fire in her brown eyes. "Why don't you understand the only getaway I want is from you?"

Just be patient with her, I tell myself. She will come around. I leave the apples on the stool, turn off the lamp and crawl beside her on the bed, facing her.

She lays down, pulling the blanket over her shoulder and facing the other way. I'm tired of this already, and I don't know how long I can keep this up. She has this insane idea that leaving me means saving me from Jaye. She never bothered to think that maybe I don't want to be saved.

I tell myself to be patient with her.

A few minutes later, I'm falling asleep when I feel her soft lips on my forehead.

Slightly opening my eyes, I see her standing over me. She thinks I'm asleep, and she's trying to escape.

Before she can move, I sit up, grab her, and pull her onto the bed.

"Miki," I say her name gently, and then bury my face in my palm for a while. I try to turn on the bed lamp, but am forced to stare into her eyes in the near darkness. "I can't do this anymore," I say in a whisper. "You may think you're saving me from Jaye, but this attitude of yours is going to kill me before he makes good on his threat."

Her brown eyes come to mine. "Then let me go. Please. If you love me at all, like you always say, let me go. They say if you love something, you let it go, and if it's truly yours, it will come back to you."

With trembling hands, I push the blankets away and walk to the door. Kicking it open, I glance back at her. "You win. Get out of my house."

"Vince..."

"I said get out of here!" I point out through the door. "Go and confront Jaye on your own. Go ahead, leave me. Jaye doesn't have to take what you love away from you— you've already thrown it away. Just get out of here and don't let me see your face ever again."

I walk back to the bed and pull the blankets over me. She stands watching me in silence, then take a few steps back.

"Vince... after everything we've been through together, I don't want us to end like this."

"I don't care what you want! You lost that right already." I struggle to get the words out. "Get out of my sight!"

She nods and looks at the floor. Laying on the bed, I face the other side and try not to look at her.

"Vince," she calls in a soft voice, "when your anger dies down, I hope you can remember the good times we had and remember me for that."

Without turning to look at her, I reply, "I'll remember you for the coward you are."

"I'm doing this so that you can stay alive and look after Tiwa. I'll be damned if I let anything happen to both of you because of me. Despite what you think, I'm doing this for you."

That's it. I jump out of bed and in a blink I'm standing in front of her, glaring down at her.

"Don't you dare say that!" I yell. "You're doing this for

you. You're a coward who doesn't have the courage to lose, who doesn't have the liver for what fighting a monster entails. Don't you ever say that you're leaving me for me!"

"You're right," she says, tears in her voice. I see tears running down her cheeks, and in the next few seconds, I can hear her sobs. Every sound pulls at my heart, urging me to hold her and tell her everything is going to be okay.

"You're right. I'm a coward," she says in between sobs as she sinks slowly to the floor. "I can't stand losing you or Tiwa. I'm just tired of everything. I'm scared. I'm exhausted."

I crouch and touch her forehead with mine, sharing in her tears and her pain.

"Miki, don't leave me, please. I'm strong enough to lift both of us." Holding her hands, I look into her beautiful eyes filled with tears. "I'll fight your battles, and if it will make you feel better, I want you to know that if I die, it's not your fault. It's not because of you." I give her hand a reassuring squeeze. "I die because it is my time to die. So, Miki, stay with me. Please, for me. You leaving me will kill me before Jaye actually does."

I keep watching her eyes, waiting for a response.

She manages a nod.

Letting out a breath of relief, I pull her in and hold her in my arms.

Chapter Twenty-Seven

Miki

I'm in the middle of a meeting with the board of directors when my cellphone rings.

"Excuse me, please," I say and quickly step aside to take the call.

"Hey, Vince," I say immediately after I press the green button.

"Got a call from Tiwa's school," his voice is so tense I can notice it through the phone. "She is missing."

My heart jumps out of my chest. "MY GOD."

"I'm heading to her school right now."

"I'm on my way."

I end the call and stare back at the others. "Emergency. I have to go."

I can't bring myself to say more as I run out of the room.

Feeling tightness in my chest, my throat, I stand frozen for a while, resting my back on the door for support. I'm not aware of how long I remain immobile until I begin to walk down the hallway in a daze. Making a stop at my office, I grab my car keys and head out.

By the time I reach my car, my hands are shaking so badly it takes more than a few tries to get the key into the ignition. When I finally start the engine, I pull onto the street, tires squealing loudly.

A few minutes later, I'm at the school. Running on my five-inch heels, I'm heading toward the head teacher's office. Seeing Vince standing in the hallway and pacing back and forth, I race up to him and into his arms, holding him for comfort.

"What did they say?"

"Nothing yet. I'm waiting for the head teacher."

Running my fingers through my hair, I rest the back of my head on the wall. I'm trying hard to fight back the tears.

God, please, let her be alright.

That's all that keeps repeating itself in my head. That's all I can think of. Nothing bad can happen to my little girl. Nothing.

Glancing down the hallway, I see two women walking toward us. One I identify as Miss Bello, Tiwa's teacher and the other, older woman, I assume to be the head teacher.

"Did you find her?"

"Is she alright?"

Vince and I ask almost at the same time.

The head teacher shakes his head slowly. "I'm afraid no. We've searched everywhere in the school. We can't find her."

Hands on my forehead, I shut my eyes and grimace, tears flowing down my cheeks.

"How did it happen? When was the last time anyone saw her?"

Vince is asking the questions, now. I'm too broken to speak further.

"I took the class to the Signature Art Gallery," Miss Bello says. "I wanted the class to take a look at some paintings, but Tiwa said she's not interested. She stays behind, and when we got back from the art gallery, she was gone."

Something is not right.

I stare suspiciously at Miss Bello and the head teacher. "Tiwa loves art. She would never say no to a chance like that."

Miss Bello averts her gaze and shrugs. "Well, she said she wasn't interested in going..."

I cut her off. "Is there something you're not telling us?"

The head teacher stands between Miss Bello and I. "Are you accusing us of lying, Mrs. Ali?"

Vince holds my waist to calm me down, but I glance at him, scowling. "I know what I'm saying. Tiwa loves art. She wants to be an artist. There's no way she would miss out on a trip to the Signature Art Gallery."

Vince tightens his hold on my waist to calm me down. He is a patient man who doesn't jump to assumptions like me. Instead, he glances at the head teacher. "You and Miki should sweep the school surroundings again and see if you can find her. Miss Bello and I will speak to some of Tiwa's classmates just to know if she told anyone anything that might help us find her."

That said, we separate and begin to look for my little girl.

We go from the classrooms to the hostels, to the dining area, the bookstore, the library, everywhere I can think of. I keep calling her name, wishing desperately for her to hear me and come out of wherever she's hiding.

I just want to believe she's here somewhere. I can't let myself believe the worst because the worst would confirm my fears.

I just have to keep hoping for the best.

After searching everywhere and still finding no trace of Tiwa, the head teacher and I head back out to meet with

Vince and Miss Bello.

Outside the building, my eyes catch a man I guess is the driver cleaning out the school bus. I'm not exactly paying attention to him or the school bus. I'm just glancing around, looking for Tiwa, though my sub-conscious takes everything in. When the driver picks a piece of paper off the ground, he finally has my full attention.

I can only hope that this is not what I think.

Walking over to where the school bus is parked, I ask the driver. "Can I see that paper, please?"

Vince and Miss Bello have joined us by now.

The driver looks at me strangely. "It's just a paper. The students littered everywhere when I drove them to the art gallery."

My anxious face quickly becomes a frown. "I just want to see that paper, please."

Lifting a shoulder in a shrug, he hands it to me.

Hands shaking and desperately hoping I'm wrong, I open the paper. A dark cloud painted on a clear, blue sky with the words 'after d dark, there's light' written below it.

Anger takes over my sense of self. I feel myself lose it as the protective mother traits in me threatens to expose themselves.

Grabbing Miss Bello, I push her against the doors of the school bus. "You lied to me. You lost my daughter at the art gallery! You were trying to cover your own ass..."

"Miki, what's going on here?" Vince asks.

Not taking my hands off her, I glance at Vince. "That painting belongs to Tiwa. It was her mid-term assignment. I helped her with it. She was on that bus, Vince."

Vince's clenched fists shake. I can see by the look on his face that he's lost all patience. He fumes, his chest rising and falling with labored breaths as he glances at the head teacher. He says nothing, but his eyes reveal more than words can say.

"I'm sorry," the head teacher pleads. "It's easier to let everyone think she ran off. It will destroy the school's reputation if we lose her on a field trip."

In a split second, I let go of Miss Bello and slap the head teacher across her face, leaving the mark of my five fingers on her cheeks.

"My daughter is missing and the first thing you worry about is the school's reputation!" I yell, my voice trembling with rage and pain.

There are so many hot emotions running through me that I raise my hand to slap her again, but Vince catches my hand before I can.

Shaking with impotent rage, I struggle to get to her as Vince tries to hold me still. "I swear to God if anything happens to my girl, I will destroy you. By the time I finish with you, this school will be burned to the ground. It will be nothing!" I promise.

"It's not time for this. Right now we need to find our daughter," he says, looking into my eyes to make sure I understand him.

I can only manage a nod.

She's probably somewhere right now, afraid, waiting for her badass mom to come save her. And here I am, I don't even know what to do. I don't know how to find her.

Tears rush down my face.

"Go to the nearest police station and file a missing persons report," Vince says. "I will go to the art gallery. Maybe I can find something that will lead me to her."

I walk into his open arms and let him hold me for a second. "Call me as soon as you find something," I say.

He nods. "We'll find her, Miki. We will find her."

I manage a nod. He seems to be handling the situation better than me.

****

Miki

I pull in front of the police station and hurry inside. There's a police officer in uniform sitting at the desk.

"I want to file a missing persons report," I announce immediately upon walking in.

The officer gives me a sarcastic look. "Good afternoon to you, too."

"I'm sorry," I try to apologize. "But my little girl is missing, and I can't think of anything else."

"You're at the right place, ma'am. We will help you find your girl," he says, making his voice sound reassuring. "But please calm down and give us all the information we need."

I nod.

"Her full name, please."

"Tiwatope Ali."

"Can you give a detailed description? A picture will be helpful."

I search through my phone very quickly until I see a picture of her and hand it to the officer.

He looks at it for a while. "This is very helpful. Do you know when and where anyone last saw her?"

"She was last seen about two hours ago at..."

He cut me off. "She's only been missing for two hours?"

"Two hours is a long time, officer."

"I know. But you can't file a missing persons report until after twenty-four hours."

I frown, losing the grip on my anger again. "What do you mean I can't file a missing persons report?"

"I'm sorry, ma'am. You can try and look for her some more on your own. If you can't find her after twenty-four hours, come back here and we will help you. But calm down. I'm sure your daughter is fine. She probably just ran off with a boy."

"She's only seven!"

He shrugs. "You'd be surprised what girls nowadays are capable of."

I stand still for a while, glaring at him. Tears begin to gather at the corners of my eyes, but I tell myself to be strong. For Tiwa.

Hands on the desk, I lean in and take a good look at his chest.

He gives me a look of disgust. "What are you trying to do?"

"Oh! I'm checking your name."

"What?"

My face close to his, I give him a bold stare. "In case you don't know, I am Miki Daniels." I can see the shocked look on his face, but that's not what I'm after, so I continue, "I have the office of the minister of police affairs on speed dial. My advice for you, start writing a resume for another job right now because you're about to lose this one."

I begin to dial a number on my phone. Before anyone can pick it up, he reaches out across the desk trying to stop me.

"Ma'am, you didn't hear me very well. I said we're going to look for your daughter. Forget about the twenty-four hour waiting period."

I look at his face to make sure he means it.

His fear-filled eyes plead with me.

And then I hang up.

"Who was she with before she went missing?"

"Her class teacher, Miss Bello. They went on a field trip to the Signature Art Gallery."

"So the Signature Art Gallery is where she was last seen. Correct?"

I nod.

"Do you know what she was wearing?"

I shake my head no. "I'm not sure. I'm guessing the school uniform."

"And what's the color of the school uniform?"

"White, short-sleeve shirt over a red, black-striped skirt."

He finishes typing and then looks at me. "Finally, ma'am, I'm going to need you to think deeply. Is there anyone you had a quarrel with, anyone at all who may want to get back at you by harming your daughter?"

Flipping through my mental file, I didn't have to think too much. The memory returns to me very rapidly in a frightening rush.

Jaye Jamal.

Everything I love shall be taken away from me.

A glancing wave of shock makes me falter. My head begin to pound heavily, my whole body shaking at the mere thought that Tiwa is missing because of me. My temperature is rising; my heart breaking into a million pieces. The thought of what Jaye might be doing to her sickens me.

"Ma'am?"

I'm hearing the voice of the police officer from afar. Taking a few steps away in a daze, I place a call to Sade and tell her to get Jamal's phone number and text it to me.

Seconds later, Sade texts me his phone number. I dial the number and wait impatiently for him to pick up.

"I was beginning to doubt that you would call."

The crisp voice crawls like ice down my spine, fanning

the flames of fire in me.

"You have something that belongs to me," I say, cutting to the chase.

"Yes, ma'am. And you can have it back when…"

I cut him off, yelling. "She's not an it. She's a child!"

"Okay. You can have *her* back when…"

"Let's end this once and for all," I interrupt him again.

"I agree. Your place. In thirty minutes."

"Good," I reply and hang up.

Very quickly, I place another call to Vincent.

"Anything?" Vince asks.

"I'm sorry, Vince. It's all my fault. Jaye has Tiwa. And I'm going to get her back."

Vince shouts into the phone. "This is not your fault, Miki. Do not take him on alone!"

"He's given me no choice!"

"No, no, please, Miki," he pleads. "We always have a choice. Wait for me."

"This is my fight, Vince. Not yours. For years, I've been waiting for someone to come and save me from my monster. I've been waiting and waiting while he gets stronger and continues to ruin my happiness. I'm not waiting anymore!"

With those words, I hang up and head to my car.

Pulling onto the street, my hands flex on the steering wheel as I fight to keep hot tears from falling. My mind tries not to think the worst. I know what Jaye is capable of. I can't let myself think about it. My eyes shut tightly in an attempt to keep the sickening memory of it all at bay. It's useless. I can hear my every cry. I can feel every pain again as if it were recent.

I can only pray that Tiwa doesn't share in my fate.

No one should have to go through what I went through.

It's too much for anyone to bear.

The blast of a car horn jerks my eyes open in time to see an oncoming truck bearing down on me. I yank my car back to my own lane and out of the truck's path with seconds to spare. My heart pumping with fear, I grip the steering wheel tightly and step on the gas pedal.

•

Chapter Twenty-Eight

Miki

Entering the passcode to my apartment, I push the door open and walk in.

I haven't been here in weeks. Vince's house has been home for me for the past month now.

My living room seems stuffy and dusty, but that's not the issue.

Jaye isn't here yet.

I need to take advantage of the situation.

Pacing back and forth, I begin to think about anything that can help me fight him, anything to protect myself with if it comes down to it.

I'm not a gun owner. I don't even know how to use one. So a gun is definitely out.

My mind goes to the knives in the kitchen, and very quickly I run to get one. It looks sharp enough to cut through his flesh if he tries to force himself on me.

But I need a place to hide it. A place where he won't see it, but near enough for me to grab it if I need to.

An idea strikes my mind and without giving it a second thought, I rush to my fridge and fling it open. Fortunately for me, I find about three oranges in there. They've been sitting in there for weeks and are soft now, no longer good for consumption. They will serve my purpose well.

Setting the oranges on a plate, I place them on my table in the living room with the knife carefully placed nearby. There's no better place to hide a weapon than in plain sight. As far as Jaye is concerned, the knife is for the oranges, while in truth, it is for him.

Arms folded across my chest, I begin to pace back and forth, waiting impatiently for him to get here.

A few seconds later, a small knock on my door almost makes my heart jump out of my chest.

He's here.

I hurry to get the door, but then I hesitate a second.

If I let him in, it means I'm ready to endure whatever it is he's going to do to me. The fear of it cripples me for a while. I stand there, contemplating whether I should change my mind. But every second I waste thinking about that is another second I could have spent saving my little girl.

Summoning a little bit of courage, I open the door. And there he is.

I stand frozen for a moment, looking at him. He's wearing a white shirt over black pants. He probably left his suit jacket in the car.

Just looking at him, he looks like a gentleman. Who would ever think he could be a monster? Who would believe that this handsome, good-looking young man is a psycho?

"May I?" he asks.

"Of course." Stepping out of his way, I hold the door open, closing it after him. He walks into my living room, taking every step gently, one at a time as his eyes dart around and giving a gentle nod of approval. And then his face turns slowly to mine.

I rest my back on the door, arms folded. I glance back

at him with fierce resentment. "Where is she?"

Hands in the pockets of his trousers, he shakes his head slowly and sighs. "You still look at me like that. Like I'm a monster."

"Where is she?" I ask again through gritted teeth, my voice louder and harsher than I had intended. Not that it matters.

"She is safe. I have my guys watching her until you and I can come to a reasonable agreement."

My brow wrinkles. "And what kind of agreement is that?"

Removing his hands from his pockets, he takes a step toward me. "First, you have to know that I'm not a monster. I took your girl just so I can have your attention. I want you to hear me out. I know I've done terrible things to you in the past, and I'm so so so very sorry."

Releasing my folded arms, I hold his gaze. Not a trace of remorse lay in his eyes. I'll be damned if I fall for his petty, gentlemanly trick.

I cover up the distance between us and stand closely opposite him. Without betraying a thread of my fear, I glare at him. "What do you want?"

"You," he replies.

"You're joking."

"No. I want you, Miki. I want to make things right with you. I want to stand by you."

"No," I reply.

"No, what?"

"No, you can't have me. Over my dead body!"

He smiles as he breaks our gaze with a glance to the floor. I know his smile has nothing to do with my marbled floor. Something is going on in his head, but I don't know what.

When he finally looks back at me, the smile is gone. He puts a hand forward, pushing away the strands of hair covering my face. I knock his hand away without hesitation.

"Miki, my father wants your company. He wants Daniels Group, and he will get it at all cost, no matter what."

"And you? You don't want the same thing?"

"I told you I want you."

I force a smile. Eyes filled with confusion, he stares back at me.

"What's so funny?"

"Oh! I must give it to you. You're smarter than your father. Your father wants Daniels Group, but you want me. And I own Daniels Group. What better way to lay claim to Daniels Group than laying claim to the one who owns Daniels Group."

He's quiet, so I continue;

"But, of course, you want more than just Daniels Group. You want to relive your fantasy because you're obsessed with me."

"Miki..."

"You want to pleasure yourself as you watch your guys tear me apart. You..."

"Miki... stop."

"...want to hear men moan as they cum on my face. It excites you. It excites the animal in you."

Palms clenched into a fist, he's shaking. Hot sweat covers him up in seconds as the gentle mask he daily wears over his steely, sadistic self begins to fall off.

"You want to enjoy the sight of it as your guys shove their dicks in my ass, another in my throat, so deep I can't breathe. You want..."

Before I know it, strong hands grip my neck, choking

me for several seconds before shoving me away. I land painfully on my butt, coughing as I try to catch my breath.

Towering over me, he begins to remove his belt. "I'm going to enjoy this."

The corners of his mouth twist into a cruel imitation of a smile. "You're still as stupid and dumb as I remember." By now he's removed his trousers and flung them several strides away. "Look how easy it is to get you alone with me."

Fuming with rage, I spit at him. He ducks before it hits him.

He smiles. He's enjoying this.

"I bet we could be here for days and no one will show up to look for you."

"You're wrong. Vince will look for me."

"Your boyfriend? I'm sure he's busy looking for his daughter."

He gives a laugh devoid of joy. It only aggravates the hatred and anger building up inside of me.

Still sitting on the floor, I shuffle back on my butt.

He closes the gap in one step and stands over me again.

"And your boyfriend's daughter." He reaches for his Smartphone in the pocket of his shirt and begins to dial.

In a split second, he's flashing me his phone and the image of my little girl stares back at me. I go on my knee, reaching up to have a closer look.

"Tiwa!"

"Mommy?"

I hear her voice.

I had thought it was a picture, but apparently it's a video call.

"Tiwa, are you alright?"

She's far from alright. I can see bruises and remnants

of blood on her face. Tears gather in my eyes.

"Mommy, I'm scared…"

I cut her off. "You're going to be okay, princess," I say, modulating my voice to sound reassuring. "Mom is going to come get you." My voice breaks off as lumps build up in my throat. I manage to speak through it. "Princess, everything is going to be fine. Nothing is going to happen to you."

"You can't be sure of that," he interrupts.

A knowing smile spreads across his face. He takes the phone away from my face and says something I don't quite understand.

In a split second, the screen of his Smartphone is back in my face.

Only now, I can't see Tiwa.

I see a man from the waist down, and he's naked. Stroking his penis, I hear his moan as he moves, the camera moving with him.

And then the camera lands on Tiwa's face, a naked man standing before her, about to shove his penis into her mouth.

Hot rage explodes through my mind, and I scream "No!" in a murderous rage

My heart clenches and my breath snags.

This can't be happening. Not again. It can't be happening again.

I can't let this happen again.

"No, no, tell him to stop," I cry, talking like a mad woman.

Hot tears run down my cheeks. This is destiny repeating itself. It has to stop. All the pain of that time returns to me, and I scream. There's no way I'm letting my daughter experience that kind of pain.

The vivid memories cloud my mind, showing me all the

painful phases of my life, letting me know this is what will become of my daughter. This is what her life will look like if I don't stop it.

I feel myself lose it as I become wild, driven by the protective, all-consuming motherly instincts in me.

"You can have me," I plead to his face. "You want me, you can have me. You can have Daniels Group. You can do anything you want with me. Me and you together in here for eternity. You can have your guys do anything to me for your pleasure. You can have all of me, but please spare her."

I realize that it may seem like I'm insane, like I'm totally out of my mind. Playing with the teeth of the lion, asking to be torn apart. I don't care, though. At this moment, I feel all my buried compassion comes back to life, and I'll do anything to protect the ones I love, even if it means I have to relive my worst nightmare.

Smiling with satisfaction, he commands the man to stop, which he does. And then Jaye ends the call and throws his phone on the couch.

I've manage to buy a little more time.

I just have to look for a way to save us all.

Standing on my feet, I lean closer to him, watching his icy brown eyes and letting him know I surrender myself to him. I'm all his.

Gently, he removes his boxers and stands naked from his waist down, his penis dangling in front of me.

Bold eyes sweep over my body hungrily as he holds me by the neck and pushes me backward until I hit the door.

Leaning closer, he watches my face with a savage hunger in his eyes. His hand moves from my neck to grab a fistful of my hair. Sticking out his tongue, he begins to lick my face like a dog.

I whimper in pain and disgust.

His eyes flicker in excitement. He's enjoying my pain.

His penis is expanding and growing bigger and harder as he watches me wince. This is his foreplay.

Still holding on to my hair, he pulls on it and begins to bang my head against the door, non-stop.

A sharp pain threatens to split my head in two, and I scream. Hot tears flow down my cheek. I didn't think I had any tears left in my eyes after all the tears I shed today. As I fight to remain conscious, my only thought is to stop this man from ruining my daughter. I might not have given birth to her, but she calls me mommy. She looks up to me, and I'm not about to let her down.

Summoning strength I didn't know I had, I raise my leg and kick his balls.

He lets out a loud cry, his hands letting go of me for a second, I try to make a run for it. Before I can, his hands reclaim me again, this time flinging me away violently, my back hitting the table before I crash down, the oranges and the knife crashing down alongside me.

I cry out loudly, and for a second my body goes numb with pain.

He stares down at me. "Oh! I'm going to enjoy this."

The knife.

My hand searches out blindly, tapping the floor, trying to find it.

Crouching over me and straddling me, he holds my neck and chokes me. I struggle, my hands flapping like a drowning bird, I try to beat him.

He's unstoppable.

My eyes wide open, uncontrollable tears crawl out and flow through both sides as I feel air crawling out of me, my whole body going numb.

As he chokes me, he's moaning, his face contorted in pain and pleasure. His whole body vibrating as he nears his orgasm, he lets go of me. I'm coughing to catch my breath when he shoves his penis into my mouth, pushing it deep down my throat, so deep I can't breathe, choking me.

I feel him spasm deep inside me as he half groans and half shouts, his hot wetness spurting inside my mouth.

There can't be a better time.

Putting all my strength into it, I bite down on his penis.

His groan of pleasure becomes a scream of pain.

He lets out a loud cry, slapping me hard across my face to get me to release him.

Despite the pain, I don't stop. I keep biting on it until I feel the metallic taste of his blood in my mouth.

Finally, letting go of him, he staggers back, landing on his butt. Blood rushes out of his penis as he lays on the floor, screaming. Sweat covers his body and uncontrollable tears flow down his face.

Spitting out the taste of his blood in my mouth, I grab the knife. The need to end him overcomes me. Every ounce of my strength goes into making the knife more deadly. Standing over him, I look into his icy brown eyes.

His eyes remind me of the deathly stare of the man who gave his life for me. For days, I lived with his corpse in the basement of Jaye's house.

Everything else dissolves in my vision. My rage is unleashed like never before by the need to make him pay for everything he's ever taken from me.

Kneeling beside him and putting all my strength into it, I let out a loud cry as I dig the knife into his stomach. His cries fill my ears, but don't make me stop. They only remind me of every time I cried like this. The time that he tore me apart when I was only eight.

The time he watched a friend take me when I was sixteen.

The times he raped me repeatedly in his basement.

I remove the knife and stab him again. And then again and again, one for every time one of his guys who pushed their penis into me while he watched, enjoying it.

He's quiet now, laying lifelessly on the ground.

But I'm beyond reason. No power on earth can stop me.

His silence only reminds me of all the loneliness and pain I had to bear, and I stab him again for it.

He lays down there, quiet. His silence becomes suffocating and I look at him. I take a good look at him, reason rushing back into my mind. He's lying in a pool of blood at my knee.

I can't seem to take my eyes off of his frozen, damaged body. The sight of him makes my stomach roll and something come spewing out of mouth and I throw up on his body.

What did I just do? Did I really just take his life? Did I just kill a man?

Oh, my God!

I drop the knife and sink to the floor.

I killed someone. I took someone's life. Nothing is ever going to be the same again. Shaking uncontrollably, I feel tears running down my face. I try to wipe them away before pulling my shaking hands back and looking at them. They're covered in his dark red blood. I have killed a man. A sick feeling crawls from the pit of my stomach. I can't believe I just took a life.

I look for my phone. Finding it near the table, I place a call to the police.

"My name is Miki Daniels. I killed someone," I continue

to speak like someone hypnotized. "I killed someone. I killed someone."

Chapter Twenty-Nine

Vince

Miki is sitting across the desk from me with her hands in cuffs. She's only been held in here for few hours, but it seems like days already. Her eyes are red and puffy, her lips dry, her face swollen. She's probably been beaten by her mate in the holding cell, but more than that, she's beating herself up for what she did.

"Miki..." I say her name gently.

She looks at me. Her eyes are weak; the spark in them gone.

"Vince, I didn't mean to kill him," she says, tears running down her face and her voice shaky. She seems so far away, beating herself up on the inside, and I just can't stop myself from putting my hands on hers to comfort her.

"It's okay."

"No, no, it's not okay. I took a man's life. How can you say it's okay? I handled everything wrong..."

Looking intently into her eyes, I give her hand a little squeeze. "This is not a question of whether you did the right thing. You did what had to be done under a dangerous circumstance. You defended yourself, and you fought for Tiwa. As far as I'm concerned, that was what happened. Now let me make this right for you. Let me get you out of here."

Breaking my hold on her hand, she averts her gaze. "No."

My brow wrinkles. "What do you mean 'no'?"

"You can't get me out of here. Have you heard the word on the streets? Everybody is saying I'm a monster. I chewed on his penis. I stabbed him twenty-six times. They say I deserve to be punished. They hate me."

"That's because they haven't heard your side of the story." I touch her hand again, trying desperately to let her see things through my eyes. "We can win this. We can fight this."

"I'm tired of fighting," she says. I can hear the strain in her voice, and it pulls at the strings of my heart to feel her suffer this much. "Maybe this is my destiny. Maybe this is the way it has to end. I don't know. All that I know is that I'm exhausted. I don't want to fight anymore."

"And you don't have to. I'm strong enough to fight for the both of us. All you have to do is do nothing and let me do everything."

"No!" she replies firmly.

Her resolution infuriates me, but I try to be calm. "I can't let you do this."

"Vincent..."

That's the very first time she's said my full name. And she's looking softly into my eyes with a sadness that hurts.

"I've had it hard," she continues. "Life has been really tough for me, but it has been good to me, too. I had everything most people could only dream of. I was loved with a special kind of love that withstood every storm. I had someone to help me and hold me through my darkest time. And no matter how cruel I became, I was able to feel loved. I love you, Vince, with all my soul. Looking back at my life,

I'm satisfied. I did okay. I was loved. So let things be, and let the law take its course."

"No!" I say, my voice harder than I had intended. "You don't get to die the very first time you tell me you love me. You don't get to die from something I can save you from."

"Vince, you have to respect my wish."

"You have a death wish, and you're asking me to respect that? I can't. Because if you don't know, they are willing to prosecute you to the fullest extent of the law. They're going for the death sentence. I'm your lawyer, and I'm telling you we can win this."

"You were first and foremost my man before anything else. As my man, you have to respect my wish."

Standing up from the chair, I button my suit jacket and glare at her. "Yes, I'm your man. If I were a good man, I would respect your wish. But I never told you I was one."

Picking up my briefcase, I walk out of the room. She continues to yell my name, but I don't look back. I hear the officers violently take her away. I only wish I were alone so I could cry.

****

Vince

I knock on the door gently and wait.

It's the door to the one-bedroom apartment that now belongs to Mr. & Mrs. Daniels after Miki chased them out of their mansion. I don't know what I'm doing here right now. I guess I'm hoping they can give Miki a reason to live.

I knock on the door again.

Seconds later, the door opened.

"You!" she shouts, almost slamming the door in my face.

I hold the door, putting all my strength into it and trying to stop her from closing it.

"Hear me out."

"How dare you show your face on my doorstep?"

"I'm not here for myself. I'm here for your daughter."

Her grip on the door loosens a bit. She goes soft, and I take the time to really look at her. Her eyes are red.

She knows. It's been all over the news.

And she's been crying. I'm right. A mother's heart is never fully closed against her child.

This is my shot at getting to her and I intend to use it. I lean closer and let her see the desperation in my face.

"The Jamals are rich and powerful. They are going to do anything to make sure Miki pays for killing their son. They will force the hand of the justice system, the prosecution will go for the death penalty, and they are going to win. Miki is going to get a death sentence if she doesn't let me help her. But my powers are limited. If she requests a change in attorney, there will be nothing I can do. That's why I need you to help me convince her that all hope is not lost. Help me give her a reason to fight, to live."

Tears fill her eyes in an instant, and she wipes them very quickly. "What do I have to do?"

"I need you to come with me to..."

"Kiki!" The voice roars way from the living room.

Miki's father.

I try to continue before he gets here. "Come with me to..."

"Kiki!" he calls his wife again.

Before I can continue, he's right at the doorway, standing behind his wife and glaring at me. "Young man, what are you doing here?"

"He's here for our daughter," she replies.

His glare deepens. "I don't have a murderer as a daughter!"

He then pulls her away and slams the door in my face.

I hit my palm on my forehead and grimace.

When I open my eyes, I know I have one more trick up my sleeve, and Miki isn't going to like it.

****

Miki

For the second time today, I'm sitting at the desk waiting for my attorney. Vince just won't give up.

I've accepted things; now, he needs to accept it too. I have to be punished for what I did. No matter what, I shouldn't have taken the law into my hands. If I can turn back the hands of time, I'd do it differently.

But it's over now. The cruelty of the officers and my cellmates are going to kill me even before I get my sentence.

I never really knew how much people despised me until I sat with them in that holding cell. One of them said she met me at a gathering, tried to say hi, but I ignored her and looked down on her. Another said she lost her job because I fired her. The sight of me disgusts them.

The door opens and Vince walks in. But he's not alone.

I'm surprise at who he brought in to see me.

"Mommy," she calls gently.

My eyes open wide, looking at Tiwa and then back at Vince.

Taking a seat opposite me, he tries to explain. "After Jaye's death, the kidnappers returned her to school. We found her."

Nodding gently, I look back at Tiwa. She's sitting next to her father.

"Hey, princess." I manage a smile.

She smiles back. "Hey, Mommy."

"Are you alright?" I ask.

She nods gently. "You saved me."

I study her face intently and notice several scars on her face. They're cleaned up, and she looks strong and healthy, but I know there's another scar deep inside her. She saw something she shouldn't have seen at her age. The memory is going to taunt her for a long time. She's going to need someone to explain things to her. And there's nobody better for that than me. I've been there. I understand what she might be feeling. She needs me.

My eyes move slowly to Vince. I understand his trick. He brought Tiwa to remind me that I'm not done yet. I still have responsibilities to take care of. He brought her to remind me that I have a reason to live.

"Vince, I know what you're trying to do, but it won't work. You've only succeeded in letting me know that my death won't be for nothing and..."

Tiwa interrupts. "You promised me."

Confused, I study her eyes, waiting for her to explain.

"You said you are going to be here forever. You promised me."

I let out a deep breath and shake my head slowly. "I'm sorry, princess. That's a promise I can no longer keep."

I can feel that she's trying hard not to shed any tears, but a tear betray her and flows down her face.

If my hands were not cuffed, I could hold her in my arms and tell her she's going to be fine. She's going to be okay. Without me.

Left to her own, though, she wipes her tears with the

back of her palm. It hurts me to see her devastated like this. And to think that I'm the reason behind those tears makes it hurt even more.

"I brought something for you," she says. Putting her hands in the pockets of her jean, she brings out a folded piece of paper and gives it to me.

Slowly, I carefully unfold it and what I see almost take my breath away.

It's a priceless gift.

She drew a picture of me.

I keep staring beautifully at it, and then I notice the quote written below.

After d dark, you are my light.

I close my eyes tight. My chest rises and falls amidst choking sobs I can't suppress.

"How many times have I told you to stop writing 'the' as just 'd'?" I ask, my lips quivering.

I'm not expecting a response, but she answers anyway.

"Several."

She reaches over and holds my hand in hers. "Is that a yes, Mommy?"

A painful smile spreads across my face and I nod. "But don't get your hopes up. I will try, but I'm not certain I'm going to win."

"You always win."

I nod and smile at her again.

And then I slowly glance over at Vince, letting him know that his little trick worked.

"First thing tomorrow morning," he begins, "I'm going to request your bail and get you out of here. And then we have four days to prepare for your trial. Every media outlet is reporting that you killed Jaye because he wanted your company. We have to put out your side of the story. We are going to have to let the people know the truth about everything. How it all started. We need the people to believe you, identify with you, and connect with you. The Jamals have the power of the government behind them. You need the power of the people behind you. When the people make a demand, even the government has no choice but to obey."

He stops and looks into my eyes to check if I follow him.

I simply nod in understanding. I don't have his optimism in the system, but I know I have no other choice.

Chapter Thirty

Vince

As soon as I finish with Miki, I drive down to the slums where Lola lives. I need all the help I can get. Knocking on the wooden door gently, I wait.

The environment is dirty and smelly, but it doesn't matter to me. I grew up in a place far worse than this.

When the door finally opens, Lola is so surprise to see me.

"Vincent?"

"Hi, Lola," I say in greeting.

"How did you know where I live?"

"Miki told me. May I come in?"

She hesitates a while, and then lifts a shoulder in a shrug. "Sure," she replies, stepping out of the way and inviting me in. I glance around and she has all her stuff neatly packed. She's moving out of the slums, I guess. If that's the case, I'm happy for her.

She cleans up the chair for me to sit. "How may I help you?"

"Miki needs your help."

Lola gives a small, sly smile as she takes a seat next to mine. "And what can the lowlife me do for the high and mighty one?"

"Don't say that." I give her a chiding expression. "She's

your friend. She might talk tough, but you know there's a gentle heart underneath that toughness."

She seems uncomfortable with my last statement.

"I don't think so," she says. "I mean, what kind of gentle heart kills someone just because he tries to take over her business?"

"Miki killed Jaye for so many reasons, but Daniels Group isn't one of them."

She looks at me in surprise. "Then why did she kill him?"

"First, because Jaye had my daughter kidnapped." I pause and sigh. "And then because he assaulted her sexually. He's been doing it to her since she was eight. When she was twenty-two, he kidnapped her and condemned her to sexual slavery for several months. She got pregnant and while Jaye was trying to abort the baby, it got complicated so much that Miki can never have a baby."

"No, no, that can't be. Miki and Jaye were lovers."

I shake my head. "They were never lovers."

Lola sits there, frozen. She can't move; can't say a word. She shakes as her wide eyes look into mine. She forgets to close her mouth.

"Lola, you okay?"

"No," she says in a broken voice, her eyes wet. "It's my fault. I was consumed by jealousy. I thought Miki had it too easy. And I hate the way she walks all over me, crippling my self-esteem."

"Lola, what did you do?"

"It's my fault. I'm the reason Jaye came back. I told Jessie that Miki and Jaye were lovers, and if Jaye were to return, it might start up old flames between them. Then Jessie would have a shot at being with you."

Lola takes on an expression of pain that makes me feel

sorry for her. Leaning closer, I look intensely into her eyes. "You have a chance to make things right."

"How?" she asks with a whining cry.

"I'm aware you have a job at ABJ TV station. I want you to tell the story I just told you to the people. I tried approaching all the other media houses, but it looks like Jamal bought them over."

"I'm sorry, Vincent. I no longer have my job at the TV station. When Miki wouldn't advertise with them, they fired me."

I sink into myself and sigh.

"But I can take it up with my boss. I no longer work for him, but I know he'll never turn his back on a good story."

I let out a breath of relief. "Thanks."

****

Miki

The next morning, I'm released on bail, four days before my trial begins. I step out with Vince by my side, and I'm surprised by the crowd standing in the sun outside the jail, demonstrating for my release.

Hundreds of people. Maybe thousands.

I can't count. And I can't look into all their faces. But I can see their struggles for me, I can read their placards.

Justice For Miki. Say No To Sexual Abuse. Protect the Girl Child. Justice for Miki means a better future for our girls. I Am Miki Daniels. Miki could have been my child. We Support Miki Daniels.

My wet eyes become blurry, and I can't see any more. I have to stop reading. My effort not to shed tears is futile. They roll freely down my face.

Why are they doing this for me?

I understand that they know my story now. They identify with my pain, with my suffering, but they don't have to do this for me. I have done nothing but oppress them. I have walked on them like a mat. Most of them are jobless because of me. I look down on them and destroyed their self-esteem.

They have no reason to do this for me.

Their love and support touch me, and I can't say a word. All I can do is cry that I'm grateful.

Vince and Wale lead me through the crowd into the car that is waiting for me.

As soon as I sit in the car, Vince offers me a handkerchief and I wipe my face. I keep looking at Vince as we drive home in silence. He hasn't had a moment of rest since I've been locked up.

How can I ever repay him?

A few minutes later, the car pulls up to Vince's house. I'm fatigued, thirsty, and terribly hungry. Not that I have an appetite for food. I just want to have a good shower and try to sleep. I know sleeping won't be easy. My memories are going to haunt me for a long time.

Vince gets out from the car, holds the door open for me, and helps me into the house. When I walk into the living room, I see the last person I expect to see sitting on the couch waiting for me to get back.

I halt, turn to the side, and look at Vince. "What is she doing here?"

"She's your mother," he replies, trying to get me close and clamp down the raging fire burning inside of me.

"That doesn't answer my question."

Before he can respond, my mother walks toward me, only to stop a few strides away, respecting my personal space. "Miki," she calls gently. She sounds like a stranger to me.

She calls me, and I don't respond.

I don't know what to say. I have too much to worry about, and my broken family isn't one of them.

"Miki, I didn't know," she says, her voice sounding genuinely hurt. "I didn't know. You should have told me. You shouldn't have kept it all to yourself."

"Are you saying it's my fault? Are you blaming me?" I ask bitterly.

She's shaking her head. "No, no. I'm saying that I'm sorry. That I'm a disgrace to motherhood, and I failed you. I am so very sorry."

I swallow hard, but stay quiet. I look away from her, feeling suddenly, unexpectedly, softhearted toward her.

"It's too late," I say in a soft voice, and then walk past her toward the stairs.

"Your father passed away," she announces. "I left him when I heard what happen to you. And he killed himself."

Her words hit me, and I stop walking, waiting for me to feel something. I don't know what I'm expected to feel, but I know there's something people feel when they lose their father. But I feel nothing. I'm neither sad nor happy. I'm just empty inside.

Without turning back, I continue to climb the stairs. When I get to the bedroom, I step out of the clothes I'm wearing. I'm about to walk into the bathroom when the door to the bedroom opens.

"Miki."

It's Vince, and I know what he's going to say.

"I have a right to miss my father's funeral," I say and look back at him. He's not trying to walk toward me, just gently resting his back on the door, his face is set in a frown of true concern.

"I'm not going to ask you to." He takes a breath, as if he's trying to remain patient. As if he's trying to teach something to a child. His expression makes me feel more than a little stupid.

"Miki, listen to me. The crowds outside the jail today, most of them are poor people and you've never done anything nice for them despite everything you have. Yet, they stand by you and support you. If you think for a moment that you deserve what they are doing for you right now, then skip your father's funeral. But if their strong, forgiving hearts touch you, then you should go. It's that simple."

I try to betray nothing with my face. I simply nod and then walk into the bathroom, stepping into the shower and enjoying the feel of the warm water on my skin.

Chapter Thirty-One

Miki

My mom and I sit side by side on the front pew, dressed in black French lace. My mom is wearing a black sunshade which I believe is meant to conceal her red, puffy eyes.

I don't shed a single tear. He doesn't deserve it.

And I don't pay attention to the funeral service either. Instead, I glance around. My eyes scan the church, and there are a lot of faces I don't recognize. It's easier to look at them the familiar faces that have betrayed me.

I look at Vince. He stares straight ahead, fully concentrating on the priest. His face is perfectly still and serious, listening intently to the sermon. I can see how hard he tries to hold it together. He's worked with my mother to plan the funeral, and he's trying to stay strong for everyone. He catches me staring at him and gives me a reassuring smile to let me know he's here.

The priest finishes the sermon and step down from the pulpit as the hymn, *God Be with You Till We Meet Again*, begins to play. My mother's sobs grows louder, and I just have to put my arms around her to console her.

I can't wait for this to be over.

Thankfully, the hymn that brought tears from my mother finishes and the priest steps forward to the front of the congregation.

"Today, we bid farewell to our friend, Mike. Father, husband, and a lover of God. I'd like to call on Miss Daniels to say her farewells."

I sure as hell didn't tell the priest to include me in the funeral service to eulogize my father.

I'm sitting there, staring at the priest, confused.

And then I feel my mother take my hands in hers and give me a little squeeze. Looking at her, I know she told the priest to include me in the service.

I want to decline, but I'd rather not cause a scene.

So I walk gently to the front of the congregation, bowing slightly to accord my respect to the priest. For one long second, I'm standing in front of the congregation at a loss for words. My eyes find Vince in the crowd, and he nudges me to speak. I have nothing prepared to say, so I have to say the first thing that comes to mind.

"There are a lot of people here today, and I believe every single one of you has something good to say about my father. And that doesn't surprise me. He was a man who took care of the needy, gave to the poor, loved his country, protected the orphans, prayed for the widows... He had a good heart. He was simply a good man. A good friend. A good husband. A good..." I hesitate, looking down for a moment. When I look back up, I have to swallow the lumps in my throat before I can continue. "He was my father. And maybe if he'd been a better father, I might have turned out better than I am. We'll never know. But I am what I am because of him, for good or bad."

Ending my speech, I go back to sitting beside my mother, not paying attention to the rest of the program. I keep staring past my father's casket to the altar.

I haven't been in church in a long time.

Fourteen years ago, I just got back from church when Jaye and his friend did what they did to me. It took the death of my father to bring me back.

By the time my attention comes back to my surrounding, I'm all alone. Everybody is gone. Perhaps to the graveside.

My eyes go to the casket still lying in front of the church. Something nudges me to stand and move forward to take a peep.

My father lies peacefully in his favorite black suit. His face looks at peace, and I envy him for a moment. It was the peace that I craved for until Tiwa made me realize that my work here isn't finished.

I keep staring at my father. For a moment, I wish he could speak because there are many things I want to hear him say. There are many questions I want him to answer. Like why he was a coward till the end and took his own life. Like why he could never look beyond wealth and fight for me.

Hearing footsteps from behind me, I glance back to see who it is.

My mother.

She comes and stands beside me, putting her arms around my waist as she peers into the casket. "He looks so peaceful..." she says, resting her head on my shoulder. We are silent for more than a minute. I'm sure both of us have something we want to say to him right now, but my father is forever silent. We will never hear him speak again.

Raising her head from my shoulder, she looks up at me. "It's time to take him to the graveside. I'll let you have a moment with him."

I nod.

She removes her arms from around me and put her

hands into her black purse. She brings out a small envelope and holds it out for me. "He wanted you to have this."

I take the envelope from her and wait for her to leave.

I look at the envelope. *To my angel* is boldly written on the back.

The last time my father called me that was when I was eight. The bond between us had been severed from that day.

Opening the envelope, I read his letter.

Dearest Angel,

If you are reading this, then you already know that I was a coward till the very end. But I can't go away without letting you know I regret deeply everything that happened.

When you were born, I had nothing. I could barely provide food, let alone provide the kind of home or nurturing that you needed. I tried to be a good daddy. Believe me, I tried. My effort wasn't enough and it left me ashamed and insecure. I internalized all my pain and insecurities until I was consumed with the thought of acquiring wealth by any means necessary and I completely lost sight of everything that matters.

And today, as I listen to the news and hear everything that you had to suffer for my greediness, all the sacrifices that you had to make, I am saddened and ashamed of my failure as a father.

Believe me, I did not know all those terrible things happened to you. I did not know. But that's not an excuse. I can't say I would do things differently if I knew. You wouldn't believe me if I said that, but I blame myself for it because if I had stood for you 22 years ago—if I had enough courage to fight for you—I could have prevented it from happening again.

And it's not just hearing your story that's gotten to me. Lately, I've been experiencing a new round of emotions. Regrets, and some sadness even.

I've had this regret since the man you brought home stood up for you and protected you, doing the things I should have done. I regret that I couldn't do anything for you on my own. I regret that you had to take up the task of providing for the family, a task that should have been mine and mine alone. I regret that you parented me instead of I you. I regret that I ruined your childhood, and ruined your happiness.

Despite all that, you have flourished beyond any parent's wildest expectations. And none of the credit goes to me. You did it all by yourself. You are a survivor. Everything you touch survives. And I can't imagine I could have done better for you than you did for yourself. I only wish I had given you beautiful memories of your childhood and beautiful memories of beautiful times with your parents.

I want to say that I'm sorry, but I know you won't accept it. I can't ask you to forgive me; it's too much to ask for. But please forgive your mother. She's a good woman. She needs you. Please look after her like you've always done.

I am sorry.

Daddy.

My wet eyes are blurry by the time I finish reading. My hand moves gently into the casket.

"Daddy..." I whisper as I touch and caress his face. My legs go weak and I sink to the floor slowly. Burying my face between my legs, I cry like I've never cried before.

Moments later, I feel strong arms around me, and I rest my head on his chest and cry against him. And he lets me.

Chapter Thirty-Two

Vince

Miki sits on the leather chair in my office while Lola sits opposite her. I'm pacing back and forth as we wait for Wale.

I need people to discuss the case with, and these are the only people I can trust with Miki's case. They are not lawyers, but I trust them because I'm certain the Jamals have bought a lot of people over to their side—and I know these people cannot be bought.

I must admit that I'm nervous and I'm afraid that after everything I've done we might lose. Miki believes in me, and I can't let her down.

A minute later, the door opens and Wale walks in.

"I'm sorry I'm late," he says.

"That's okay," I say and point to a seat across from Lola.

He says his greetings to Miki before sitting.

"Lola, this is Wale, my friend. He's a doctor who works at the National Hospital." I glance at Wale. "She's Lola, a friend of Miki's. She used to work at ABJ TV and has been mobilizing the public to support Miki."

Wale keeps taking a good look at Lola, staring at her with the kind of glance I understand so well.

I know my friend likes women, maybe a little too much. He will bed anything as long as it has a hole between the legs. But despite his uncontrollable desire for women, I don't think now is the right time for that.

I'm about to caution him when he speaks.

"Lola Williams?" he asks, still staring unbelievably at her.

She nods. "Yes, and stop staring at me like that."

"Like what? The last time I saw you eight years ago you were..."

She rolls her eyes at him. "Shut up, and nice to meet you, too."

Wale leans closer to her, trying to say something, but he seems not to have the word for it. And the look on his face is priceless. It's a look of pain and happiness joined in one. Something tells me Lola is the woman who showed my friend the painful side of love. She's the reason he's going through women so fast he cannot be fully committed to anyone but himself.

Ignoring the tension between them, I sit on the desk with one of my legs resting on the floor for support.

"Miki's been charged with murder. The prosecutor will be arguing that Miki killed Jaye because he was trying to take over Daniels Group, which is, in fact, a very good motive. People have killed for less than a billion-dollar company. I'm going to try to throw away that motive and find a way to include everything he did to Miki in the past. I will try to appeal to the emotions of the jury. And that won't be difficult because five of the ten people on the jury are women, and I am so certain they've had an experience with sexual assault, and if not personal, then through daughter, a cousin, or good friend. The five men on the jury are older and have a sense of responsibility and the urge to protect. It's going to be easy to appeal to their emotions, but we still need evidence to back up the claim. The problem is that we have none."

The room is silent for another minute. Heads down, everyone deep in thought.

"What about a witness?" Lola asks. "There has to be one person who knew about it."

"There was someone who knew about the incident that happened at eight years old. Her father."

"And he's dead," Lola says, and then sighs. "That's convenient."

"Did she not get medical attention when it happened?" Wale asks.

I nod. "Yes, she did. At the National Hospital."

"Well, maybe they still have the records."

I shake my head. "It happened a lot time ago. Even if we're able to get our hands on that record, it will only prove that Miki was sexually assaulted. It won't prove that it was done by Jaye."

Everyone is quiet again. Miki sits there, saying nothing. I'm not even sure she's paying attention. I told her to do nothing and let me do everything, and she's doing exactly as I said. I'm only afraid I might not be able to save her. For once, I wish she'd go back to her old ways and disobey me.

"Wale," I say, "see if we can get our hands on the records from the hospital. I'll see what I can do with them. And Lola, keep mobilizing the people to demonstrate. You did a good job with the *Justice For Miki* hashtags on social media."

With those words, I dismiss them. I need to be alone. I need to think.

****

Miki

I'm sitting inside the dock when my trial begins. I try

not to pay attention to anything. You know how they say if you don't expect, you don't get disappointed. That's exactly what I'm trying to do right now. I pleaded not guilty to all the charges and am hoping for the best, but I've made up my mind to accept the worst if it happens.

No matter how I try not to pay attention, the prosecutor's first witness catches my attention.

She takes the oath and then the prosecuting attorney approaches the witness stand.

"Please, can you tell this court your name and your relationship with the deceased?"

She clears her throat. "My name is Bose Wright, and I am the executive assistant of the deceased."

"Thank you, Mrs. Wright. I'm aware you had an encounter with Miss Daniels, correct?"

She nods.

"Can you please tell this court what happened the day you met Miss Daniels?"

"I was sitting at the front desk when Miss Daniels walked in. I tried to say a greeting and welcome her, but she ignored my greeting and asked me if my boss was in. I told her yes, but I didn't want to let her in because she had this wildness in her eyes that tells me she is angry and can be violent. I tried to stop her, but she pushed me aside and forced her way into my boss's office. I wanted to push her out, but Mr. Jamal stopped me. He was a gentle soul. He told me to let her be, so I did. I walked out of the office and went back to my desk. A few seconds later, I started hearing voices. Loud, angry voices that mostly belonged to Miss Daniels. I listened. And from what I heard, it looks like Miss Daniels was mad because my boss had tried to sabotage her business. The arguments continued for a long time. And I heard Miss Daniels threaten my boss, saying that she would kill him, cut his body into pieces, and feed it to the dogs."

"Can you repeat what you just said?" he asks.

She nods. "If you ever come near my business again, I'll kill you, cut your body into pieces, and feed it to the dogs. Those were her exact words."

"Thank you, Mrs. Wright," he says and walks away from the witness stand to the front of the judge's bench. "My lord, Miss Daniels threatened to kill the deceased and cut him into pieces, and that is exactly what she did. She stabbed him twenty-six times and…"

"Objection, my lord," Vince cuts in.

"Objection overruled," he replies, and then points to the prosecutor. "You may continue."

"Thank you, my lord. Miss Daniels had a good motive to kill the deceased, and from the testimony of the witness, we know she wanted to kill Mr. Jamal. She brilliantly planned everything out and delivered death unto Mr. Jamal exactly the way she threatened."

"Defense counsel, any cross examination for the witness?"

"Yes, my lord," Vince says and approaches the witness stand. "Mrs. Wright, please tell me if I'm wrong. You said Miss Daniels forced her way into your office. You tried to push her out, but your boss said to let her be. So you went back to sit at your desk, am I right?"

She nods. "Yes."

"Can you please tell this court the distance between your desk and your boss's office?"

She's quiet for a while, probably thinking of what to say. "About fifteen strides apart."

"And you were able to hear every discussion they had, word for word, from that distance?"

"I never said I was sitting at my desk when I heard…"

Vince cuts her off. "I think everyone in this courtroom heard you when you said you were sitting at your desk, and do not forget, Mrs. Wright, you're under oath to say nothing but the truth."

She nods.

"How long have you worked for the Jamals?"

"About twelve years. I worked for the father and then worked for the son after the father retired from business."

"And I believe you have a good relationship with the Jamals, and would be willing to do anything for them, or if not for them, for Jamal Corporation, to which you have given twelve years of your life."

"Yes," she replies, and then Vince turns to the judge.

"My lord, Mrs. Wright cannot remember where she was when she heard the threat that my client supposedly made. Even if she did remember, it would be difficult, if not impossible, to hear a discussion going on behind closed doors from about fifteen strides away. I ask this court not to base the fate of Miss Daniels on this witness."

Vince pauses and studies the face of the jurors for a moment before he continues.

"My colleague was right about something. Miss Daniels, in fact, killed Mr. Jaye Jamal by stabbing him twenty-six times. It is indeed a cruel sight to behold. But my colleague failed to mention that Miss Daniels also bit his penis, which makes me wonder why his penis was in her mouth in the first place."

The prosecutor jumps to his feet. "Objection, my lord!"

"Objection overruled."

The prosecutor sits and Vince continues.

"We know that Mr. Jamal and Miss Daniels were not in a romantic or sexual relationship. That means his penis had no business being in her mouth. Since Miss Daniels did not consent to this act, it could only mean that Mr. Jamal was sexually assaulting my client. But I'd like this court to hear the story from the victim herself."

He begins to walk toward my stand.

He's going to make me tell the tales. No matter how many times I've told the story of what Jaye did to me, it doesn't make it easier.

"Miss Daniels, who is Jaye Jamal?"

I steal a look into his eyes before speaking. "He was a family friend. And he was someone that used to be like a brother to me."

"He used to be like a brother. What changed?"

God, I wish he were not making me tell it again. But I can't blame him. He's doing his job. Swallowing hard, I try not to look at anyone.

"I was eight years old. As a child, I was naïve and quick to trust. I wasn't the only one who trusted him—my parents did, too. And on that day, they left me home alone with him. And he came into my room and... he raped me." My voice breaks off as a lump begins to build up in my throat.

"And then he did it again when I was sixteen, but my parents were too afraid to fight because his parents were rich and powerful and we would stand no chance against them. And then he did it again... and again..." My voice grows softer and weaker until it fades away and my face reflexively takes on an expression of pain.

I try to continue, but my voice is choking up. So Vince continues for me.

"He kidnapped and subjected her to brutal sexual slavery."

The prosecutor hits his fist on the desk and jumps to

his feet.

"Objection, my lord."

"Objection sustained. Mr. Ali, you..."

Unable to mask his anger, Vince continues, unwilling to be stopped by anyone.

"He watched as several men tortured, raped, and tore her apart until her very life almost bled out. He kidnapped a child that she cares about."

"Mr. Ali!" the judge cautions.

Vince throws caution to the wind, his chest heaving with anger. "He violated her because he thought he could get away with everything. His father is powerful—the senate president of this country—and because of that he thinks he is above the law. And it is in the hands of this court to prove that no one is above the law. Miss Daniels might have killed him, but she did what anybody would have done in the face of an impossible situation: protected herself from being violated again and protected her daughter from suffering the same fate."

"Mr. Ali." The resounding noise of the gavel hitting the block roars throughout the courtroom. "I will have you thrown in jail for misconduct if you don't stop."

He bows slightly as the rage grows calms and he gathers his composure. "I'm sorry, my lord."

Chapter Thirty-Three

Miki

There's a reason why they don't let a doctor take care of a patient who is family. Same reason why Vince should have stayed away from my case.

As we proceed with this trial, he gets more and more agitated as it dawns on him that we're closer to losing than to winning.

Another witness takes the stand and I know that this person has nothing nice to say about me.

"Can you please tell this court your name and your relationship with Miss Daniels?" the prosecutor asks.

"My name is Ola Mathews, and I work for Miss Daniels."

He raises a brow. "How is that? You used to be the CEO of Cashmit PLC."

"Miss Daniels bought Cashmit PLC, but she let me stay and keep working for her."

"And would you say letting you stay and keep working for her is out of the goodness of her heart?"

He replies without a moment of thought. "No. I believe she did that to spite me."

"Please tell this court how Miss Daniels negotiated the buying of your company."

"It wasn't really a negotiation. She invited me to her office and told me she's going to start the production of sanitary pads—the same business Cashmit was into. She said she wanted me out of the market, and so she wanted to buy my business. When I declined, she threatened to tell the public that I use cheap products which can cause cancer, even though we both know that Cashmit did not use cheap products..."

He cuts him off. "Maybe it was just an empty threat,"

"No. Miss Daniels will do anything to protect her business, including blackmailing me to sell my business to her."

"Thank you, Mr. Mathews," the prosecutor says, glancing at the judge and then the jurors. "This man is one of the many who have suffered at the hands of Miss Daniels. The only difference between him and Mr. Jamal is that this man lived to tell the story while Mr. Jamal isn't so lucky. Miss Daniels is a vicious woman who would do anything for herself and her business, including lying that the deceased tried to rape her and kidnap a child she cares about."

Vince slams his fist on the desk. "Objection, my lord!"

"Objection overruled."

The prosecutor continues. "Miss Daniels is a woman incapable of caring for anyone. Her defense that she was trying to protect a child is a complete fabrication and I can prove it to this court."

The judge gives his consent.

"I call the next witness, Titi Idris."

The court clerk keeps calling the name again and again. The name troubles my mind, but I can't remember how exactly I know her. I need not bother myself. I know no one can have anything nice to say about me. Jaye did many things to me, but my bad relationships are completely on me. It's my fault and my fault alone.

The witness steps into the stand and takes the oath.

"Can you please tell this court how you came to know Miss Daniels?"

"I applied for a position at Daniels Group. Miss Daniels interviewed me for the job."

"And did you get the job?"

She shakes her head no.

"Why is that? Did she say you weren't good enough?"

"She admitted that I was good enough, but she couldn't hire me because I had a child."

"What do you mean she didn't hire you because you have a child?"

Vince jumps to his feet. "Objection, my lord."

"Sit down, Mr. Ali. Objection overruled."

My heart breaks. The judge is being unfair, sidelining Vince and not giving him a chance to speak. He didn't even give him a chance to cross-examine the last witness. We have no chance of winning with a judge who isn't bought, but now that he is...

The prosecutor continues. "Miss Daniels is a woman and she understands what it is to have children. Why did she refuse to hire you because you have a child?"

"I don't know. She told me that she can't have a child. She comes across as someone who doesn't like children."

"Thank you, Miss Idris." And then he turns to the jury. "How can someone who doesn't like children claims that the deceased kidnapped a child she cares about and then killed him to protect that child? I don't see how that is possible."

I shut my eyes and grimace in pain. When I open my eyes, I just keep staring into nothingness. It's over.

My mind is in a faraway place thinking of the things I'd like to do before I die. I need to prepare a will. And then I need to spend some more time with Tiwa.

Tiwa.

It feels like I'm hearing her voice in the courtroom.

"My name is Tiwa Ali, and I think of Miss Daniels as my mother."

The prosecutor nods, and then looks her in the eyes. "I'm going to be asking you some questions. Is that okay?"

She nods.

"If it gets uncomfortable for you to answer, you can decide not to."

She nods again.

And then he begins. "I'm aware that some strange people took you away few days ago. True?"

"Yes."

"Tell me, how did it happen?"

Her eyes move slowly and hold my gaze. I nod and let her know it's okay.

She swallows before she begins. "We went for a field trip at school. I needed to pee, so I stepped away from my teacher and my friends, and then two men came and took me away. I tried to shout for help, but they covered my mouth."

"These two men, if you saw them again, would you recognize them?"

She hesitates a while and then nods.

The prosecutor walks to his bench and grabs a picture of Jaye.

"Is he one of the men who took you away?"

Tiwa takes a long look at the picture and shakes her head gently. "No. He's not one of them."

"Objection, my lord!" Vince yells. "He is confusing the kid. It's very possible that Mr. Jamal made other people do his dirty work and the victim never got the chance to see him."

"My lord, my colleague is making a baseless accusation without evidence."

"Mr. Ali, objection overruled," the judge says.

Vince's palm folds into a fist as he shakes with impotent rage.

"Thank you, my lord." The prosecutor continues. "I have to ask you again—is he one of the men who kidnapped you?"

"No, he's not. I've never seen that man before."

"Thank you," he replies, but before he can continue, Tiwa interrupts him.

"I know what everybody is saying about my mommy. They are saying she's a bad person, but she's not. She can say mean things, and she can be tough. She can yell and scream and threaten to do terrible things, but she would never hurt anyone. She's a good person..."

Hearing what Tiwa said, I feel... satisfied. Whatever the world thinks of me: a murderer, a cheat, a bully, it doesn't matter. Someone remembers me for something kind, and that is enough for me.

The prosecuting attorney has said a lot before I pay attention again.

"I have been able to prove that although Tiwa Ali was missing, she wasn't kidnapped by the deceased. But my colleague raised a very important question that I would love to answer. Why is Mr. Jaye's penis in Miss Daniel's mouth?" He pauses and bows slightly to acknowledge the judge. "If I may, I'd like to call another witness to the stand."

"Go ahead."

He walks back to his desk and reads from his papers. "Lola Williams."

"Lola Williams," the court clerk calls again, inviting her

to the stand.

Lola is my friend. She has mobilized the masses to support me, but when it comes down to it, she's not going to have anything nice to say about me.

If only I had more time. I was changing. I was becoming a better person. Vince was helping me become a better person. All I need is more time to show everyone I can be better. If I had a chance, I'd do things differently.

"Miss Williams," the prosecutor begins, "tell this court how you know Miss Daniels."

"Miki is my friend. We've been friends since childhood."

He nods. "Good. So you know that about eight years ago, Miss Daniels went missing for four months."

"Yes. I was the one who found her and called the ambulance."

"Can you please tell this court how you found her?"

"Someone dropped her off at the house."

"Did you see a face?"

"No," she replies firmly, "but I saw a customized licensed plate customized JJ3, which I know for sure belongs to Mr. Jaye Jamal."

The prosecutor's quiet for some time, pacing away from the witness stand and then glancing fiercely back at Lola. "What did you think of the situation at that time?"

"I thought they were lovers. I thought that Miki ran off with him, and Jaye only brought her back when her sickness got out of hand."

"And why would you think they were lovers?"

She hesitates. "Because there was this tension between them at work. And there were rumors everywhere that they were... you know... sleeping with each other."

"And did you believe that rumor?"

She lifts a shoulder in a shrug, forcing herself to answer even though it's so obvious she doesn't like what her answer will be.

"Yes. I believed the rumor, but that was before I knew the truth."

He lifts a brow. "And that truth you now claim to know is the story Miss Daniels tells about a sexual assault"

She nods.

"Thank you, Miss Williams. That will be all." And then he glances at the judge. "My lord, we now know that there were rumors that the relationship between Miss Daniels and the deceased was sexual. Which means his penis inside her mouth might be an act of two consenting adults. I know this court cannot give judgments based on rumors, but sadly, Mr. Jamal is not here today, so we cannot hear his side of the story. We also have no evidence. We only have Miss. Daniels to tell her own tale. It's her words against a dead man—a man she has admitted to killing. So, can we believe her words? Is Miss Daniels a trustworthy person? Before we decide if she can be trusted, I'd like this court to listen to what people say about Miss Daniels' character."

The judge gestures him to go on.

"I'd like to invite to the stand Miss Sade Ojo."

The court clerk announces the name again and again until she steps forward. After taking the oath, the prosecutor approaches the stand.

"Can you tell this court who you are?"

She clears her throat. "My name is Sade Ojo. I am Miss Daniels' executive assistant."

"How well do you know Miss Daniels?"

"I spent twelve hours a day, six days a week over the last three years working for her. I think I know her well enough."

"Good. So what can you tell this court about the character of Miki Daniels?"

Hesitating for a second, she pulls her brow together in a frown. "I'm sorry I don't understand your question."

The prosecutor glares impatiently at her. "Miss Ojo, I'm asking you to tell this court about her character. You've seen her relationship with people over the years, and you can tell what kind of person she is."

She's shaking now. She glances at me and my heart races in anticipation of what she might say.

"Miss Daniels is a bully," she begins.

My head lowers in defeat. There's no coming back from this.

"She's condescending, supercilious, and finds no one indispensable. She cares about nothing and no one. Not even herself. Only Daniels Group. That company is her life. She gave her soul to build it and will do anything to protect it. She fights dirty. She threatens, blackmails, and destroys people just to protect Daniels Group. Whatever the cost, she's willing to pay to see that the company thrives. It was the only thing that made her happy. But all that began to change a few months ago."

"That will be all, Miss Ojo." He cuts her off, and then glances at the jury and the judge. "Every witness who has taken this stand has only one thing to say about the deceased. He was a good person, a gentle soul. He does good for everyone and respects the law. He was incapable of hurting a fly, let alone raping and subjecting someone to torture and sexual slavery. Also, every witness today has said the same thing about Miss Daniels: she's a person who cares for no one but herself and would do anything to protect her business."

He turns his gaze toward me. His gaze feels like a death sentence already. "I dare say that Miss Daniels killed Mr. Jaye Jamal by stabbing him twenty-six times because the latter tried to take over her business. She killed Mr. Jamal and tried to cover it up by lying to this court that the deceased tried to rape her."

"Objection, my lord!" Vince hits the desk and jumps to his feet.

"Sit down, Mr. Ali. Objection overruled," the judge says and gestures the prosecutor to go on.

"A life was taken because of one woman's lust for more money and power. Section 220 of the penal code and section 320 of the criminal code says and I quote, 'Whosoever causes death – (a) by doing an act with the intention of causing death or such bodily injury as is likely to cause death; or (b) by doing an act with the knowledge that he is likely by such act to cause death; or (c) by doing a rash or negligent act to commit the offence of culpable homicide is guilty of murder.' I ask that this court uphold the law and punish Miss Daniels accordingly with death by hanging for the murder of Mr. Jaye Jamal."

He bows in acknowledgement.

"I rest my case."

The prosecutor slowly walks back and takes his seat.

The judge lets out a deep breath and clears his throat. "Defense attorney, do you have anything to say?"

Vince rises to his feet, covering his displeasure as much as he can with a blank face. "Nothing, my lord."

The deed is done. Any further argument is pointless.

"Very well then," the judge says. "We will take a break for the jury to reach a verdict. The court resumes in an hour."

Hitting the gavel on the block, he rises to his feet and

court is dismissed.

****

Vince

Throwing the folder in my hands on the desk, I scream in anger and kick the table. I'm so unnerved that I begin to pace back and forth. Covering my eyes with both palms, I let out another scream. This time, hot tears fill my eyes, and I try so hard not to shed it, but I'm crying deeply inside.

I feel a touch on my shoulder. I don't have to look. I know who it is.

"You tried all you can." Her voice is soft and gentle. "You did your best. We never stood a chance, and I've accepted things. You should, too."

I feel an agony born of compassion and love for her. I feel for what she's going through and what she has gone through—and the fact that I can't do anything about it. I feel the ache of defeats, even though I know it wasn't exactly a defeat. We never stood a chance. The trial wasn't a true hearing; it was a one-sided argument. Hours of listening to the prosecuting attorney rant on and on while I was given little or no time at all to actually defend my client. The judge has been bought.

Miki tried to warn me. She tried to make me understand that it was over. She wanted to save me from the pain of expecting the best and getting the worst. Why couldn't I have listened? Why did I have to be so foolish to think that I'm smart enough to figure out a way to win this for Miki?

I know why.

I care too much for her. I love her so much that I can't

imagine living without her for a second.

I walk slowly away from her. I never want her to see my tears. I keep swallowing over and over again so that I can talk.

"I can't lose you, Miki. I can't," I say, shaking my head.

Ever so gently, she walks toward me. Holding my shoulder, she watches my face, looking so lovingly into my eyes. A tear betrays me and drop down my face.

The dam breaks.

I give in to the itch to cry. Shoulders moving as I sob softly, I break down and share my vulnerability with her.

She holds my head against her breast, close to her heart.

"I'm happy I met you, Vince," she says, caressing my head as she tries to console me. "I never knew love like I've known it with you. Nobody can love me like you, and..."

"It doesn't have to end." I cut her off, looking deep into her eyes. "We can elope."

Her eyes open wide. "Vince."

Holding her upper arm, my eyes penetrate hers, pleading with her. "Run away with me. Let's leave everything behind: Daniels Group, my law firm, everything. Let's leave it behind and run. We can be together. Start a new life, a new page."

She shakes her head. "No, Vince..."

"Miki, we can finally move away from this mess. You don't have to face death. We can be together."

"You're not thinking about Tiwa." Her voice breaks with emotion as she tries to keep herself from crying. "We will be disrupting her life, taking everything away from her."

"She will start afresh. She will make new friends, and we will work hard to give her a good life."

"But it won't be the kind of life she's used to. We will be giving her less than she is used to."

"She will survive."

"No, Vince. No. It's not right."

Running my fingers through my hair in frustration, another angry scream escapes my mouth. The system is messed up. Good people don't always get justice; I know that for sure. It seems okay when it happens to somebody else, but when it happens to you or to anyone close, it burns like fire on your skin.

"You've lost hope from the beginning. You really wanted to die. It seems you are going to get your wish," I say and hide my face from hers.

I know it's a bad thing to say. Hell, it's a terrible thing. But I'm burning, and I'm not giving a thought to anything I'm saying right now. I lost a woman I loved once before. It's beginning to feel like death is always waiting to take the woman I love away from me. It's beginning to feel like I'm destined to grow old alone.

I can hear her crying behind me. "I don't want to die, Vince. Despite what you think, I don't want to die."

It's the first time she's really showing an emotion—her true emotion about her imminent death.

Still looking away, I wipe my tears and then close my eyes tight. Pain tightens my chest, and I struggle to breathe.

"I can't let you die, Miki. There has to be another way."

With those words, I open the door and walk out of the room, bumping into Sade in the hallway right outside the door.

"I promise I just got here," she says. "I wasn't eavesdropping. I came to apologize about what I said on the stand."

I manage to feign a smile. "It's not your fault, Sade. You only said what you were asked."

I'm about to walk past her when she speaks again.

"I've listened to the news. I heard everything he did to her."

I shrug my shoulders. "Well, they're just stories we can't prove."

"But what if..." she stops abruptly. I gaze into her eyes as she continues. "What if we find someone who was an accessory to the crime, would it help?"

"To some extent, yes, if the person is willing to testify and name Mr. Jamal, but that would be difficult because the person would be confessing to being an accessory to a crime. He might be facing jail time. Why do you ask?"

"There's this priest who's been sending apology notes to my boss for the past three years now. My mind keeps telling me that whatever he's sorry for has something to do with this mess."

"Who is this person?"

"I don't have the full name, but he always signs his notes as Father Paul."

Paul... Paul... I've heard the name before. Miki said something to me about a Paul once before. I flip through my mental files, and my eyes open wide when I remember him.

"He wasn't just an accessory to the crime—he committed the crime with him!"

Paul and Jaye raped Miki when she was sixteen.

With every sense of urgency, I take a look at my wristwatch. "It's thirty minutes before court resumes. We have to find him!"

She desperately searches through her handbag. "I have the address that's always on his letters. It's a small parish about ten minutes from here."

I take the letter from her. "Thank you, Sade."

Chapter Thirty-Four

Vince

"Bless me, Father, for I've sinned exceedingly in thought, word, and deed. It's been five months since my last confession."

The priest opens the window. "That's a very long time. Would you like to tell me your sins?"

His voice is gentle and soft. And for a moment, something pricks at my heart that this man is not the same person he used to be. He's a changed person with a bad past. But the thing is, a past doesn't always stays in the past.

"I'm not here to confess my sins, Father. I'm here to confess the sins of another."

"You cannot confess on behalf of another. Confession has to be done with a broken spirit and the contrite heart of the sinner." He pauses for a moment. "I'm sorry I can't take your confession."

"I'm sure you will want to hear this confession. Fourteen years ago, a man by the name of Paul raped a sixteen-year-old girl with his friend. They tore her apart in her own home and went scot free without any punishment—not from the law and certainly not from God. And today, this man sits in front of me as a priest."

"Stop!" he yells. "You think God did not punish me? In the nine years that I've been a priest, not a day goes by that what I did doesn't weigh on my conscience. Even though God tells me he has forgiven me, I've spent every day of my life asking for forgiveness over and over again. I've punished myself, serving a penance..."

"That is not enough!" I cut him off. "The girl you raped is about to be sentenced to death because she dared to kill the man who tormented her from childhood. No one will believe anything she says about that monster but if you... if you..." my voice breaks off.

"If I testify," he finishes for me. "You want me to testify. Do you know what that means for me?"

I lean closer. "You're the one who talked about serving a penance."

He lets out a breath and then moves away from the window. "I'm sorry. I can't," he says with tears in his voice. "God has forgiven me. And that is enough."

"God forgives, but he doesn't always take away the consequences of those sins. You and I both know that, Father."

****

Miki

The court is about to resume when Vince comes back. I wonder where he has been. I know he's having a hard time accepting this, and I've made it worse for him by breaking down and telling him that I don't want to die.

I've been acting strong for him, pretending as if the thought of my imminent of death does not scare me to the bone. As I sit in the dock, waiting for my sentence, I'm shaking, my heart beating really fast as if it's about to jump out of my chest.

After the court has settled in, Vince rises to his feet.

"My lord, if I may I crave your indulgence, I'd like to call one last witness."

"I'm afraid we've past the hearing stage, Mr. Ali."

"Please, my lord. It's important that this court listens to the testimony of this man before making a final decision.

"Does the prosecuting attorney agree to this?"

The prosecutor stands on his feet. "I believe there are no further words that can change the facts that we already have on ground. I say let my colleague call his witness."

He bows and sits.

"Very well then. Mr. Ali, call you witness."

Vince bows. "Thank you, my lord."

The court clerk calls the name, and when he steps forward, surprise is an understatement for what I feel.

Why the hell is Vince bringing him in into this? I forgave this man. I told him to be happy. Why did he have to drag him into this? He is a changed man. He made a mistake. We all do, but we don't have to keep paying for it for the rest of our lives.

"Please, tell this court who you are," Vince says.

"My name is Paul Ebele. I am a priest at St. Patrick Parish."

"Tell us what you know about Mr. Jaye Jamal."

"A long time ago, before I thought of going to seminary school, Jaye and I were very good friends. We were best friends. Inseparable. We did many things together. We got drunk, smoked marijuana, used drugs and... violated Miss Daniels at her home fourteen years ago."

The judge scowls. "Do you know what you're saying?"

"Yes. I'm saying that Jaye and I raped Miss Daniels at her home fourteen years ago."

"You're confessing to a crime. You could go to jail," the

judge continues. "You're looking at fourteen years imprisonment for the rape of an underage girl."

He nods gently. "A friend once told me God forgives, but sometimes he doesn't take away the consequences of our sins."

The judge looks down at the papers he has on his desk, shakes his head, and clears his table. "We'll take a break, and this court shall resume in twenty minutes."

I'm counting the seconds until the court resumes.

The court resumes and the judge begins;

"In the light of the testimony of Father Paul Ebele and the signs of a struggle at the scene of the crime, it has proven that it's quite possible that the deceased attempted to forcefully have sexual intercourse with Miss Daniels. This court, therefore, asks the police department to continue the investigation of Mr. Jaye Jamal and the kidnapping of Miss Tiwa Ali."

The judge is quiet for a second, but it seems an eternity.

I'm holding my breath as if breathing itself will be the end of me.

"The jury has reached a verdict," he says. "Miss Miki Daniels is found not guilty of the charges of murder, and all charges against her have been dropped from this moment on." The gavel hits the block and the judge rises.

The sounds of joy and triumphs fill the courtroom.

I can't believe my ears. I am free!

I feel several arms around me, trying to hug me and share in the happiness of my freedom. But my eyes are fixed on only one person. He's looking at me, holding my gaze as tears fill both our eyes.

He saved me.

I just want to run into his arms and kiss him thank you.

I want to thank him for fighting for me till the end, for never giving up on me. Even when it looked like we'd lost all hope, his love remained undying.

There are people pulling me left and right, trying to congratulate me. And his colleagues are pulling him, too, to complete the papers.

We continue to hold our gaze and my lips curl into a small smile. He nods and smiles back. I might not be able to run over to him right now, but the silence and distance between us speaks volumes. I don't have to say it. He knows. He can see it in my eyes, and he can feel it in the hot tears running down my face.

As I step out of the courtroom, I'm surprised by the crowd. They've been protesting and demonstrating, asking for justice. I stand before them to speak, but I'm short of words. I can only cry.

When all of this is over, I'm going to pull down every building that belongs to Jamal Corporation. Why? Because destroying people makes me happy. Old habits die hard.

I'm kidding. I've learned my lessons the hard way.

I'm going to pull down Jamal Corp because I can't think of a better venue to build a shelter home to protect young girls from any kind of abuse.

Dear Reader,

I want to thank each and every one of you who has followed Miki's journey. Mostly, I want to thank Miki for choosing me to tell her story. Her tears, pains, sufferings and redemption have touched my heart.

I wrote Miki's story about two years ago, but I could never share it with the world because I thought it was controversial and might turn off so many readers and open me up for bad reviews.

But when I heard about the 276 schoolgirls that were kidnapped and raped in the town of Chibok, Nigeria, I feel compelled to share Miki's story with the world. No matter who is going to love or hate the story, I feel the urge to tell people who suffered any kind of abuse that there's light after the dark.

Thank you again for reading After d Dark. If you enjoyed it, I would appreciate it if you would help others enjoy it, too.

Review it. If you enjoyed it, leave a review on one of the major retailers. It can be two to three sentences. Nothing fancy.

Tell others. Help other readers to find this book by recommending it to friends, families and book clubs.

Much Love,
Aderonke
Facebook: @AderonkeMoyinlorun
Twitter: @IAmAderonke
Website: www. authoraderonke.com

Other Books by Aderonke